THE FALL
OF ONAGROS

SAGE:
BOOK ONE

Books and stories by Marian Allen

Novels
Eel's Reverence
Force of Habit
SAGE Book 1: The Fall of Onagros
SAGE Book 2: Bargain With Fate
SAGE Book 3: Silver and Iron
Sideshow in the Center Ring

Short Story Collections
Lonnie, Me and the Hound of Hell
Turtle Feathers
The King of Cherokee Creek
MA's Monthly Hot Flashes: 2002-2009

Visit the author at
http://MarianAllen.com

THE FALL OF ONAGROS

SAGE: BOOK ONE

A Novel
by

MARIAN ALLEN

Per Bastet

The Fall of Onagros Sage: Book One

Second Edition

Copyright © 2014 Marian Allen

Published by Per Bastet Publications LLC, P.O. Box 3023 Corydon, IN 47112

Cover design by T. Lee Harris

ISBN 978-1-942166-50-4

DEDICATION:

Many thanks to my mother, Genarose Turner, to my husband, Charles Allen, and to my youngest daughter, best critic, and dear friend, Sara. Without you three, SAGE would never have survived its rewrites.

THE FALL OF ONAGROS

SAGE:
BOOK ONE

prologue

Unicorn pressed a hoof into the yielding earth, leaving a moss-lined hollow. Phoenix shook a tiny iridescent feather into the impression. Tortoise spat upon the feather; the droplets dissolved it, swelled, burst their surface tension, and filled the shallow bowl with shimmering liquid. Dragon breathed gently on the water, and a vision appeared.

Two rounded beehives of woven straw – skeps, as the beekeepers call them – one skep painted green and blue, the colors of The House of Onagros. The other is stained with the red and gold of The House of Sarpa. The Sarpan bees grow larger while the Onagrans dwindle. The Sarpans attack the blue/green skep, killing or driving out the Onagrans, piercing brood cells and dragging half-formed bees into the dry and pitiless sunlight, taking the hive and its honey for themselves. But the weave of the assaulted skep still glows blue and green.

Tortoise yawned. "This is pointless. Who cares about their squabbles?"

"I care," said Dragon.

"Not enough to do anything."

Dragon did not reply.

"I only watch," said Unicorn. "It's all the same to me."

Tortoise cocked an orange eye at Phoenix. "And you, brother? Does this interest you?"

Phoenix ruffled his wings. Sparks flew, sizzling as they hit the watery vision. "Is there any reason why it should?"

"I think it does," said Tortoise. "I think it interests all of you. I think you'd like to dabble in this pool."

"I only watch," Unicorn repeated.

"As do we all." Dragon sighed, agitating the liquid, erasing the scene of strife.

Dragon disappeared.

Tortoise grinned maliciously. "Suppose I chose to involve myself?"

"We're all involved." Unicorn stirred the water with a horn-tip, leaving a silvery sheen upon the troubled surface. "*They* involve us, whether we 'choose' to act or not. Yet it is all the same."

Unicorn vanished, as well.

Tortoise took a gray-green step toward Phoenix. "What about you? How about a game?"

"I've had enough of your games." Phoenix lifted his head and gave a ululating cry.

"You won't interfere with me, then? You promise?"

"Oh, yes. I promise." Phoenix rose into the air and was gone.

Tortoise gazed a while longer into the pool and then, with a slow blink of his orange eyes, faded away.

So there was no one to see the speck. It represented a man of small character and petty mind, a man of no more importance than a grain of sand. It fell into the silver swirl as a grain of sand might enter the shell of an oyster, and with the same results: irritation and the accrual of superior matter. But first, the speck.

The old woman stood in her doorway, one ear cocked toward the sound beneath the trees, and waited.

chapter 1
the roll-keeper's tale

Dreams of death and the bodies of the dead haunted him for fourteen years. The day he decided to go see the old woman, Darcy rose early, and the spirit of his child rode with him.

Elsie, he thought. *"Little" Elsie.* These days, Darcy thought often of Elsie. He thought of her as a child, curled up like a hedgehog, sleeping so deeply he wondered if she might never wake; or when she was eight, in her first long gown, charming His Grace's Chamberlain. And now: fourteen and marriageable; amber hair, brown eyes, pointed chin; spoiled by his own indulgence, trained in the skills of a manor-wife and a public scribe by his wife's insistence.

Darcy thought of another name now. The name of the old woman he was on his way to see, the one who lived in Fiddlewood. He remembered the first time he had ever heard of her, and the first time he had ever seen her. After Elsie's coming…. After his promotion and transfer to the capital…. It was ten years ago, but as clear as this morning.

Ten years ago, he had been only Deputy Roll-Keeper of the Unified Realm of Layounna. Not yet granted room in the royal stables for his horse, he walked the winding streets from his manor to the castle. It thrilled him, as it always did, to see the wooden palisade at the hub of the city, its gate lowered across the protective ditch, and know that he would enter as a titled official. Inside the wall of massive, sharpened logs, he crossed the bailey to one of the wooden structures which lined the palisade. He looked across at the steep rise of the earthen motte, at the inner palisade atop the rise, and at the wooden tower showing above.

The royal pennants snapped in the wind. Darcy felt his life justified at that moment.

He walked in on his superior's conversation with the Deputy Roll-Keeper from the Eastern District, walked in as casually as a man might take the first step onto quicksand. The ground seems firm; only after too many subsequent strides is the mis-step clear.

"Who counted her this time?" the Crown Roll-Keeper asked.

"A widow. Burll – her oldest boy – had a horrible wet cough for more than a month, and his mother went to her for a cure."

"Did it? Cure the boy?"

"Something did. I wouldn't like to say it wasn't her."

Darcy stroked his drooping blond moustache to hide an arch smile. He turned to his superior and winked a blue-gray eye.

The Crown Roll-Keeper either failed to pick up the condescending signals or chose not to return them. "This widow is known to you?" he asked the man. " Her word can be trusted?"

"Oh, yes, absolutely."

The Crown Roll-Keeper nodded and dismissed the man, while Darcy frowned and twitched the skirt of his robe to underline his disapproval.

When the man had left, Darcy asked, with a faint snicker, "Local hob-goblin?"

"Who?"

"'Her.'"

"You can laugh," the old man answered him sourly. "You haven't seen her. And I'd advise you not to, if you've got something on your conscience."

"As who has not," Darcy said weakly. Then: "But we can't count her like that – by hearsay. One of the Eastern District people must be made to identify her."

"They can be told to do it, but they can't be made. They would only count her by hearsay and lie about it. I'd rather take the word of an honest widow than a lying official, wouldn't you?"

He handed Darcy a sheaf of papers, his fingernail beneath one name.

"'Salvia Zglaria,'" Darcy read. "'Called Moder Zglaria.' – But that's wrong. No one has a name like that. It should read Salvia beren Moder or Salvia beren Zglaria. If she's a local matriarch, or very old, or the mistress of a baby farm, I can see her being called Moder Salvia. But Salvia Zglaria or Moder Zglaria – that doesn't make sense. That's like saying she was born of no mother, or she's her own mother, or she's mother of her own mother."

The old man shrugged. "There has always been a Moder Zglaria – a Salvia Zglaria – on Wild Ass Island in Fiddlewood River in the Fiddlewood. Always, since records have been kept. Longer, if oral history can be trusted. You're from Bahari, aren't you? That's not far from Fiddlewood – haven't you ever heard of her?"

Had he? It almost seemed he had, but had dismissed it as servant's prattle. After a pause, Darcy said, "That isn't the sort of thing I'd hear of, or take notice of if I heard it. It's nonsense."

The old man shook his head and tapped the papers in Darcy's hands. "Look at the records, back to the oldest. It's always been listed like that."

"It's nonsense," Darcy repeated. "Someone will go identify her under my administration, if I have to escort one of them myself."

By the next year, Darcy Aminta beren Valda was Chief Roll-Keeper of the realm of Layounna.

He appointed a new District Roll-Keeper in the Eastern District. He requested and received permission to ride with the new man to Pazni, to collect a handful of local villeins and see this "Salvia Zglaria" for himself.

The villeins protested. One offered to turn in her badge of office and find other employment.

"It isn't safe to work for the crown anymore," she said. "Why this new District Roll-Keeper? And what's become of Helena beren Marna?"

"She was inefficient," Darcy said. "She failed to follow proper counting procedure. She had to be replaced. As to what's become of her, I suppose she went elsewhere."

"You do, do you?" asked the woman. "And you suppose counting Moder Zglaria is as easy as counting anyone else."

"If she exists," said Darcy. "If she isn't one of many paper people on your District's Rolls. Paper people don't eat their bread allotment, do they? What would that extra bread buy out here near the Kozabir border? Mercenaries, perhaps?"

The villeins didn't like the way Darcy Aminta's mind was running. Not that Kozabirian mercenaries were on any of their shopping lists or that their Rolls were full of paper people, but it had been known for a death to go unreported for a month or two or for a still-born child to survive until the next official count.

"I'll go with you, and gladly," said the woman who had offered to resign. "I want to see this."

Others volunteered then. Darcy Aminta left the new District Roll-Keeper to look over the books and followed the villeins, on foot, into Fiddlewood.

The path was narrow and faint. Leaves and twigs crackled under the delegation's feet. Crows screamed and flapped, and other birds too swift to be seen shot deeper into the woods, making enough noise in their passage for so many bears.

"I always thought the woods were quiet," said Darcy.

Nobody answered him.

When they reached the river, the woods simply stopped where the land dropped off.

"The tide's not out yet," one of the villeins, a man, said. "Should we wait half an hour, or wade?"

Darcy was wearing his riding boots. "Wade," he said.

"Let him through," said the man.

The villeins stepped aside.

Darcy Aminta saw that the path didn't end at the river bank, but continued at a gentle slant into the water. He could see the narrow bridge of land now just under the water's surface. Twice in twenty-four hours, the bridge would be exposed.

On the other end of the path was Wild Ass Island, about three miles from end to end.

"The maps say it's a quarter of a mile across at the north," said the man at Darcy's elbow. "Tapers to a point at the south like it was pointing at the capital."

The island was rimmed, at least on this eastern side, with cedar trees and brush.

"It looks uninhabited," said Darcy.

"She lives there," one of the villeins said.

"Let's go see." When the others hesitated, looking from the watery bridge to their own skirts, hose, and low wooden clogs, he said, "Now."

Darcy led the way across and into the stand of cedar. There was hardly more than a double line of trees, then a small clearing populated by geese and goats. A covered well stood in the clearing; on the far side was a low stone hut. A cream-colored goat lay in the shade chewing a mouthful of something. Honey bees hovered and darted, ignoring the meaningless humans.

The livestock braced themselves at first sight of the intruders, then the goats bleated in rude chorus. One black and tan let out a "maaaa" like the blast of a horn. The geese spread their wings and hissed, advancing, heads forward, to do bloody battle.

Darcy led his troupe no further; he nearly stepped on them, backing up.

Then the door opened and the old woman stood in the doorway.

"Moder Zglaria," said the woman who had threatened to resign.

Moder Zglaria was draped and swaddled in shapeless black clothing. Her hair was twisted up in a black and white scarf tied in a knot over her forehead. She held a blackthorn stick in one hand, leaning on it, and a long-stemmed clay pipe in the other. She was white, whiter than Darcy, a color-less white, like an albino. But she wasn't an albino; even from across the clearing, Darcy could see the shocking blue of her eyes. This blue, with a tinge of green.... It was like a candle burning behind aqua glass; alive and clear and fiery. And it focused on him.

The old woman spread her pale lips, showing teeth so broad and blunt Darcy couldn't tell her canines from her incisors. She made a sound, and the livestock wavered and relaxed. The geese gave final honks and shuffled their feathers back into peaceful alignment. The goats resumed feeding.

"There's a lot of you," she said, in a voice like sand over stone. "Come in."

The others waited for Darcy to move first. "Geese can bite," he said, to cover his hesitation. His heart thudded, and his palms were wet. They prickled, and so did his scalp and his armpits; they prickled to the point of pain.

He forced down his reaction. He had forced down worse.

The inside of the hut was surprisingly bright. There were windows in two of the walls, covered in oiled skins that were worn to near transparency with age.

Moder Zglaria sat on a stool near the smoldering hearth. She pointed with the stem of her pipe to a stone bench that ran between the hearth wall and the door.

"Room for all of you there," she rasped, "if you're friendly."

The villeins sat. Darcy looked down at her, his long white-blond hair falling around his bony face. "I am Darcy Aminta beren Valda," he said. "Chief Roll-Keeper of the realm of Layounna, by the authority of His Grace, Landry Oliva beren Ada. Your name?"

"Salvia Zglaria," the old woman said.

"What sort of a name is that? That's no proper name." Darcy heard the villeins protesting his tone, his words.

"It's no sort of a name," said the old woman. "It's mine. And, as for proper, at least I'm entitled to it, which is more than I could say for some."

"What do you mean?"

The old woman drew on her pipe and let out a cloud of aromatic smoke along with the word, "Nothing."

"I'll mark you down by the name you've given me. You'll be counted every year after this, personally, by one of the local Roll-Keepers. Do you understand?"

Moder Zglaria flicked her gaze down the row on the stone bench, and back up the row of puddles around their wet underpinnings. "I do."

"If they fail His Grace the Kinninger, I'll be back. Do you understand that?"

"You'll be back," said Moder Zglaria.

"These locals may be afraid of you, but I am not."

Moder Zglaria took another draw on her pipe and said, through the smoke, "Afraid of me? You're afraid of my geese."

The villeins coughed and tucked their mouths into their collars.

Darcy decided it was time to go.

His exit was spoiled by the villeins, who rose and filed out the door ahead of him, leaving him the sole object of Moder Zglaria's attention.

"Now you know my name, Darcy Aminta beren Valda," the old woman said. "And I know yours."

~*~

She knew his name: born Darcy beren Aminta, married to Devona beren Valda, now called Darcy Aminta beren Valda. Heartily and often, he wished he had left the old woman a disembodied name in the Rolls.

Many times, after that meeting, he woke from a nightmare to find her name on his lips. Sometimes he came across it while hunting for another. Then a picture of the old woman would rise in vision before him – tall, stout-boned, thick-skinned, raspy-voiced, with eyes like azure scorpions and a tongue like a rawhide whip, always thrusting at him with the knot of her turban or her blackthorn cane or the stem of her clay pipe. She would rise, fixing him with a glare of savage understanding, leaving him drenched in salt sweat, leaving him weak and with all his sins scoured off him. He could almost sense the mind of her out in the woods, knowing his knowing her name, and he'd have tricked himself into forgetting it, but he clutched it as a man adrift would clutch a floating coffin.

And now, ten years after that first visit, he stood once more on the bank of Fiddlewood River, telling himself he was waiting for the tide to go out, although he wore his riding boots again.

He was alone, this time; what he had to say must have no witnesses.

The tide went out, and Darcy crossed to the island. The trees were the same, the clearing was the same, the bees hummed and buzzed as before; a different goat lay in the shade, that was all.

Moder Zglaria stood at the well, drawing water.

"You're just in time to be useful, Darcy Aminta beren Valda," she said. "Here's something to prove your worth."

Darcy flinched.

"The water, Darcy Aminta," said the old woman.

"The water?"

"Fetch in my water."

Darcy took the well's bucket and emptied it into two earthenware jugs. Moder Zglaria plugged them with rags and cinched the bucket up close to the crossbar.

"Carry those in, if you please, My Lord Roll-Keeper."

Darcy followed with the jugs and held them until she came and put them on the table.

He said nothing. He stood under the old woman's gaze as a man with no shelter might stand under a stinging rain, and clung to his dignity as such a man might cling to a sodden cloak.

"Thirsty?" the old woman asked. "Throat a little dry?"

"No. Yes. Yes."

The old woman took two wooden tumblers from a shelf and brought them, both in one big hand, to the table.

"You pour," she said. "Then sit."

Darcy poured carefully, but he spilled some despite himself.

He took a stool across from Moder Zglaria. She dragged her hearth stool up by the toe of one black leather half-boot, sat, and lit her pipe.

"Ten years ago," he said, then stopped.

"Ten years ago," the old woman said, "something happened."

Darcy's blood rushed from his face to his heart. His very hands felt numb. "How did you know?"

"All I know is that you have something you want to tell."

"Why would I want to tell you anything?"

Moder Zglaria shrugged. "People do," she said. "Don't, if you've changed your mind. It isn't as if I'm interested. You came to me."

She started to rise.

"Wait," said Darcy, almost touching her wrist to keep her. "Ten years ago…."

Moder Zglaria sat back down and leaned her elbows on the table. Darcy could see some of her hair, escaped from the turban. It was red – dark red, almost black.

"A terrible thing happened…," Moder prompted.

"A terrible thing," said Darcy. "Our child, Elsie, took a sudden fever. She convulsed. She died. She was only four." Hot tears ran from Darcy's eyes; he let them fall, scarcely noticing that he wept. He took no shuddering breaths and gave no sobs; all his effort went into his speaking. "I hardly knew her. …I was busy. I was only a District Roll-Keeper then, but I meant to do better for myself. I didn't have time for the child; that was her mother's job. That same night…. The same night she died…."

Moder Zglaria smoked in silence.

Darcy took a gulp of the well-cold water. "A man came to the house. One of the Kinninger's Swords. He was hooded; his face was deep in shadow. 'It's time to make yourself useful, Darcy Aminta,' was what he said. 'Come prove your worth.' The words you spoke to me outside, just now…."

Darcy raised his eyes from the table to Moder Zglaria's face. Her gaze followed the curl of smoke from her pipe; she seemed unimpressed by the echo.

"So," Darcy went on, after a heartbeat, "I saddled my horse and rode with him, out of town, toward the Inland Sea."

"Leaving your wife…."

"Alone, with the corpse of our daughter, with the heat of the fever still in it."

"You'll go far under Landry Oliva," said Moder. "You were made to serve the House of Sarpa." She ignored his clenched fists and prompted him, "And then…."

"We rode till we came to a horse-drawn wagon, half-hidden by the side of the road.

"'There's cargo in the back,'" the Sword said. "'Drive it to Lands End Point and throw it over. Keep the cart and horse. You'll need them, when your transfer comes through. Your promotion, I should say. Kinninger Landry Oliva beren Ada forgets no one, neither friend nor enemy.'

"The man turned his horse and galloped away. I tied my horse to the rear of the wagon. I drove to the Point, above the Inland Sea. The light was dim, but I saw that the wagon was filled with wooden barrels; thirty-six in all."

"You didn't wonder what was in them?"

"Of course I did, but it was none of my business. I wouldn't have been asked to dispose of them this way, in the middle of the night…."

"If there hadn't been something wrong about it?"

"If my Kinninger hadn't trusted my discretion," Darcy said stiffly.

"Discretion," the old woman muttered, and watched another curl of smoke.

Darcy watched it, too. When it had disappeared, he went on.

"I expected the barrels to be heavy, but they weren't. They felt nearly empty. When I rapped them, they even sounded nearly empty. There was something in each of them, though; I could feel the weight shift as I rolled them out of the wagon and off the Point. They were old – still strong, but with pin holes and hairline cracks. They smelled…sweet and bitter at once, and some…of urine and…body soil."

Darcy fell silent.

"You weren't tempted to open one? What would make such a smell, do you think?"

Darcy was still. When he spoke, he said, "Finally, there were only two. The moon was still up, though it was low in the sky. The sun was just below the horizon, there was a mist rising from the sea, and the air glowed pearl gray. I tripped on my way back from the edge and fell, with my hand on a pointed stone."

"Lucky you didn't trip on the way," said Moder Zglaria. "You might have gone over, yourself."

"There was nothing to trip me on the way. A big tortoise had crawled into my path; that's what I tripped on."

The corners of Moder's mouth turned up, her eyes narrowed, and she grunted what seemed to be a laugh.

"Why is that funny?" Darcy asked.

"To think how something so slow could be so troublesome," she said. "Go on."

Darcy took another drink of water. He would rather not go on. He would rather forget the rest. But the rest was what he had come to tell.

"I picked up the pointed stone and broke into one of the barrels."

The cottage was silent, except for the crackle of the hearth-fire.

"He was dead," said Darcy Aminta, staring across Moder's room into the flames. "There was a bit of rag tied around his face. That was what I had smelled: something on the rag and his – what he couldn't hold in. I untied the rag, but he was dead. He was blue."

Darcy looked at the old woman, as if his pain made her eyes safe to meet. "He was only a baby. Less than a year, I'd say. Naked, and dead."

"Strangled? Cut?"

"No, nothing. I think it was the rag that killed him. Something on it to make him sleep, I think, to keep him quiet until it was too late. So I wouldn't hear him cry. So I'd throw him off the Point for them, and never know what I'd done."

Moder Zglaria blew a mouthful of smoke toward the ceiling. "Him?" she said.

Darcy took more water. "Or them. There may have been a child in each of those containers. Thirty-six of them. And some of them may have been alive. I threw them into the sea." He gasped as if he were about to sob, but mastered his breathing. "There may have been only the two, and the boy was dead when I found him."

"Yes, there were two. Go on."

"I was afraid of the other, but I opened it. There was a girl in it, huddled in a ball. She had torn the rag away, but she was deep in sleep. Naked, like the boy. Older."

"About four? The age of your daughter?"

"…They were right about you."

"Everybody's right about something. Go on."

"I left the boy's body in the barrel. I took the girl out, and threw those last two containers over the Point. I wrapped the girl in my cloak and put her in the cart and took her home."

"And gave her to your wife. She was delighted, of course. She forgot all about the dead child you'd left her to mourn alone, and blessed you for this one."

Darcy didn't bother to contradict such ponderous sarcasm.

"We buried our little Elsie in the garden, before the sun was well up. I never told Devona where I'd been, or where the child had come from. I only told her we had it in our power to save a life that had been lost, that we owed it to our Elsie. She agreed. We called the child Elsie beren Devona. We kept her 'in quarantine' until my promotion came through: I was promoted to Deputy Crown Roll-Keeper, transferred to Kudasad, with a house in the very shadow of the Kinninger's castle."

"That must have given you a nasty shock," said the old woman.

"It *was* a shock," he said. "At first, I didn't see what was to be done. I almost told Devona – my wife – everything."

"But you did not."

"No."

"Not surprising. A woman who would hide the death of her baby for the sake of another woman's child, simply because it lived…. She'd think nothing of expecting a man to throw over a choice promotion to keep that child safe. No point in even asking her."

Darcy scanned Moder's face for a trace of understanding or scorn, but found only blandness wreathed in smoke.

"By the time we received notice to relocate," said Darcy, warily, as a dog approaches a bone in the presence of a man with a stick, "I was clearer in my mind. I keep my own counsel, and make my own decisions."

Moder only nodded.

"The child's memories – which we told her were fever dreams – didn't indicate contact with royalty. I decided she and… and the others… were the children of rebellious serfs or… disloyal…."

Not even Darcy could go on.

"In short," said Moder Zglaria, "you decided the reward was worth the risk and took the transfer. The child could always be jettisoned if necessary. She'd be no worse off, in that case, than she would have been if you hadn't opened the cask."

"…True." The word was barely audible, as if it had been dragged through Darcy's lips by a power just barely stronger than his will to keep it back. This was his greatest torment. This was the blackest spot in his soul: that he had saved and raised and cosseted the child, all the while willing to sacrifice her to his own safety whenever that seemed necessary.

"And you've lived in the shadow of the castle for ten years," Moder said at last. "The girl is fourteen, and marriageable, and within the Kinninger's notice, and he's done ten years of mourning – if you want to call it that – mourning the loss of Kinninger Karol beren Ada. He feels secure on the throne, now, and he's ready to remarry."

In defense of his liege, Darcy said, "Karol beren Ada is dead. She left no heirs."

"You should know," said Moder. "But you were saying –"

"What do you mean, I should know?" Darcy's voice grew shrill.

"You're the Crown Roll-Keeper. There should be thirty-six children missing from your books – or two, if it pleases you to think so. Were you too loyal to see what children had disappeared from the roll-books?"

"There were none."

"Ah," said Moder. "Go on."

"His Grace does wish to remarry. He doesn't want a Thane, or a Thane's daughter –"

"Can't say I blame him: He's a Thane's son, and he knows what came of Karol's marrying him."

"– and he doesn't want to ally himself with a foreign throne –"

"Because this time he wants control of his wife and her offspring."

"How can you say these things?" said Darcy Aminta. "How can you know these things?"

"I'm old," said Moder Zglaria. "Not stupid. So Landry Oliva beren Ada looks to you to make yourself useful again."

Darcy dropped his gaze. "He wants to marry Elsie."

Moder lowered her pipe to the table between them. Smoke rose in curls and tendrils, blown like the mane of a running horse up and across the divide, from her hand to Darcy's head. She said, "He wants to marry a girl he hired you to kill. The girl is probably the child of an enemy. She could even be an heir of his wife's body. An heir of…?"

"Landry's?" Darcy shook his head. This interchange – this impossible interchange – came to his ears as if from a distance. Neither he nor the old woman was actually, audibly suggesting that Landry Oliva had murdered the heirs to the throne. It wasn't possible that such a thing had been done. It wasn't possible he, himself, had connived in it, and it was utterly impossible to speak of it. Still, from that distance, he heard his voice say, "If Karol had a child-sire, it wasn't Landry Oliva beren Ada. Those at the court during

Karol's time concur on that, in their gossip and in their insinuations."

The old woman raised her pipe to her mouth and blew smoke toward the hearth. "So the Kinninger wants to marry your so-called daughter. And you object? Darcy Aminta, you surprise me."

Darcy drew a deep breath and sighed it out. "She no longer remembers anything before she woke with us. As I said, we've always told her it was the fever, that sometimes people can't remember afterwards, or they remember their fever dreams as if they were real."

"A clever use of one tragedy to mask another. But, if she married the Kinninger…."

"She might hear something, or see something, or meet someone who would bring it all back. She might remember at last what happened before she lost consciousness."

"And she might suffer?"

"She might tell."

"Ah, well, there would go your promotion, I'm afraid."

"How can you make light of this?"

"It isn't my problem, you see. What does your wife think?"

"I haven't asked her. She still knows nothing about that night, or where Elsie came from. She… hardly speaks to me anymore."

"Has she a business? Or is being wife of His Grace's Roll-Keeper enough for her?"

"She's a scribe. A public scrivener. Copies documents, writes and reads letters for those who can't, copies books, sometimes."

"A clever woman. But she pays you no attention?"

"I didn't say that. She pays me great attention. She wears these spectacles. She's little, with brown hair and large brown eyes, and these spectacles, and she's always watching, always listening. It's like living with an owl."

Moder rose and went to the hearth, knocked her pipe out into her hand, and threw the dottle into the fire. She packed her pipe with a fresh load of tobacco.

"Why did you come here, Darcy Aminta? What do you want?"

"I want you to help me. Stop the marriage, with no danger to me or my career."

"Or your wife or your child?"

Darcy fluttered an impatient hand. "Yes, of course."

"What makes you think I can help?" the old woman asked.

Darcy had no answer. "You can," he said.

Moder Zglaria stuck the end of a straw twist into the fire and lit her pipe with it. "Let me think," she said. She sat again, and smoked, while Darcy Aminta turned his tumbler in his hands.

"You wouldn't consider throwing it all away – tell your wife everything, take your family and leave Layounna altogether?"

Darcy blinked slowly, at a momentary loss. "Of course not."

Moder nodded.

"Do you have a garden?" she asked at last.

"Yes, several: a kitchen garden, a flower garden, and an herbal."

Moder nodded again. "Are any of them walled?"

Puzzled, Darcy said, "They're divided by low walls, yes; walls about as high as my chest. There's a high wall around the manor – Why?"

"Privacy. Here's what you must do: Pick a garden, any one will do. Go into it – the same one – just at sunset, every day for a week, and tell what you've just told me."

"Tell it to Devona?"

"If you choose; that would be best, but tell it to the air, if you won't tell her. – Do you keep bees?"

"…Yes. My wife does."

"Then tell the bees. The bees will hear you. Listen to them hum. You'll hear your answer in your heart."

After a moment of silence, Darcy thrust himself out of his seat, kicked away his stool and threw his tumbler toward the fire. He missed, and it bounced back to roll at his feet.

"You fraud!" he shouted. "I came to you for help!"

"Uninvited," said the old woman. "Do it or don't, it's up to you."

"Folk tales! Children's fancies!"

"What did you expect – magic? You should have gone to a Tarkastrian adept, if you wanted that."

Darcy left without another word or backward look. Fuming, he waded across the causeway. Fuming, he claimed his horse from the District Roll-Keeper in Pazni, thundered south, and reached home about sundown two days later. He would have ridden through day and night, but thrift dictated he rest his only horse.

Both Devona and Elsie rushed out to meet him when he clattered into the manor court.

Elsie threw her arms around Darcy's neck. "I'm glad you're back. What did you bring me?"

Distracted, eyes on the low wall and the arch which led to the gardens, Darcy patted Elsie's head.

"Nothing this trip, my pet." Responding to the pout he didn't have to see to know was there, he went on, "But you shall have a new ribbon, as long and fine as this will buy," and drew a coin from the purse at his waist.

Elsie squealed and hugged him again, showed the coin to her mother, and ran into the manor.

"Dinner –" Devona began, but Darcy motioned the talk away.

"Begin without me, if it's ready. I'll be in…later."

"I'll see Jehan's made comfortable."

Darcy nodded. He felt Devona's stare, felt it leave him as he heard Jehan's weary hoofs strike the court's paving.

Tell it out again. He had hardly been able to tell it once. Listen to the bees. What a stupid idea! A rustic notion his family had scorned and mocked, even in the provinces. Yet the gardens drew him.

The kitchen garden? No, cabbages and turnips were too common for Darcy's trouble. The flowers? Prettiness was offensive, with such a story to relate. That left the herbs. The herbs; curative, wholesome, pungent…. That seemed right.

He threaded the paths and archways to the herbal garden. Then he sank to his knees on the gravel path, clenched his hands in his lap, averted his face, and talked. He told the tale straight through, with none of the interruptions and side-trackings that had so disturbed him when he'd told the old woman. Around him rose the odors of sage and rosemary, of the creeping thyme he'd crushed in kneeling. Around him, leaves and stems whispered against each other, stirred by a soft breeze. A bee buzzed over the daisy-like chamomile and a hummingbird hovered among the scarlet spikes of bergamot. Below the bushes, Elsie's tortoiseshell cat stretched and purred. A blue-tailed lizard basked in the last rays of the sun. And Darcy talked.

When he was done, he listened. He could hear nothing – no sound of bees. He raised his eyes to the straw hives, ten of them in niches built into the back wall of the manor house. A straggler flew into one, another into another. Of course…they would be homing at sunset. He listened harder and heard – or thought he heard – the communal buzz of swarms gathering themselves in the darkness.

He felt light; lighter than he had for years. Perhaps this had been good advice, after all. Perhaps nothing could stop the marriage; still, with a clear head, perhaps he could see himself through.

He could hold to the "fever" explanation. Any memories the new "Elsie" might bring up were certain to be muddled; he would explain them away somehow. If Devona told the truth? She would not. She would stand by him. This recognition of her loyalty twinged his conscience.

In the night, he woke to doubt. He couldn't sleep again; the next day, he couldn't attend properly to his work. He stayed late in the bailey to catch up, and came home as the sun touched the horizon.

Elsie rushed out to show him what she had bought with his coin.

He hardly saw her, barely heard her. "Later," he said, and went to the garden like a young man to a lover, to kneel among the plants and spicy odors.

The next day was better, but the fourth, when he was kept till sunset looking up information for Rhu beren Robia, Landry Oliva's Chamberlain, he thought he would go mad. Whenever he was in Devona's presence, Darcy felt her eyes on him, peering at him through her round spectacles as if the words he spoke in the garden lingered around him, as if they were a scent she could see and read.

On the eighth day, he received a notice summoning him to present his daughter, Elsie, to the castle. The date named was less than a week away.

Devona beren Valda took the note and double-checked the address. When the Kinninger had first broached the match to Darcy, Devona had sniffed and said, "When did it become proper to propose to a woman's father, not to the woman or her mother?" Now, she said, "Directed to you, indeed. Our new Kinninger does things differently."

"Careful, woman," said Darcy. "The Kinninger may do as he pleases."

"Yes, of course," said Devona, and closed her mouth very tightly. Then she said, "I'll be the one to tell her, at least. The Kinninger doesn't dictate what's proper in our private house, as yet."

"Yes, all right." Darcy felt once more out of his depth and short of control.

~*~

Suddenly, his pampered daughter was as removed from him as his wife had long been. Elsie, having been informed of the Kinninger's intentions toward her, took to her room, and would see no one but her mother.

When he asked if the girl objected to the marriage, Devona said, "On the contrary. The honor overwhelms her. She's eager to be off."

On the morning Elsie was to be presented to His Grace, Darcy was kept waiting while Devona closeted herself with the girl. Below, in the sitting room, Darcy's fatherly advice fermented within him until he was dizzy with it. At last Devona led the bride out of her chamber and down the stairs, just as the time came to leave.

Elsie was lovely. Her rippling amber hair was too coarse to stay neatly in a formal dressing, but a silver net held it scooped away from her long brown face. Her lips were unnaturally red; Devona must have stained them somehow. She wore a gown of black, covered with a tunic of white interwoven with silver, bound in at her waist with a sash of black silk.

"Black!" Darcy cried. "You've dressed the child in black! It isn't a funeral she's going to, it's a bridal!"

"It's her richest gown," said Devona. "When did you ever see a funeral gown covered with a tunic of silver? When did anyone go to a funeral with a net of silver filigree on her hair? Besides, black suits her."

Elsie beren Devona fluttered long eyelashes, making Darcy laugh.

"Well, so it does," Darcy agreed.

Devona and Elsie embraced with nervous smiles. Devona pressed the girl's hand.

"I wish you well," she said. "I'll see you soon."

"Very soon," said Elsie. She turned to Darcy. "Shall we go?"

A hired chair – open, so all of Kudasad could see the Chief Roll-Keeper taking his daughter to be the Kinninger's bride – took them to the castle. On the way, Darcy held Elsie's hand, which lay unresponsively in his, and uncorked the platitudes he'd bottled up all morning.

The palisade gate was down for the day, bridging the ditch around the castle grounds. Darcy and his "daughter" were carried across into the bailey. There they left the chair and were greeted by Rhu beren Robia, the Kinninger's Chamberlain.

"Welcome, Elsie beren Devona." He was a tall man, broad-shouldered, with high cheekbones and hollowed cheeks, as dark as Darcy was light, as taciturn as Darcy was eloquent. His crooked smile was obviously forced, on this supposedly festive occasion, and even Darcy noticed that he didn't look straight at Elsie when he spoke to her. "Our castle will be sweetened by your presence in it."

"Thank you, Rhu beren Robia," said Elsie. "I hope so, although my presence will be brief."

Rhu beren Robia cast a sharp look at Darcy.

"I thought it best not to tell her," Darcy said.

"You did?" The Chamberlain's smooth, rich voice sounded diplomatically bland, his face looked diplomatically blank.

Darcy felt his moustache tickle as a faint sweat broke out on his upper lip. "Tell me what, Father?"

Rhu beren Robia answered. "First, let me say that the death of Karol beren Ada was a terrible blow to His Grace. If she had kept to the castle – *been* kept to it, if necessary, she might be alive today. If she had taken her Consort, Landry Oliva, for her child-sire – been *made* to take him, if need be, there would be an heir on the throne today."

"So I may not return to my home after the bridal," said Elsie. "I may not return to my home…ever?"

Darcy Aminta put an arm around the girl's slender shoulders and squeezed a bit. "For a visit, someday, surely. When the throne is secured for His Grace's line – and yours. You'll have a House, too, my dear; as Kinninger's Consort, you'll surely be given a Household."

He looked at the Chamberlain, hoping to hear that, in fact, *he*, Darcy, would be given the Household, with Elsie descending from it. No such promise came forth. No promise came forth at all. The Chamberlain's face remained impassive.

"My mother was afraid of this," said Elsie. "She said there was no other reason for the Kinninger to marry the child of a minor official."

Darcy didn't like that "minor," still less the emphasis with which Elsie had said it.

"She was wrong, there," said Rhu, looking at her directly for the first time. "Your beauty would be reason enough."

Elsie smiled and fluttered her eyelashes at him.

"Shall we proceed?" said Darcy.

They walked up the steep incline of the earthen motte, through the lowered gate of the tower palisade, and up the stairs into the great hall of the tower itself.

There, they were met by the Chief Sword, Guthrie beren Melanell. Four of his men stood behind him; they were all dressed in black boots, hose, and tunics, shirts of polished mail and sword belts of black leather.

"Welcome, Elsie beren Devona," said Guthrie. "My honor guard will escort you to your chamber."

"Where is His Grace?" Darcy asked. "The bridal…."

"The woman will wait on His Grace's convenience. You may go."

"But—"

"His Grace's orders. Leave her and go." The Chief Sword turned to Elsie and motioned toward a door in the corner of the room. "Up those stairs. All the way."

There was a sheen of moisture on Elsie's face, but she kissed her father's cheek and nodded to Rhu beren Robia. With the four armed Swords behind her, she passed through the door in the corner of the room and up the tightly spiraling staircase beyond.

Darcy wondered if he had seen the last of his foster daughter. He was surprised at the pang the thought caused him.

"You have His Grace's thanks, Darcy Aminta beren Valda," said Guthrie. "Your obedience will not go unrewarded."

"No reward was thought of," said Darcy. "And none is required."

Rhu beren Robia's lips twitched. "Your selflessness on His Grace's behalf is inspiring," he said.

A shout from the staircase stopped all talk. Five Swords – and no Elsie – burst into the hall.

One of them made himself heard above the babble: "She's gone!"

"Gone!" said the Chief Sword. "Gone where?"

"Disappeared! Vanished, with a flash!"

"It's true!" said another Sword, an older man with streaks of silver in his hair. "I was coming down the stairs as they were coming up. Just as the girl turned into my sight – flash!"

Rhu beren Robia turned to the castle steward, who stood near the door to the first-floor storeroom.

"Round up as many villeins as you can quickly," he said. "Search this tower from turret to cellar. Let no Sword interfere with you."

The Swords looked to their Chief, who nodded.

"This is none of my men's doing," he said. "This is some sorcery."

The older Sword stepped forward. "Shall I search the girl's home?" he asked.

"You are…?" asked Guthrie.

"Jehan beren Marcia," said the Sword, with a slight lift to an eyebrow, as if to say, *don't you remember*? "Promotion and transfer from the Southern district."

"Ah, yes."

"Shall I go, sir?"

The Chamberlain nodded.

"Good man," said the Chief Sword. "Yes, go."

The Sword left at a trot.

"This is impossible!" said Darcy, his voice rising to a shout. "They've killed her! My innocent child!" Then his mouth clamped shut.

For she wasn't his innocent child. What did he know of her, after all, but that His Grace had wanted her dead? Perhaps those hadn't been children he'd thrown into the sea but Creatures of Power. Perhaps he hadn't murdered....

Darcy breathed thanks he had shared his secret with no one. No one but the old woman of Fiddlewood.

A honey bee buzzed through the hall, circled Darcy's head, and flew away to the north.

chapter 2
the false consort

Fourteen-year-old Karol beren Ada sat by her mother's bed. On the wall above the bedstead hung the device of the House of Onagros: A sprig of Clary sage in its proper colors of green with pink-tipped white flowers, upon a blue field. The bedstead was carved with the same device and painted with the same merry colors, muted now in sickroom dimness. Her Grace, Kinninger Ada beren Cinnie, was dying and Karol, as was her right as elder daughter and heir to the throne, attended her.

Karol beren Ada had grown to look much as her mother had at the same age – a woman's age of fourteen. Dark brown curls tumbled over her shoulders, glinting with red highlights where it hung free, glowing dully in braids on either side of her heart-shaped face.

She had wept herself temporarily dry, and now listened with apparent dispassion to her mother's reminiscences.

"Your father – may he rest in the peace at the heart of the Way… he was all the man I ever wanted or needed. My consort, my child-sire, my friend…."

"I know," Karol said.

"You know, you know!" said the dying woman pettishly. "Do you know that I've mourned him these twelve years since his death?"

"Yes, Moder," said Karol patiently.

"Do you know that I've been faithful to his memory?"

"Yes, Moder."

"Well, I haven't."

Patience and apathy alike dropped from Karol's face and manner.

The Kinninger's petulance melted. "I shouldn't have put it like that," she said. "It was cruel. Forgive me?"

The younger woman took her mother's hand, so frail now, so sturdy months ago. "Of course. It was a lie, then?"

The Kinninger shook her head. "True. But cruelly spoken. Let me say it again, more gently." She drew a long breath, collecting her strength. "Seven years ago, in Agra, a small village in the Southern Province, I met a man, a widower, named Gils Nara beren Ailith. A silversmith. He and his son, Cameron beren Osa – a boy about your age, a little older – brought me some trinkets as a gift of the village."

She smiled, and rubbed a thumb along the raised markings of a silver ring she wore on her index finger. "It was a brief presentation but, in the time it took, something about Gils Nara touched the deepest places in my heart. I returned to the village soon, then again. I began to leave more of the affairs of state in the hands of my Chamberlain, and to spend more time 'among the people'; that is, in retreat with Gils Nara."

"Secretly? Why secretly?"

"When you fall in love, you'll know. For a time, you want your love all to yourself. Not just the man, but the feeling itself seems too precious to share with anyone. That would have passed, in time…. But there wasn't time."

"What happened?"

Ada beren Cinnie turned a palm up on her blanket and moved her hand in an attempt at a sweeping gesture. "This."

"Does he know? About your illness?"

"I'm sure the word has reached him."

"And he hasn't come?"

The Kinninger's eyes shone in the candle-light. "I told him if anything ever happened to me I would send you with a message. Will you go?"

Karol again took her mother's hand. "You needn't ask. You know I'll go. Gils Nara beren Ailith, in Agra, in the Southern Province. The message?"

"Tell him I love him."

"He knows that, but I'll tell him."

"Tell him to keep the child by him."

"The child?" Karol beren Ada stroked her mother's hand. "If he's older than I, he's hardly a child."

"Not that child. *Our* child. My child by Gils Nara."

Karol's grip nearly tightened, but didn't.

Ada's cold fingers twitched, as if they felt her daughter's checked impulse. "He's five years old, now. A beautiful child."

"How could you – How could you hide that? It isn't…."

A trace of smugness touched the dying woman's face. "No one ever knew. No one even suspected."

"How? Why?"

"How? Loose, bulky clothing, a Kinninger's right of privacy, a long retreat away from the capital – it's easily done. It's been commonly done. Look to your history again: I'm the first Kinninger in many generations to keep all my chicks in one coop."

"Almost all."

"His name is Kinnan. Kinnan beren Ada. I visit him as an aunt, under a false name. He has a false name, too – the name of his half-brother's mother. Look after him – but quietly. See that he never wants. Leave him with his father. He'll serve you better, when he comes of age, if he knows the people from the inside out. Will you do this?"

"I will. Does Sorcha know?"

"If I didn't tell the elder, why would I tell the younger?" said Ada, querulous again. "No, Sorcha doesn't know. Tell her or not, as you think best. Now, call my ladies back in. Call them in. I'm tired."

~*~

If there was talk about the heir's retreat in the Southern Province during her mother's final illness, none of it reached the castle.

She found Gils Nara easily, and he was much as Karol expected: a handsome man, physically powerful, with delicate hands. He wept openly when he saw Karol, because he knew her at once and because his beloved Ada had not forgotten her promise to him.

The child, Kinnan, was much as Karol expected, as well. He had Ada's curls and was as slender as Karol's sister – his half-sister – Sorcha, had been at his age. He had his father's gray eyes and somewhat outsized nose.

He bowed to the lady, and stared boldly into her face, but left without a backward glance when Gils Nara sent him outside to gather herbs for the supper pot.

Karol longed to take him with her.

Cameron beren Osa, however, was not what she expected, at all. He was large, like his father, and well-muscled, but he looked more like a soldier than a silversmith. In fact, he had spent some years in the militia. He had scars on his face and arms, and a nose that had been broken at least once.

Karol longed to take him, too.

She left both sons with their father, and returned to her mother's bedside.

Within a month, the Kinninger was dead, and Karol beren Ada ascended the throne.

~*~

After a year's mourning, Karol's grandmotherly Chamberlain advised taking a consort. So the still-new Kinninger retreated to the south, "to think it over."

Gils Nara beren Ailith looked much older than he had a year earlier. He had lost flesh, his smile had gone watery, and his work took longer to complete to his satisfaction.

"It's been a long time," he said. "Not that I blame you. I'm nothing to you."

"You're my mother's last love," said Karol. "That makes you something to me. Something most dear."

"Well," said Gils Nara. "Well…. You haven't come for my boy, have you, Your Grace?"

Her heart leapt, but she said, "Don't 'Grace' me, Gils Nara. I'm 'Karol' to you and yours. No, I haven't come for the boy, although I want to see him. I've brought him a present."

"Too much will spoil him, Your – Karol. He isn't to know of his birth, yet."

"I know. Look, and tell me if this would spoil him."

Karol unwrapped a bronze spiral. Outlines of birds were beaten into the metal; behind them they drew long tails, or possibly trails of fire. "May he wear this bracelet, for the sake of his…aunt, who hopes to pay him visits now and then?"

"Of course." Gils Nara took the bracelet in his hands. "Lovely work," he said. "Lovely."

"It was part of a chest of trinkets sent from Kozabir in honor of my birthday."

"Is the writing Kozabirian, then?" He showed her the line of script running the length of the bracelet's inner side.

Karol smiled. "Yes. I chose the present for the inscription. It says, 'I am here when you need me.'" Karol touched the bracelet. "The spiral can be unwound as he grows. I'd like to watch the turns unraveling for many years with you."

"I'd like that, too. – But you'll be wanting to see him now. He's out in back, with Cameron. I'll show you the way." He handed her the gift. "You give it to him."

They found Cameron beren Osa teaching his six-year-old half-brother the art of armed defense. He lowered a staff – slowly, but too quickly for Karol beren Ada's taste – toward the child's head. Kinnan raised his little stick and blocked it. He never tired, and he never flinched.

Cameron saw the guest, and stopped the practice.

"You're a brave boy, Kinnan beren Osa," said Karol, using the name they had agreed to give the boy. "But, of course, you know your brother wouldn't hurt you."

Kinnan brandished his stick. "Let him try!" he roared, and Karol laughed.

The boy loved his bracelet, so much so that he even remembered to thank Karol for giving it to him. It thrilled him to have something from exotic Kozabir, a land on the northern border of his country, as far from home as any place imaginable.

Gils Nara took him into the house, and Karol was alone with Cameron.

"It's good to see you again," he said. He sat on an upended bucket and motioned Karol to a weatherworn wooden bench nearby. "I've drunk your health many a time at the tavern."

"But you don't call me 'Your Grace.'" Karol pointed out.

"I do at the tavern. Should I now?"

"Call me Karol," she said.

"I liked your mother," Cameron said. "You look like her. I miss her visits." Cameron glanced toward the house. "It's been very hard on my father. Kinnan helps him bear it."

"I know."

"You won't take Kinnan away?"

"Not him."

Cameron rubbed a thumb along the scar on his chin, his eyes on Karol. "What do you mean?"

"They tell me I should choose a consort," she said.

"You're looking at *me*," said Cameron.

"Are you spoken for?" She held her breath.

"By myself. Karol…Your Grace…I am not consort material."

With a tentative smile, she asked, "Will you consider it?"

"Consider it?" He shrugged uncomfortably. "That's fair, I suppose."

"I'll say I want a year, so I can choose properly. Will you think of me for a year?"

Cameron smiled, then. "That won't be difficult. Will I see you at all during that time?"

"As often as you like. Bring some of your father's work to the market in Kudasad. I'll ask to see silverwork from the south. I'll like Gils Nara's best, and dismiss the others."

"When?"

"You say."

"The third Market Day in the month."

"Agreed."

Cameron rose and held out a hand.

Karol took it, and he pulled her to her feet. She thought he would pull her into his arms, and she was willing to go, but he stepped away from her with a solemn face.

Market Days seemed longer apart every month. Karol acquired a boxful of southern silverwork along with detailed news of Gils Nara and little Kinnan.

Every day, Cameron grew dearer to her. Every Market Day, she could see in his face herself grown more dear. And nobody knew, not even Karol's sister, Sorcha beren Ada.

In the meantime, potential consorts were passed before her like so many bolts of cloth. The sons of Oliva beren Audre, Thane of the House of Sarpa, paid court, each to a sister.

The younger one, Hayward beren Oliva, courted Sorcha. The elder, Landry beren Oliva, presented Karol with his prospectus.

Landry had served his mother as bailiff since her husband's death some years before. On paper, and according to witnesses questioned in secret, he had done a fine job of it.

Karol agreed to bear him in mind.

At the end of the year, Karol rode again to Agra.

Kinnan remembered her well. He threw his little arms around her waist and tried to lift her off the ground.

"Look!" he cried, and waved his fist in the air, showing off his brace-let, as shiny as the day he'd been given it.

"Do you only wear it when I come?" asked Karol, admiring the gleam of the metal.

"I wear it all the time."

"He never takes it off," said Gils Nara.

"I *refuse*," said Kinnan. "Except to polish it. But I put it right back on."

"It looks smaller than it was."

"No," said Kinnan. "I'm bigger."

By and by, Karol and Cameron were left alone, in cushioned chairs, on either side of a cold hearth.

"Have you considered?" she asked.

"Carefully," he said. "Shall I tell you what weighed with me?"

"Yes."

"In favor of accepting your offer...." Cameron leaned forward and took Karol's hands, which she leaned forward to give him. "I love you dearly."

"And I, you," Karol whispered.

"You never tried to tempt me with power or wealth or luxury or leisure."

"It wouldn't have worked."

"You understood that about me. That was the most tempting thing of all." He released her hands and leaned back. "In opposition –"

"Nothing more in favor?" Karol's face was bleak.

"No. In opposition, there are my father and my brother. They need me here. If Kinnan is to be kept from the court until he comes of age – and I think he should be – he must stay here with my father. He's a lively boy, and your mother's death has left my father old beyond his years."

"A consort needn't live at the castle –"

"But a consort should live close to the throne. If not in Kudasad itself, in one of the nearby Thaneholds."

"You could be made a Thane, or Gils Nara could."

"At whose expense?"

"Crown lands...."

"At the expense of the people then." He shook his head. "No, I thank you."

"My consort can live where he wills."

Cameron shook his head. "I drink in taverns, remember? I was hard pressed to hold my tongue, the last years of your mother's life. The people complained that she let her Chamberlain rule from behind an empty throne. I wished I could defend her, but I had to keep her secret – and I agreed with those who complained. You need a true consort; one who can administer in your name when you can't be reached."

"Where would I be, that I couldn't be reached?"

"Your mother was here."

There was silence between them.

"What are you suggesting?" Karol asked.

"That you find a consort. A suitable one. I'll come no more to the market, and you come no more to visit. – Not forever, but for a while. For years. The people must know you better. They must know your consort, and trust him."

Karol flushed. "I know my duties."

Cameron spread his scarred hands with a smile. "I told you, didn't I? I'm no man to run tame in a strong woman's household. I would be equal, if not master; a consort must always bow."

Karol scowled, but she granted the truth of what he said.

"When Layounna can run a while without you," Cameron went on, "come see us again. My father will understand your absence, and Kinnan will forgive you. Then, perhaps, you and I…. Your mother found a husband for her heart here. Perhaps you will, too."

"And if I find a consort I can love? If I choose not to come again?"

Cameron's gaze caressed the Kinninger's face and slid into the empty fireplace. "I know the risk," he said. "I have no choice."

So Landry beren Oliva became Landry Oliva beren Ada, Kinninger's Consort. He was an able assistant, although he was better with the books than with the people. He brought Rhu beren Robia, his manor steward, with him; a tall, dark, crag-faced man with a baritone voice as beautiful as his face was plain. Ada beren Cinnie's old Chamberlain retired to write her memoirs, and Rhu beren Robia took her place.

Landry Oliva beren Ada's brother, Hayward beren Oliva, assumed Landry's old duties as their mother's bailiff. Oliva beren Audre and her youngest child, a grown and widowed daughter named Corvina, came to live in the castle. Hayward's courtship of Sorcha, Karol's younger sister, prospered, and he became Hayward Oliva beren Ada.

At first, the novelty of having a Consort absorbed Karol's attention. Landry was eager to learn the business of managing the realm, and he was able. He was attractive, as well: Slender, with full black hair which he wore loose to his waist, light brown eyes, fine features, hands as delicate as Gils Nara's, and olive skin. He had a weakness for jeweled ear baubs and bangles, and an impudence underlying his deference, both of which Karol found charming, at first.

But he wasn't Cameron. Landry Oliva seemed to have no desire to be master in Karol's house, but he looked to his mother as its mistress. Karol tolerated this fantasy – a fantasy Oliva beren Audre shared – because the villeins did not. Any instructions from Oliva or her son were checked against Karol's own; if they coincided, the Consort or his mother was obeyed. If they did not, the instructions were ignored and the reason was courteously given.

Karol put the realm in order. She executed reforms that pleased the people but pinched the Thanes. Though Landry often argued against these reforms, he always conceded to her judgment, saying that he had only argued to help her muster her defense against real opponents. Gradually, Karol placed more administrative duties in Landry Oliva's hands, and supervised him less.

~*~

So five years passed.

At last, Karol knew the time had come. She announced her intention of going on a retreat, to refresh her spirit and mind. She left Landry Oliva in charge of the realm's administration, and rode to Gils Nara's shop.

Kinnan opened the door to her. He was nearly twelve; almost as tall as Karol, already strongly muscled in spite of his slight frame, his curly hair a darker blond than in childhood, his nose just as prominent.

"Aunt Karol!" he cried. He embraced her, drawing her through the smithy into the parlor.

"What's pressing my back?" Karol asked, taking his arm from around her. "Why, this isn't…?"

"It is." He held his arm and turned it, so she could see how the bracelet she'd given him still gleamed. "Almost completely uncurled," the boy said proudly. "Well, only a little more than one more twist."

"You've kept it well."

"I was taught to care for fine things."

Karol laughed. "It's only bronze. And you the son of a silversmith?"

"It's made of bronze." The boy frowned at Karol's laughter. "But it's more than that."

Karol put a hand on the boy's shoulder. "It was more than that when it became a gift. You've made it a fine thing by your care."

Cameron came in, then. "The shop stands open and empty, boy. Do you –" He stopped speaking and walking, both, when he saw the guest.

"It's Aunt Karol. Shall I go tell father?"

Cameron nodded. Kinnan went, not back to the smithy, but up the dark narrow stairs at the back of the parlor.

Karol watched him.

"Is Gils Nara unwell?"

"It comes and goes," said Cameron. "He grows weaker."

"I've been away too long."

"No."

Kinnan came far enough down the stairs to say, "He wants to sit up and visit."

Cameron wouldn't let her stay more than a few minutes. She left when he drew her away, though she longed to take off her mantle and her shoes and spend long hours by his bed as she had by her mother's.

She and Cameron returned to the parlor, leaving Kinnan to ease the old man to rest.

"I think I'll never see him again," she said.

"I think not often," said Cameron.

There was a space of silence, then Karol said, "It's been five years. Do you… Do you still bear only your own mother's name?"

"My mother's name, and no woman's hopes," said Cameron. "Unless I still bear yours."

Then Karol's arms were around him. He held her and stroked her hair.

"We're promised, then?" he whispered.

"Promised. When Gils Nara is better, we'll take some time together. A retreat, away from here; maybe in the East."

"We will. Let it be soon."

~*~

But Gils Nara was never better. Karol came for a day now and then, when affairs of state permitted, and when she wasn't covering the importance of these visits to the Southern District with visits to the other four.

She knew, now, what her mother had meant; Karol held this other family close and in secret. It was as if she shielded them from something – from what, she couldn't have said. Still no one knew of them, not even her sister, Sorcha.

When Kinnan was fourteen, Gils Nara beren Ailith died.

Cameron sent Karol word, and she attended the burial.

Afterward, she sat in the parlor with Cameron on the other side of the fire from her and Kinnan on a stool by her feet. Between them, Karol and Cameron told the young man the truth of his birth, only to find that Gils Nara had told him years before, when he first realized his illness was a final one.

"You're of age now, Kinnan beren…." Karol's voice trailed away.

"Beren Osa, for now," said the young man. "Beren Ada, if you ever need me."

"You will not come home with me now?"

"I am home," said Kinnan. "I don't desire the court."

"You don't know it."

Kinnan set his mouth, and Karol laughed gently.

"How I know that look," she said. "I've seen it on my mother's face; next you'll tell me to take the answer I'm given."

Kinnan laughed, too. "You're right, though," he said. "I don't know the court. I ought to, I suppose, in case you ever call me to it."

"Why not use our old Market Day strategy?" said Cameron. "Take samples of our wares to the Market in Kudasad."

"The third Market Day of the month," said Karol. "Remember?"

"Is that why you went so often, yet sold so little?" said Kinnan. "You went to meet Aunt Karol? – I mean, my sister?"

"That's why," said Cameron. "How about it, Kinnan? A glimpse of life at court?"

"If you like it," said Karol, "but still want to remain unknown, you can have a shed within the bailey as the crown's own silversmith."

"And leave Cameron to drive our father's business into the ground? That, I could not do."

So he came every third Market Day, while he and Karol and Cameron observed a year of mourning for Gils Nara. He brought Karol beautiful things of silver, and carried messages of tender regard from one chaste lover to the other.

At last he carried a message home to Cameron that Karol had purchased a small cottage and some land in the Eastern District, near Pazni. She would be on retreat there, at such-and-such a date. If Cameron came then, he would find her there.

~*~

Seven years flew by. Karol beren Ada, like her mother before her, left more and more of the administration in other hands – the hands of Landry Oliva, of the House of Sarpa. The royal treasury gradually fattened. The castle villeins gradually learned to obey Oliva, Landry Oliva, and even Landry's sister, Corvina beren Oliva, without question. The Kinninger's mixed-gender Guards, established as a ceremonial body, became the all-male Swords and trained for combat, a small standing army.

Karol and Cameron began to quarrel, never more bitterly than on their last night together.

"But the smithy doesn't need you any more!" Karol said. "Kinnan is twenty-two, and does most of the work now. He could pay someone to fill your place."

"I've always done my share."

"You've always done your best," said Karol. She stood behind the seated man and tried to smooth his brow with her hands. He jerked away.

"What is it?" Karol said. "Have I asked you too often? I won't stop asking. I want you to come to Kudasad, or to here, or let me put you in a house in Agra, if you like. Or stay at the smithy, if it pleases you to play at work, only let me acknowledge you. I want to visit you openly, not in secret, as if it were wrong for a Kinninger to have a child-sire other than her consort."

Cameron rose and grasped Karol's shoulders. "If I'm your child-sire," he said, "where are my children?"

"Wh-what children?"

"That's my question. Your mother hid one of hers; don't I know that? Have you hidden ours from me?"

"Why would I hide a child from you?"

"Because Kinnan has no more use for the court than I do. A child I raised would be too much mine. The Kinninger's children must be all her own. Where are they, Karol?"

"Where should they be? Why should there be any? Many women are barren for seven years. As seldom as we come together, why should there have to be a child?"

They were shouting, intent upon it, so they heard no one approach.

The door was only on the latch. It opened softly, and three armed Swords came in. Without a word, they drew their weapons.

"Put up your swords," Karol commanded. "What do you want? How dare you walk —"

Cameron blocked the first cut with a chair, and knocked the second aside with a fist to the Sword's forearm.

"Put up your weapons!" Karol shouted. "This man is not to be harmed!"

"We don't answer to you," said one of the Swords, "but to Landry Oliva, Kinninger by right of merit."

"Go back to Landry Oliva and tell him I'm coming. I expect a thorough explanation – Stand back! What are you doing?"

"They're assassins, you fool!" cried Cameron. "Run!"

Cameron grabbed the poker and swung. One Sword fell to the floor with a broken head. Cameron dragged the lantern from the mantelshelf and flung it at the other two. While they jumped back and slapped out drops of liquid flame, Cameron threw down the poker and picked up the fallen man's sword.

Karol snatched a knife from the sideboard.

"Run!" Cameron cried.

"I'll fight by you, or die."

"If we have a child anywhere in the world, woman, run! I forgive you for it. I forgive you anything. Just run!"

Cameron reached for the knife. Karol pressed its hilt into his hand. His fingers curled in hers one final time, then she turned and ran. She heard the clash of steel on steel as the Swords tried to follow her and met Cameron at the door. She stumbled across the grounds, blinded by panic, by the sick surety that she had left her only love to die for her sake, and for the sake of the child she carried within her.

She ran, hoping to reach Pazni, to raise the alarm, to lead a rescue back, to be in time....

Horses screamed behind her. She whirled and crouched, facing the danger. She could see the Swords' horses, pulling up the bushes to which they had been tethered, plunging into the night. She saw them by the light of the fire. It roared from the thatch of the cottage. There was no movement within but that of the flames.

Karol rose from the spongy ground. She could see nothing but the fire. She could hold nothing else in all her mind, nothing but the fire.

At last the flames died away, and the surrounding darkness grew more light with its going.

She would have been too late, anyway. She would never have found help, not in this direction. Her witless flight had led her in a spiral toward Fiddlewood, not Pazni.

Cameron dead, the Swords disloyal, Landry Oliva untrue to his trust....

With these facts taking the place of thought, Kinninger Karol beren Ada walked into the Fiddlewood, and her false Consort sat upon the throne.

chapter 3
WAYMASTER

Andrin beren Tooli, Royal Waymaster to the House of Onagros, woke with his heart pounding. The same dream, three nights in a row; a sure sign that the "dream" was no dream, but a vision.

The old man opened his black-purple eyes and let himself be comforted by the familiar shadows cast by the banked temple fire.

There was fire in the dream. In the dream, he faced roaring flames – not he, Andrin, but the someone else he was in the dream. The flames were consuming his heart – he reached for it, trying to pluck it from the heart of the blaze but though the fire didn't burn him it kept him from his prize. He was frightened and ran…threw himself into a river. Bubbles brushed his face as he swam slowly under the water. The water became air and the bubbles became leaves. He moved slowly through heavy undergrowth; his clothing snagged on twigs and thorns. His own self tried to regain control of the dream, to run from the danger he felt at his back, but he couldn't – another proof that he was dreaming a vision.

The first night he dreamed of the fire he wakened normally, soon after entering the forest. The second night he jerked awake, struggling against the restraining brush. This night, he felt his own terror being swallowed by a lifelessness that, his dream-self knew, was caused by the loss of his heart to the flames. His real heart strained to assert its existence and power, and it was this that wakened him this morning.

Andrin beren Tooli folded back his blanket and sat up on his pallet. His body was blocky, heavy, his dark skin concealing unobtrusive muscle. He slept only in a breechcloth; the early-morning chill felt good after the fiery vision. He ran one trembling, long-fingered hand over the silver stubble on his shaved head. He crossed his legs tailor-fashion and let his hands rest loosely on his knees while he breathed away his panic.

The old man wasted no thought on the meaning of the vision; that would come when it was ready. Attempting to puzzle it out would only court misinterpretation.

When he was calm, he rose. According to his water clock, it was nearly his usual time, anyway. He stirred up the central fire, laid on some blocks of charcoal, and filled the three-legged kettle which straddled the fire-pit with water from a jug.

He lit a candle and stood before his herb-cabinet, debating which to choose for the central pot. The taste and scent of it would color his day; so, it must harmonize with the day. Perhaps he should take his vision into account when choosing.

Common sage, to soothe his nerves? Clary sage, to sharpen his vision? He chose the dried leaves of the first, the salted pink-and-white flowers of the second. He carried a handful of each to the open kettle, meditating on their qualities and natures, and dropped them into the heating water.

He folded his blanket and rolled up his pallet and stored them in a cabinet carved with the device of the House of Onagros.

As he performed the exercises which kept his aging body strong and supple, the smells of the sages filled the room; the Common was rich and bitter and astringent, the Clary was camphoric and piney. A strong smell, medicinal, and not entirely pleasant.

Andrin took some of the scented water out into a shallow bowl, washed himself and shaved his head, pouring the used liquid into a trench which led outside and into his garden. He dressed in his yellow silk robe, and slid his feet into red leather shoes.

Still the dream haunted him.

He shook his head and reached for a book at random. He would lose himself in commentary on one of the major texts of the Canon.

The book his unguided hand chose was THE SHIFTING PATH, the Wayfarers' ancient book of divination. Then he realized that his effort to put the vision from his mind had become discordant; his harmonious path now lay through the vision, not around it.

The Waymaster put the book on a long low table next to an ebony box, poured himself a cup of sage tea and sat on a pillow before the table. He would drink his tea while he regained his balance, then would cast the pebbles, and follow the shifting path to wherever it would lead.

Outside the shuttered temple, dawn was breaking. Outside, the world began to stir. Inside, it was very still.

Andrin beren Tooli's temple – or Waystation, as temples of the Way were called – was within the castle bailey. It was, like all the bailey buildings, a simple wooden structure. Like the other buildings, it had one small unglazed window cut into the outer wall. A heavy wooden shutter slid onto a sill inside; a thick bar held the shutter in place. Unlike the other buildings, the temple's window was always shuttered and barred, refusing the world entrance.

The Waystation was smaller than most other buildings within the lower palisade; it only needed to be big enough for Andrin and the occasional private Wayfarer. When the crown wanted the Waymaster's counsel or aid, the Waymaster went to the crown.

The crown hadn't wanted him for quite a while. Karol beren Ada had been absent more often, and for longer times, every year. She gave various reasons, but one didn't need to be a mystic adept to see the truth; she had a heart-husband, possibly a child-sire, probably both the same man. She had that look about her, and that sound to her voice.

Landry Oliva and his family never called Andrin to the tower. Pure scholarship was held in slight regard by Oliva beren Audre, Landry's mother. She followed the mystic adept Tarkastrus, one of the misguided fools who believed the Way could be manipulated and controlled by controlling and manipulating the Divine Spirits.

According to the oldest texts, which all true scholars (like Andrin) agreed were purely symbolic, the Way was served by four Spiritual Animals: the unicorn, the tortoise, the phoenix, and the dragon. The unicorn was the spirit of unity, longevity, wise administration, illustrious offspring, perfect good; the phoenix, of virtue; the dragon represented generosity, vigilance, and safeguard; and tortoise, strength and endurance. Tortoise was also known as "the creature that forgets the eight rules of right and wrong." Tortoise was a dark symbol, and a dark focus for those who practiced the Tarkastrian arts. It was to Tortoise that Oliva made her sacrifices and supplications. It was to Tortoise that Landry's sister, Corvina, dedicated her powders, brews, and elixirs, her drugs and her poisons.

Andrin heard, faintly, the sound of the palisade guards shouting to someone outside, then the rumble of the massive bolts and the lowering of the gate. A rider galloped in and past the temple, up the slope of the motte.

Karol? A messenger from her, or from a Thane, or a village? He would learn, later, probably from one of his gossips. Unless it was, indeed, Karol, he wouldn't be told anything officially.

Sometimes Hayward Oliva beren Ada, Landry's brother and the husband of Karol's younger sister, stopped by on his way to or from the castle, but only to pass on Sorcha's greetings. Andrin sensed in Hayward a pull toward the Path, as a compass needle pulls to point north, and is kept from it by placing it near certain stones.

The stone keeping Hayward from harmony was his mother, Oliva beren Audre. She –

From the tower yard came a long, high, "Ohhhhhhhhh!"

Andrin knew the sound of that, and he was outside with the last echo of it still in his ears.

It was not repeated. Worse and worse.

That cry of horror and despair was the hallmark of Biddi beren Anna, the chief kitchen maid and his chief gossip for many years. All disasters, as soon as Biddi heard of them, called it from her. One could judge the extent of the trouble by the number and volume of Biddi's cries. This one had been loud – piercing and shot with pain.

But only one. Only the deepest, blackest fear could have stopped the rest of Biddi's keening.

Andrin took off his leather slippers, the better to run up the motte boardwalk.

The tower gate was down for the day. Andrin ran over it, around the tower and through the kitchen garden.

There he found Biddy, crouched behind the chicken coop, where she couldn't be seen from the tower windows. She had both her large, rough hands clamped over her mouth. Her eyes, pale blue as the sky seen through thin clouds, streamed with tears.

Andrin sat in the dust beside her and took her in his arms, stroking the heavy auburn braid of her hair as if it could take comfort from his caress.

"Karol?" he said.

Biddi took her hands from her mouth, small, like the mouth of a painted doll. Biddi's sun-brown skin was unnaturally pale, the masses of her freckles seeming to stand away from the whitened skin.

"He's killed her," she said. "I know it. I know it. You know I know things," she thumped her chest, "in here."

"It was a messenger I heard, then? What was the news?"

Biddi whispered, her voice hoarse with the strain of holding it down. "Her retreat burnt to the foundation stones, and a man burnt up in it, but they found no sign of the Kinninger."

"A man burnt up…. Her man?"

"So *I* think. But why not her? Because she's dead, too, and *he* doesn't want it known."

"Why wouldn't he, Biddi?" Andrin argued with the woman against his own instinctive knowledge, spoken to him in her words.

"Because he's shifty. He has some reason. Mark me, when the time suits him, she'll be proven dead."

It could be so. It could be Landry's doing, and not news to him at all. It would serve him to have Karol's state and place uncertain; alive, she was still Kinninger and he was still Consort and in full control during her absence. Dead, and an heir would have to be found; if there were no heir, the throne would devolve onto Sorcha, Ada beren Cinnie's surviving child.

"No," the old man breathed, and patted the kitchen maid's back. "She's foxed him for now."

Biddi sniffed mightily and sat back, eyes red, nose-tip red. "How?" she asked.

"This must be the meaning of my vision. Fire, consuming her heart…. She must have seen it happening, but couldn't stop it…couldn't help. She's cold inside, but she's alive. She escaped into the woods."

"What woods?"

"To the East, near – what's its name? The town near her retreat? – Pazni. Fiddlewood."

"Will she die there?" Biddi blew her nose into a rag from her apron pocket, content to lay her fear and sorrow at Andrin's dusty feet.

"I don't know," said Andrin. "I can't see into the future. *I* don't claim to."

The maid "humphed" at this reference to Oliva beren Audre's Tarkastrian practices.

"This vision is our secret, Biddi, and your suspicions, too. Don't tell, don't even hint. Not even to the people you trust. Not even to the hens. You must promise me."

Biddi nodded and dried her eyes.

The divination Andrin had planned went undone, and his tea went untasted.

~*~

Days passed, and Karol wasn't found. Landry Oliva sent Swords galloping over the Five Districts – North, South, East, West, and Central – with the news of Karol's disappearance and offers of rewards for news of her.

He prowled. He could be seen on the tower battlements, or in the upper windows above the tower palisade, sometimes even in the bailey yard itself, pacing, his long black hair streaming behind him or blowing wild.

Andrin had the flaming dream no more. He sometimes had another one, of an island nestled in a river, like a baby in its mother's belly, which was harmonious in itself, and didn't ask for understanding.

And then, one day, Andrin stood at the temple door watching the Kinninger's Consort range the enclave, and Landry turned, and the two locked gazes.

Landry spoke softly to the Sword nearest him. He strode past the temple and back to the tower, his head turning as he went as if to keep Andrin transfixed.

When Landry finally broke his stare to look before him, Andrin found the Sword at his elbow.

"You're to go up at once," the Sword said. "To the Hall."

"Am I to take anything with me?"

"He didn't ask for anything."

Andrin thanked the Sword for passing the message and followed Landry up the boardwalk.

Landry Oliva was already in the Hall, seated in a carved and padded chair, when Andrin entered. His mother sat in another ornate chair at his left hand. His sister, Corvina beren Oliva, sat on a high-backed bench made soft with pillows and rugs.

The castle Chamberlain, Rhu beren Robia, stood behind Landry's chair and to his left; the Chief Sword, Guthrie beren Melanell, behind and to his right.

Although he despised all of them, Andrin had to concede that Oliva beren Audre and her children were – superficially – very beautiful.

Oliva herself was small and slim, her hair a softly shining pewter gray. Her skin, once almost as dark as Andrin's, had faded to the color of weak tea. Her eyes were the same color, but a darker shade. Her lips were always pursed, at least when Andrin saw them, her eyes always half-shut, as if she concealed a secret, like a snake in a wicker basket.

Corvina was slim and tall, with hair so black it was almost blue, soft and with a very fine kink to it. Her eyes were dark mahogany, almond shaped. Her skin was the same olive shade as her brother's. She held herself with an arrogance improper in one possessed of no apparent form of power.

"Come forward!" Landry called, as soon as Andrin came into his view. "We have news, and want your insight."

Brother and sister watched the old Waymaster approach with amused contempt, Landry's tempered with determined hope. Rhu beren Robia nodded courteously to the old man.

As Andrin neared the group, he heard the zip of cloth rubbing cloth, and a pillow landed on the floor, just before him.

"For your comfort, Adept," said Corvina.

Landry held out a hand, palm up, toward the pillow, as if it had been placed with proper deference and ceremony.

Andrin stepped over the silken insult and sat upon it.

When he was settled, Landry said, "You know that our Kinninger, Karol beren Ada, cannot be found, by Sword or by report?"

"I have heard," said the Waymaster.

"It seems she had a heart-husband, kept in her Eastern retreat. I sent a messenger to her there, with some questions pertaining to matters of state, and he found the retreat in ruins, the lover dead."

"I have heard something like this, as well."

Oliva beren Audre said, "You have long ears, Adept."

Andrin bowed to her. "The ancients have it, 'Better long ears than a long tongue,' My Lady."

Oliva drew breath, but was silenced by the voice of her son.

"First, where is Karol beren Ada?" Landry asked. "Why was she not at that cottage? Why has she not come home? Where can I send to find her, now?"

Andrin appeared to be considering his answer. Beneath this appearance, he considered his questioner. Although his Sight told him that Karol beren Ada lived, he also saw that Biddi had been right in essence: Landry Oliva had meant for Karol beren Ada to die with her lover. He had meant to pretend she was alive but missing, long enough to secure himself in her place, confident that she would never return to dislodge him. Now, though, he was genuinely desperate to find her. A truly missing Karol was worse – much worse – than a truly dead one, to Landry Oliva. But a missing Karol found would become a dead one, as soon as the Swords could strike.

"These are questions not approachable by insight," Andrin said. "The answers must be ferreted out by active search and asking, or waited for, or done without."

Oliva gave a short, scornful laugh. "I told you it was useless. 'Ask a Waymaster for answers and he gives you riddles.'"

"A true riddle is more useful than a false answer," said Andrin.

Oliva flipped a dismissive hand. "Words," she said.

"I'm asking you these things," Landry said to Andrin, though it was clear he was really speaking to his mother, "because I *must* know. If I can have no facts, I must have opinion and conjecture. My mother has used her arts in this service, and told me what she found...."

Told you what she wanted to have found, Andrin said to himself. Followers of Tarkastrus, that self-deluded, self-indulgent fraud, never learned what their Master had never learned: attempting to control the flowing Path diverted it. Trying to force the Way to give up its secrets could only fail; Oliva had learned nothing but that which she had told herself.

"...and now I want you to tell me what you can."

Had Biddi betrayed the vision? Did Landry know – rather, did he believe he knew – that Karol was alive and hidden?

But Landry continued, "Perhaps you've had a message from Karol, and haven't passed it on, thinking we've had it, too."

So it was Hayward he suspected, Hayward and the Kinninger's sister, Sorcha.

"I have had none."

Oliva leaned forward. "Do you swear on your Sight?"

"I do not."

"Then –"

"Moder, he tells the truth," said Landry.

Andrin felt a new respect for the Consort, and a new fear of him. A man driven by greed and ambition is a kind of fool, and dangerous. A man who harnesses greed and ambition, and drives them before him with caution and clear vision, is a fool of no kind, and is very dangerous, indeed.

Andrin had to tell the truth; he dared not lie, and Landry knew it. The

only thing which held Andrin beren Tooli – or any Waymaster – within the
fabric of the Way itself was modesty of spirit. To lie would be to assert the
self and to find oneself outside the Way's tight warp and weft, like a stray
thread plucked from a tapestry.

"You said 'First' when you asked about Karol beren Ada, My Lord
Consort," said Andrin. "Have you another question?"

Landry smiled. "Surely you can guess," he said. "If Karol can't be
found…. Has she any heirs? What children has she left, and where? They
should be here, training to take my place."

This statement fell so false from Landry's lips, Andrin looked to the
floor, half expecting to see it lying there like a dead fish.

"You can tell me nothing?" Landry asked.

"I cannot tell you *now*. I can only meditate, and walk the shifting path,
and contemplate what I find along the way, and tell you the result."

"I don't need contemplation, I need –" Landry began, then cut himself
off, as if stopping on the brink of a mis-step.

"I can't provide you with *facts*, if that's what you mean," said Andrin.
"All I can offer are truths. You must make of them what you can."

Andrin's scalp tightened as he said this; looking into Landry's cool
brown eyes, he knew that the Consort would make of them all possible
practical use.

"I will look for answers," Andrin said.

"Quickly," said Landry.

Andrin rose. He picked up the pillow and tossed it back onto Corvina's
bench.

"I'll offer prayers for your courtesy," he said.

"I want none of your prayers," Corvina said to his back.

He walked slowly down the boardwalk, the Consort's questions clack-
ing against one another in his mind. He recalled his dream of fire and loss,
and Biddi's premonition of Landry's duplicity. If he had doubted either vision before, the interview he had just endured would have ended any un-
certainty.

The temple smelled of rosemary that day; rosemary, for a clear head,
calm nerves, a quiet heart.

Andrin took some tea. He sat before his easel, blank paper pinned to
it, dry ink block by his side, dry brush across his knees. He reached to his
right, and lifted the lid of his pebble-box.

He pulled out a handful of pebbles and scattered them on the table. Staring at the pattern they made, he allowed the chaos of his thoughts to find alignment with the random pattern of the stones.

The Waymaster scraped a pyramid of tiny flakes from his inkstone and dribbled some tea into the powder, then mixed the ink with his brush, his eyes on the scattered pebbles.

A few more seconds, three strokes, and the pattern was transferred to paper, in one of the traditional stylized forms recognized by THE SHIFT- ING PATH.

Andrin gathered the pebbles and shut them back in their box. He opened the book of divination to the section of commentary which dealt with the pattern he had painted: Between Male and Female. It was a pat- tern of bonding and contention. Children came into it, and extremes, and negation, and enhancement, and various interpretations of strength and weakness. It was Andrin's task to use his specific knowledge and personal dream-visions to sort the truth of this current situation from the greater truth of the pattern as a whole.

And, gradually, as the sun passed and began to lower, the smaller truth came clear. Karol had escaped the death Landry Oliva had planned for her. She was hidden, with a child or carrying one. Her life would never be safe, nor would any life standing between Landry Oliva and the throne, as long as Landry Oliva could end that life.

What was he to do? Tell Landry that the threats to his power were as real as he supposed? Watch Landry turn upon the realm as if it were his enemy? Live with Landry's thanks, and with the blood of who could say how many on his hands, including Karol's own?

The temple door opened, the outside light all but blocked by the man who entered.

It was Hayward Oliva beren Ada.

"Sorcha sends her greetings and her love."

Hayward Oliva had only his siblings' coloring in common with them. He was plump, with muddy brown eyes and a heavy chin, a soft mouth and pudgy hands like paws. He kept his hair, more tightly kinked than his sister's, cut to a velvety fuzz.

"You're on your way to the tower?"

"From there. Landry sent for me late this morning."

That would have been before my own interview, Andrin thought.

He called for Hayward, heard me, then decided what to do with his brother and his brother's wife.

"You're on your way back to the manor, then?"

"I'm to bring Sorcha and the children. There's some sort of trouble brewing. We're to move into the castle for safety."

Andrin's mouth went dry. He held up his teabowl; Hayward took it, filled it, and handed it back.

"Mind if I join you?" the younger man asked.

"Please," said Andrin.

Hayward took a bowl himself, and sat by the adept. In silence, he looked from the pattern on the easel to the open book, to the face of the Waymaster.

"You've been reading the pebbles?"

"Landry wants to know who stands between him and the crown."

It was more than the heat of the tea, more than the effect of the herb on his system, that beaded Hayward's face with perspiration.

"What shall I do?" he whispered.

"What you must," said Andrin. "Does Sorcha want the throne?"

"No. She says not, anyway."

"Would she support another claimant? Suppose an heir of Karol's body turned up. Would she support one against your brother?"

"She says she doesn't care. She says she wants no part of any of it, and wants no part of it for our children. I agree."

"Does Landry know your wishes?"

"He knows them, yet he doubts them. Nothing would convince him…."

Hayward stopped speaking. He took a long draught of tea and put down the bowl.

"Goodbye, Adept." He pushed himself awkwardly to his feet.

"Come and see me when you bring Sorcha and your family back."

"I will. Though we'll both have aged a bit by then."

That night, Andrin dreamed again of the island nestled in the center of a river, water flowing ceaselessly around it in a shining, shifting path.

~*~

The next day, carrying the knowledge of what he did like a stone in his breast, Andrin went to Landry, looked into his eyes, and lied.

"Karol beren Ada is dead," he told him. "Karol left no heirs in any foster home, or they would have been put forward by now. Although you didn't ask me this, the pattern tells me that Sorcha beren Ada's interests lie elsewhere. My Lord, the throne is yours."

"As I told you!" cried Oliva beren Audre. "*Now* are you content?"

Landry held Andrin in a longer gaze, then eased back into his padded chair.

"I am content. You may go, Adept."

Andrin left him planning a dinner for his Thanes. He would assure himself of their support, then declare Karol dead, then rule in her place.

The Waymaster returned to his temple and washed for the second time that day. He had done what he felt he must; he had chosen to lie, to hide the lives he held within his Sight, to hold them safe within himself as a mother's body holds the body of her child. In doing so, he had seen himself as separate from the Whole and, apart from it, had lost it.

Chapter 4
Flight of a Kinninger

Karol beren Ada wandered in Fiddlewood – her body did, rather, for her spirit had been burnt alive. Twigs and thorns, tree roots and branches caught at her clothes and her hair. Sometimes she stopped, held by wild growth, and didn't try to free herself while minutes passed and mice took shelter from owls and hawks beneath her hem. Then she would move again, breaking her hair and tearing her gown, and the morning birds gathered the soft scraps into their nests, high above searching eyes.

She came to the river by daylight – Fiddlewood River. She put a hand to her rising belly and turned aside, following the river downstream.

Sometime during the day, she heard horses floundering along the narrow, root-crossed path just visible through the trees, and riders cursing. Instinct or the memory of Cameron's last words to her made her sink to the ground and listen with her whole body. The riders passed her, seeming to ride dry-shod over the river. Sounds of an angry barnyard came thinly on the air.

Too weary to move just yet, Karol stayed hidden, and heard the riders pass again, going the other way. Later still, she heard the sound of many men in many places in the wood.

Karol felt, or thought she felt, her baby stir within her. She pulled herself to her feet and moved on, toward the path the horses had taken. They had gone somewhere, her mind coldly said, and searched, and had not found her, and had left that place. So she would go to that place, and there she could rest.

The nest her body had made in the bankside ferns was warm; before she was out of sight, the place was taken by a family of otters, who tussled and groomed one another until the men came too close. Then they slid into the water, leaving nothing behind them but the clear signs of their romp.

Karol found the narrow path where it led into the river. Water slipped over it but the men were behind her, still distant, moving slowly because they were searching so carefully, but coming all the same. She removed her belt of leather tooled in gold and kilted up her skirts. She waded into the water.

She came ashore and hid herself behind some trees. Behind the trees, like a welcoming bed behind green curtains, were a clearing and a cottage. Goats and geese and an old woman in the doorway all stared at her. The only sound was the hum of honeybees flashing through the air like bubbles in disturbed water.

The old woman took a clay pipe from her mouth and smiled with more teeth than good humor.

"Well done," she said.

"Let me rest a while. Then I'll go on."

"Go back, you mean," said the old woman. "You're on an island, you know."

"I didn't know."

"Wild Ass Island, in Fiddlewood River, in Fiddlewood, near Pazni, in the realm of Layounna, blessed under Her Grace, Kinninger Karol beren Ada. Did you know any of that?"

"More than that. Her Grace is dead."

"Is she, now? Then why were those men looking for her?"

Karol didn't answer.

"I knew they were fools before I saw them," the old woman said, making no move from her doorway. "I could hear them cursing their horses for stumbling on ground the men wouldn't walk. Making enough noise to drive any quarry to earth, alive or dead."

"May I stay here until they've gone? Until they've gone, and the path is open again?"

The old woman drew on her pipe, while her eyes of dreadful blue met Karol's. Karol felt that gaze almost physically; she felt it reach inside her, down into her heart, and shock it into thumping life.

"My name is… Cinnie," said Karol. "Cinnie beren Moder."

"'Beren Moder'? You're an orphan, then?"

"Yes. Yes, I am. Please…. Shelter…. Just for a little while."

The old woman moved, and Karol saw she walked with a cane.

"Come in," the old woman said. "Dish me up some supper. You have some, too, and we'll find you somewhere to sleep. Moder Zglaria is what I'm called, so maybe you belong here, Cinnie beren Moder."

The old woman chuckled, and went into the cottage.

Karol followed her. It was dim inside, the windows shuttered against the coming dusk. A low fire burned in the hearth, and a large candle lit the central table. A stone bench ran along one wall. Stone and wooden shelves were packed with everything from bottled herbs to blankets. A wooden bed with a thin mattress stood in one corner.

A stockpot simmered over the fire, held there on an iron pothook. A shallow earthenware dish on the hearthstones held a crisply baked sheet of flatbread.

"Serve me first," said Moder, "then help yourself. Half that bread was for my breakfast, but we'll do with something else; you have the other half now."

"Thank you."

"Don't thank me, girl. You'll earn what you have from me."

Karol swung the stockpot off the fire and removed the lid with the skirt of her tattered gown. The rush of food-smell nearly made her faint. The pot was full of a thick stew of soft roots, tender leaves, berries, nuts, cress, and strings of once-dried meat.

"Pour some water in it, when you've taken yours," Moder said. "Tomorrow, you can find something to thicken it up again."

Karol took the old woman a brimming bowl of stew and half the bread.

"There's butter and cheese in the cold room," Moder said. "Fetch some. Through that curtain."

Although she was suddenly so hungry she could have eaten the curtain itself, Karol lifted the heavy drape and looked behind it. Seven broad steps led down to a set of shelves cut into the living rock of the island. Karol took a candle, lit it from another, and descended.

It was cool behind the curtain, much cooler than in the cottage. Crocks and sacks stood on the floor and on the shelves, along with stoppered jars of glass frosted with age and use. String sacks of fist-sized cheeses coated with beeswax hung from knobs of rock.

Karol made a pouch of her overskirt and dropped two of the cheeses into it. She found the butter in a small glazed pot and brought that, too. She put the butter and cheese on the table before the old woman.

"What shall I fetch you to drink?" she asked.

"There's water in this jug. Pour some for the two of us. The tumblers are on that shelf."

The Kinninger of Layounna brought two wooden tumblers and filled them with water.

"Serve yourself, now," Moder said. "When you finish, wash our dishes – and yourself, if you like. Bank the fire, sweep the hearth, and make yourself a pallet on the warm stones. There's a bit of sacking somewhere you can make into a shift while you mend your gown. *Can* you mend?"

"Yes," said Karol, for her education had been meant to prepare her for unexpected needs. "…But I'd rather put these clothes away, and wear the sacking."

"Please yourself. Better wash those before you pack them up. Do it tonight, and dry them on the firescreen, and store them in the morning."

Karol took a bowl and a spoon…slowly, her eyes and mind on the old woman who sat in the fat candle's light. Did she know who she ordered about so casually? Surely, she guessed. Surely, at least, she supposed it possible. Men come looking for a missing lady, and a lady comes behind them, begging shelter, asking to change rich clothes for rough….

Yet the old woman behaved with neither respect nor discourtesy, but as if she knew of Karol only what she had been told, and suspected nothing more.

Karol sat on the stone floor; warm, here, from the fire's heat.

She felt she should fear the crafty, fierce old woman, but she didn't fear her. From the moment she had stepped into the clearing, she had felt… not "safe"… not quite "befriended"… At any rate, she felt she hadn't made an error in coming to the island. After all that had come before, and all that must follow from it, having made not-an-error should count as a victory of some kind.

Karol took a spoonful of the stew, a small one, so it would cool faster, and broke off a corner of the bread. She was starving. She was ravenous. She was dead, and she wanted to be dead, but the life inside her wouldn't let her die. It was hungry, and the Kinninger ate to feed it, sitting on the stones before the fire.

There was movement behind her as she ate her stew and took out more; movement, sound, and a passing chill. As a sign of her trust, she didn't look around.

A cup was held before her.

"Fresh milk from the cold room," said Moder, shaking the cup impatiently. "Hasn't quite cooled yet. Hasn't separated. I ate all the butter. You have this."

Karol took it, feeling she had passed some sort of test, wishing she could care.

She drank the thick milk and, while she waited for her second bowl of food to cool, turned the cup in her hands. It was fired pottery, made of green-gray clay. Copper filigree was fixed around the stem and half-way up the bowl, the copper forming figures. Figures of....

"Where did you come by this, Moder?" she asked.

"Don't remember. I've had it this many a year. Why?"

"I've seen this pattern before." Birds spiraled around the cup, the head of each half-lost in the flowing tail of the one before it. "No, not this pattern, but something like it. On a bracelet from Kozabir."

"Not surprising. All sorts of things find their ways here, Cinnie beren Moder. All sorts of things find themselves all sorts of places, and the tales of how they got there would be mad. Use the cup while you're here, if you fancy it."

"While I'm here...." The words were bleak. "When must I leave? Tomorrow?"

"Do as you please," said the old woman, lighting an after-dinner pipe, and settling herself on a stool across the hearth from Karol. "But if I was a lone woman, I wouldn't walk about while the land was full of men hunting a woman alone. They might mistake you for the Kinninger, and hurt you when they found out they were wrong."

~*~

So Karol stayed and worked as the days grew into weeks and Landry's hunt swirled through the land. She fashioned a gown from a pair of sacks and, from some scraps of stiff leather, sandals for her tender feet. She hunted mushrooms, plants, fruit, roots and bark; some for the stockpot and some for Moder's medicines. She gathered goose eggs, milked the goats, made cheese, made butter, cooked, and cleaned, and washed. She fished. She helped Moder harvest honey from the hives behind the cottage. She ate and grew larger.

Sometimes people came to visit Moder, to ask her for advice or pay her for past help. Payment was seldom in money; more often it was food, or carded wool, or trade goods.

When people came, Karol took to the cold room and hid until they left. She did this grudgingly; she did it for Cameron's child. If she were only free of that life, she could be done with all life, altogether. How tired she was of living. Breathing was hardly worth the effort.

One day, when she came back up, Moder said, "There's news from the capital today."

"What is that to me?"

"It seems you were right, Cinnie beren Moder. The Kinninger is dead. And her sister's put away."

"Sorcha...."

"Is that her name? Karol never thought of that, did she, the day the men were hunting for her? Took to her heels, and forgot that her sister stood behind her."

Karol was stung by the justice of this reproof, and the impertinence. "She had other considerations – no doubt. How dare you judge her?"

Moder Zglaria shrugged.

After a moment's silence, Karol said, "What other news of... of her sister?"

"They say she isn't dead, just locked away somewhere. They say she renounced the throne."

Karol's voice was bleak. "Landry Oliva has her, then."

"No, they say she put herself into a Waystation. What do you think?"

"It could be so. Power frightened her."

"Maybe she knew her limits. Maybe she knew her strengths. Still...," Moder shrugged again, "she could hardly have done worse than Karol, could she, now?"

Karol met the old woman's eyes, then looked away. "Not in the end. Karol did her best. She would have done better, in time. She loosened her grasp, for just a little while. She left her charge in someone else's care, and turned her back. And it was gone."

"Well...better people have done worse, I suppose. Her sister's safe, at any rate, and they say Karol left no heirs. The House of Onagros is dissolved. Landry Oliva's declared himself our Kinninger under the lion flag of the House of Sarpa. We're all invited to rejoice."

Karol felt her face swelling with outraged blood. *Why such fury?* she asked herself. She knew, when the Swords drew on her, that Landry would wear her crown; at least, had plotted for it. But it hadn't been real. Nothing had been real but Cameron.

What a fool she had been! She felt less anger and contempt for Landry than for herself. She had betrayed her House, and the country, and Cameron; she had placed her love above her honor and she had murdered both.

Moder spoke again. "A boy who called himself a son of Ada tried to take the throne –"

"Kinnan?"

"Kinnan. That was it. Kinnan beren Ada, he called himself. Landry Oliva said he lied, and sent the Swords to arrest him."

Karol sat heavily on the stone bench and held herself in her own lap. Her time was very near.

"Arrested Kinnan?" she said faintly.

"The people say he ran."

"Ran away?"

"I've known it to be done, haven't you?"

Karol only nodded.

"Some say he ran to Istok," Moder went on. "Some say Kozabir. They say he'll come again, leading an army. But that's because they don't like Landry Oliva. I don't, myself."

~*~

That night Karol's water broke, and her labor began.

Moder moved her own blankets to the floor, and made her bed fresh for Karol. She bathed her with water from the cold room, and dosed her with blackhaw tonic, but the birth was very hard.

Karol did her part with patient courage, with moans and gasps in place of screams.

"This is not your first," said Moder, but Karol didn't hear or, at any rate, didn't answer.

When the child lay in her arms, alive, clean, fed, and sleeping, Karol closed her eyes and wept, soundlessly, until she slept, too.

The next day, Karol moved herself and her child back to the hearth. She did some work that day, and more the next. She made a pouch for the baby with some rags, and tied it to her body. She took it with her every-where.

Moder Zglaria offered to hold the child sometimes, and sometimes Karol would let her, but not beyond arm's reach. With the old woman cradling the child on her lap, and Karol at her side, they seemed to be a family, bound close by love. But Karol's eyes never left her baby; if Moder shifted, Karol took it back.

~*~

One day, when the weather was warm, and the air was full of fresh scent and birdsong, Karol said, "We leave today."

Moder was seated on the stone bench, turning some fleece into yarn with a drop spindle. Karol's baby, still un-named, watched happily as the shaft spun and the cone of yarn grew.

"I said, 'We leave today,'" Karol repeated.

"I heard you, Cinnie beren Moder. You were welcome to stay, and you're free to go. Do you remember where you put your clothes?"

Karol glared at the old woman. She was determined to go, but she would have preferred a little opposition to her leaving.

"I'd rather wear these," she said. "Keep the others, in payment for them, and in gratitude for the shelter – although I earned it. Didn't I?"

"You did." The old woman jerked her head toward the cold room. "Carry something for your journey. Water, and cheese, dried meat, flour. There's a tinderbox about here somewhere; you might take that. But perhaps you won't be going far."

"I don't know. Kozabir is close, but its border is long. I don't know how far I'll have to look before I find him."

"Who?"

"My brother."

The spindle hummed as Moder drew strands out of the wooly rolag and let them twist with the strands she'd drawn before.

"You know who I am," Karol said. "You've always known."

Moder showed her blocky teeth, her eyes still on her work.

"It's a long, uncertain journey for a child," said Moder.

"I know my business."

"Do you?"

Karol didn't answer her, but said, "I'll find Kinnan first, in secret. Together, we'll buy an army with promises in my name. We'll march home, raising rebellion as we come. Then I'll put Kinnan on the throne, and go to join my sister."

"Give away the crown?"

"Give it away again. I gave it to Landry by default. By what right could

I hold it, now?"

"By what right do you take it back covered with the blood of your people?"

Karol flushed. "I abandoned my people to Landry. You've seen to it I know how he uses them. Do you think they want me to leave them in such peace as that? Do you?"

So Moder fashioned a pack by gathering the edges of a woven rug. In it, she put cloths for the baby, food, the tinderbox, a skin of water, and a small iron pot.

"Take this, too." Moder held out a plain wooden knife case.

Karol opened the case and took out the knife. The handle was ebony, and shaped like a horse, all four feet tucked to its belly as if it were leaping. A slender blade with a single edge curved from its forehead.

"It's beautiful," Karol said.

"It's useful," said Moder.

"I can't pay you for what you've given me. Someday I will. Do you believe me?"

"Sometimes I wait a long time for it, but I'm always paid. Do you know the price for what I've given you?"

Karol felt her deadened spirit stir again. "No. But I'll meet it."

"That's a rash promise. I don't ask for payment."

"Then I'll weigh the value myself. I promise you good measure."

Moder picked up the gray-green cup with its copper spiral of birds. "Fill this with fresh water for me."

Karol fetched water from the well and filled the cup.

Moder Zglaria put the cup on the table and pointed to it. "When this cup is dry," she said, "you'll have paid your reckoning. Not by my accounting; but by yours."

She walked with Karol and the baby across the land bridge and along the river's edge.

Neither woman spoke until Moder said, "I leave you here. Keep to the paths, and mind where you step. Snakes will be active now."

"I haven't seen any."

"Not around here. I don't permit them." She stroked the baby's head.

"I'll bring the baby with me, when I come back to pay you."

Moder's piercing eyes met Karol's. Karol felt their power again, to tell her secrets she already knew.

"I will come back, won't I?"

"How do I know?"

"If I…. If word comes of my…my death….You have my gown. Use it as you see fit."

"I will." Moder turned and left, her blackthorn cane leaving a tiny footprint beside her larger two.

Karol watched her go, then started north again.

She followed the river till the ground became marshy, then moved northeastward, skirting the bog. She spent the night near a peat-charcoal kiln, its smoke and ashes masking her own small cooking fire, its warmth adding to the warmth of her carpet-bag, which she unpacked and wrapped around herself and the baby.

She left Fiddlewood by the peat-cutter's wagon track, following it until it joined the road to Bahari. The road passed very close to the Inland Sea; she could hear the breakers on the rocks below. The Kozabirian border curved away north; she was further from it now than she had been at Pazni, but it was from Bahari she would start. Bahari was much larger than Pazni, and had something Pazni didn't have.

Karol bypassed the town to the south, around a hill and into a hollow.

A wooden house stood there; a wooden fence enclosed a large and grassy yard. A garden was outside the yard, and a chicken coop, and a pen holding two cows with one she-calf between them.

Five children, all under the age of eight, played inside the boundary of the palings.

This was Karol's first stop; the Bahari baby farm. Ada beren Cinnie herself had established five of them, one to each District, for the relief of abandoned infants. At the age of eight, the children were placed in foster homes or apprenticed. The Moders at the farms were held to strict accounting for the well-being of their charges, both while in residence and in their placement. Karol had maintained her interest in the baby farms, even after other official business had been eclipsed, and knew all this.

One of the children saw Karol, and shouted. Then all of them shouted, and waved their arms at her. One ran into the house and came out towing a woman by her apron.

The woman met Karol at the gate.

"Come in, my dear," the woman said. She saw the child, awake, and twisting its head toward the new voice. "The pet!" the woman said. "The darling! You're never going to leave it?"

"It was my mistress'," Karol said. "She died, and the master won't have it in the house. He bid me bring it here."

She untied the rag which bound the baby to her and handed it – baby, rag, and all – to the woman at the gate.

"Come in," the woman said. "There are papers to sign."

"I neither read nor write."

"Suppose your master changes his mind? Suppose he wants the child again? How will he know it? How will I know him?"

"I'll come back for it. I'll ask for it by name. Call it… Call it Gosling."

"Gosling? Like a baby goose?"

"It's the child of two fools. Call it what you will, but Gosling is who I'll ask for."

"Gosling," the woman cooed to the baby. "The downy little dear."

"If… If I should not come back…. If my master shouldn't send for it again…. Be good to it. Take care of it."

"I will, you may be sure," said the woman. "Look at my children." She smiled around at those still at play and down at those who clustered near her, standing on tiptoe for a look at the new baby. "Do they look ill-fed? Do they look ill-used? I was abandoned, myself, and brought up in the Western House. Masheva beren Moder, my name is, and proud to say it. I have a letter from the Kinninger herself – the real one, I mean, Karol beren Ada – naming me Moder of this house. Now, do I know how to treat abandoned babies, or don't I?"

"I'll take care of it for you," said one of the children, a girl of around four. She had a dirty white ribbon tied around her wrist, and she smiled shyly at Karol.

Karol stepped through the gate, knelt and embraced the child, and kissed her. Just as quickly, she stepped back and closed the gate again.

Masheva beren Moder rocked the infant in her arms and said, "Won't you come in and talk a bit? I'll make some tea, and we'll have some anise biscuits –"

"Yes! Yes!" the children chanted. "Biscuits! Biscuits! Biscuits!"

Masheva shushed them, and they ran back to their play, all except the one with the ribbon around her wrist.

Karol shook her head. "I have a long way to go."

"You're not from Bahari, then?"

"No."

"Where are you from?"

Karol shifted her pack to a less uncomfortable position. Without answering Masheva's question, not even with a lie, she gave the children a final look and walked away.

She felt sick with cold. Her mind and arms sought constantly for that other part of herself that she had put aside.

Moder Zglaria had said that this was not her first; Karol knew it would be her last.

The task she'd set herself seemed enormous – impossible. She nearly turned back, mad schemes in her mind of taking refuge at the baby farm and hoping Landry's people never found her there.

But she went on. She back-tracked to the Bahari road and went northeast, toward the border. The sun was still high but a breeze tumbled flower-scent through the salty air.

On Wild Ass Island, the setting sun drove a ray through the cottage window, catching the gray-green cup in its path. As Moder watched, the cup crumbled to powder, leaving only a copper filigree of birds with flowing tails.

chapter 5
prince anam in exile

Children pelted into the marketplace, caroming off stalls and people with cries of "Farukh! Farukh is coming!"

Farukh Suria'Apa-dan of Sule, they meant. Farukh, the Storyteller His clothing was colorful even by Sulian standards: black-and-white striped trousers, yellow sandals, a red blouse with loose sleeves, and a thin wool tunic the same bright blue as his eyes. A soft red brimless hat sat upon the thick yellow waves of his hair. The tips of his yellow mustache and beard were shaped to points.

Farukh found a clear space to stand, swept his arms above his head, and raised a loud ululating cry that pierced the air of the marketplace. By the time he lowered his voice, he was surrounded by a jostling crowd. Most of his listeners were adults, for the stories of the marketplace were not the stories of the nursery. There were some youngsters on the outskirts of the quieting group. They would listen, and think about what they heard, and pester their elders with awkward questions.

Farukh's listeners fell into his stories as if they fell into a well; for a time, the universe was limited and firmly constructed and out of their control. The storyteller seemed possessed by his own narrative, his face taking on other people's passions, his throat sounding other people's vocal qualities.

"Listen," he said.

~*~

Once, my children, there was a young prince. Although he was a prince, he lived as a common boy, for his parents had so decreed. They hoped that when he should come to rule he would know the hearts of his people, and their wants and their needs. In this, my children, they were wise.

Know, my dears, that in the land where the prince was born, the marriage bond is only a legal form, and love and offspring may be had in other quarters. It was through his mother that the prince came by his royalty. When his parents died, his older sister took the throne. She fell in love with the brother of the prince, and this was a respectable relationship, because they were each half-blood to the prince, but shared no blood with each other.

When the prince – Let us call him Anam, for a prince must have a name, even if it is not his own – When Anam was a man of twenty-two, he expected to move into a full partnership with his brother, who was a skilled artisan. He had served his two years with the citizen militia, and another two for money to put into the business. Anam was already handling all the work and all the accounting when his brother was away, trysting with his love. A partnership was what their father had always planned for them, and it had been arranged between them before Anam's brother left for his final rendezvous. Instead, Anam was left alone in the world.

The local reeve came to the shop, closing the door behind her.

"I'm sorry," she said. "Your brother…. It was an accident. A fire. In a cottage in the east. It burned to the ground." Anam said nothing, and she went on. "They found his ring. The people there knew him. They recognized the ring and they knew he spent time in the cottage. I'm afraid it's certain."

"He was not alone. There was a woman with him."

"No woman's body was found."

His brother was dead, his sister had disappeared.

~*~

Farukh paused, his hands spread to show that the story was not over, but giving his listeners time to feel the young man's pained bewilderment, his sense of loss that was worse because it was unexplained. The story continued:

~*~

Then he found a letter in the few papers his brother left. It was in his sister's hand, signed with the royal titles, and it named Anam as her mother's son. It was sealed with the royal impress, a sprig of dried sage in wax.

He must take this letter and go to the capital. He must tell them of the fire. He, Anam, might be the only person in the world who knew of that fire's importance. He must go and tell. It was time, he thought, to put an end to his family's hideaway love stories and bring the airy romance firmly into reality.

And – the realization struck him so unexpectedly he sat, stunned, gazing into a dying hearth-fire – he was heir to the throne. If his sister failed to reappear, her little brother – he – was heir.

But word came to all the towns and villages, all the farms and hermitages, that the ruler was dead. Since she had left no heirs of her body, the proclamation said, her Consort held her throne.

The audience stirred uneasily. Thrones were passed through lines of blood or the spilling of blood. Since this consort had not been identified as kin to the dead ruler, his claim was not through lineage.

Farukh fisted his hands on his knees, his eyes widening slowly, his head easing forward. When tension crackled between himself and his riveted listeners, he said:

Two men faced each other across the rush-covered floor of the Great Hall: the Consort, slender and dark and confident on the throne at twenty-eight; Anam, twice his size, and even more assured.

"I'm told you claim the throne," the Consort said, the bluntness of his words softened by a charming smile.

Anam gauged his reception by the coldness of the court's faces, not by the Consort's apparent warmth.

"Naturally," the dark man went on, "you have proof?"

"I have a letter from my sister, the late ruler, stating the truth of what I claim."

"What else?"

"…Nothing else. I can tell you when my brother went to meet my sister. I can tell you where they met. The people there will bear me out. Your own steward can tell you when Her Grace was absent from court – the dates will coincide. I can describe Her Grace's person and quirks in familiar detail."

"Of course you can," said the smiling Consort. "You were often in her presence, with your silver goods. My Chamberlain remembers you well, he tells me."

The Chamberlain, a tall, harsh-featured man whom Anam remembered kindly, nodded to him.

Anam held up his wrist, encircled with bronze. "She gave me this bracelet. Surely there's a record of it in the royal treasury – who removed it, and when. My sister gave it to me sixteen years ago."

The Consort smiled. "We are willing to concede that Her Grace may have given you that bauble some time or another. It does not, you must surely see, make you the ruler of the realm."

The handful of courtiers around the throne chuckled mildly, except for the Chamberlain, who looked silently from Anam to the Consort and back.

"My letter proves the truth of what I say!"

"Your letter could prove that you know an excellent forger."

Anam could feel his temper rising to his face. "You call me a liar?"

"I say the tale is a pretty one, no more." The Consort smiled again and held out a propitiating hand. "Did you think you could walk in and claim the realm, and I would step down for you? Be reasonable. Your story will be investigated. Nothing would give me more pleasure than to find a true heir of Her Grace or her revered mother. In the meantime, there is always room for an... enterprising and energetic man with the Swords. What do you say to that?"

Anam turned on his heel and strode out, the laughter of the court following his exit.

~*~

Farukh sat back negligently, rubbing his palms on his striped pants.

"What happened then?" someone asked.

"The Consort kills the prince – see if I'm wrong," said someone else.

Farukh laughed, his teeth surprisingly white in his pale face. To the groans of his audience, he slowly removed his hat and sat it on the paving before his crossed legs. "A man must live." He grunted as he stretched his back and arms.

Coins were tossed and passed. They clinked together in the hat. They missed and rolled and were chased and retrieved by the children, who relished this excuse to pass close to the storyteller, to catch a private glance from his glittering eye.

When the coins had stopped clinking, had begun again and stopped again, Farukh resumed the story.

~*~

Later, in his room at the inn, Anam cursed himself for a fool. It was natural for the Consort to insist on proof. He had been generous, offering a challenger place within the bailey. Investigation of Anam's claim was not only sensible, it was necessary, if the people were to accept Anam as a legitimate successor.

Was it too late? Could he sue for audience again, this time with proper – though galling – humility?

A turn through the dark streets of the capital might clear his head, he thought.

Soft footsteps followed him through the night, but their maker hid in shadows. Anam made sure his dagger was loose in its casing. He hoped his stalker would strike and give him a chance to release some of his tension.

At length, though, Anam returned to his room. It was in shambles. He pounded downstairs to demand an explanation from the landlord and found, instead of his cheerful host, two soldiers, their weapons drawn.

With a savage grin Anam asked, "Aren't there any books in the castle's library? Does the Consort want my 'forgery' to read himself to sleep?"

The soldiers attacked from two sides at once, but Anam had agility allied with muscle and size. He was also intelligent enough to know his danger; terror increased his speed and strength. He dodged, drew his dagger, rolled and struck and danced out of reach. Neither he nor his attackers concerned themselves with rules and niceties of style, but Anam proved an important fraction more creative: A handful of hot ashes from the hearth blinded one opponent, and a slate game board cracked the skull of the other. He left one man cursing and one unconscious. He fled – with nothing but the clothes he stood up in and his precious letter – to Istok.

~*~

The storyteller's posture altered, as if a stage were emptying of players. He had nearly finished.

"Anam hired his sword to Istok, in the east, and to Sule, in the south. He gained the trust and admiration of his fellow mercenaries, but only mockery when he tried to hire them with promises."

"What happened?" cried several voices.

"Go on!"

The storyteller shook his head and rose, tucking the hat that was now a money pouch into a pocket of his tunic.

Giving the crowd one last brilliant grin, he said, "That, my children, is another story."

chapter 6
dreams of the innocents

The castle was full of dreams. Waking and sleeping, the dreamers moved through their days like wanderers in mist, with only their dream-lanterns to guide them.

Landry Oliva's daylight security was shaken by terrors he imperfectly remembered in the morning.

Andrin beren Tooli dreamed of a snake with Landry's face swallowing a mouse who cried out in Karol's voice. He thought this might mean that Karol was really dead but, his Sight compromised by his willful obscuring of it, he could not know.

Corvina beren Oliva dreamed of being named her brother's administrative consort, failing to see how women in power were disappearing from the court, or perhaps rejoicing in the attrition of her potential rivals. Once beside him on the throne, she mused (gloved and masked as she handled certain vials from a locked cabinet in her workroom), she could sit alone, shortly following any given meal. Not that she would ever harm her brother, she told herself; it would be enough to know the opportunity existed.

Thane Oliva beren Audre struggled for days to combine the right ritual, the right petition. There were dreams, but none of Karol.

It must be a sacrifice, then.

Oliva walked through the kitchen garden and into the fowl-run, where one of the villeins – Biddi, Oliva thought – was scattering feed from her upturned apron.

"Girl," said Oliva, though the woman was at least as old as Corvina.

Biddi jumped, lost hold of her apron, and dumped the feed in a heap.

"Yes, Thane Oliva."

"Are these all of our birds?"

Biddi stepped around the yard, as gawkily graceful in her pattens as the birds themselves.

"Yes, Thane Oliva."

Oliva beren Audre pointed to a peacock. "Catch me that bird. Not that one, girl, the white one."

Biddi caught the bird and held him against her.

"Shall I carry him to the kitchen, Thane Oliva? He's plump and heavy."

"I'll take him. He isn't going to the kitchen."

Biddi's face went blank as she handed the peacock across the fence.

Oliva grasped the neck of the thrashing bird and tweaked it just so. He went limp. Oliva lifted the head and felt the breast. Alive. Perfect.

She took her peacock, his body under her arm, and carried him into the castle and down the back stairs. In her other hand, she carried a lamp which burned oil rendered from the fat of young goats and perfumed with Everlasting.

Below the well-room, below the storerooms, deep in the heart of the motte, were dungeons. They were little-used since the Five Nations were united as the Five Districts of Layounna centuries before. The stony rooms were cool and silent.

A grated door, made to lock, though unlocked now, opened onto an anteroom. Out of this led three doors, solid, also made to lock.

One was Corvina's workroom, where she mixed her powders and brewed her syrups.

Oliva carried a tin of one of Corvina's mixes now, in a pocket: a blend of scullcap, lady's slipper, hops, saxifrage and catnip, sewn into a cheese-cloth packet.

Another room held the library Corvina and Oliva shared, and to which they added as they learned things the books didn't teach.

The third was Oliva's temple.

Into this third room, Oliva carried her burden. She hung her lantern by a hook and pulled the door shut behind her. She put the peacock onto the altar, a stone slab where once human bodies had been stretched for punishment or questioning. She tied the bird's head and feet with thongs that once fixed human hands; tightly, so he could neither move nor take an easy breath.

Oliva looked at him with fellow-feeling. She was as tightly bound as he, and she had tied her cords herself.

As the eldest daughter of the House of Sarpa, she valued family above all else. She had Sarpa Thanehold from her father, his mother's only child; he had died before Oliva came of age. Her mother, Audre beren Oda, was a younger daughter of a House even older than Sarpa or Onagros, a House of no dishonor, but no ambition. When Oliva beren Audre married, she retired her mother to the lesser estate of Oakwood Thanehold.

As Thane of her own lands, she had been free. She had taken a husband who wouldn't interfere with her or with the raising of their children. When he had died, she had truly mourned him, as one might mourn an inoffensive pet. With a bailiff to administer the Thanehold and a steward to run the manor – both under her strict direction – she had been free to study, to worship, and to perfect her spiritual control. She had initiated her children from their births.

Then she had seen them fall away. Not even one by one, but nearly all together.

Landry, at fourteen, had suddenly declined to attend the rituals. His interest shifted from the spiritual to the mundane. He studied the running of the household, then the estate. He gradually took over from her the duties of directing the steward, then the bailiff; then he took over the steward's duties, and then the bailiff's.

Hayward, at twelve, later that same year, had begun to play truant, spending his days with the cattle herders and the fish farmers, the gleaners and the shearers.

Corvina had not abandoned Tarkastrianism, but her talent lay in alchemy. She indulged her mother's spiritualism, but she produced her powders and elixirs for their physical effects, not for the supernatural powers they controlled. A bad brief marriage had taught her bitterness but no reverence.

Then Ada beren Cinnie had died, and Karol beren Ada had come unmarried to the throne.

Oliva had used all her powers of persuasion, on her sons and on the Divinities, to graft her family onto the royal line. If Karol married Landry, Oliva had reasoned, no doubt her oldest son could charm one child at least out of his wife. In this, Landry had disappointed her. Still, Hayward wed Karol's sister, Sorcha, and Sorcha gave him children – there was hope for the future there.

Then Landry had shown himself to be his mother's son, and master of his fate.

He had shown himself master of his mother's fate, as well. With Landry's marriage, Oliva had given her Thanehold into Hayward's keeping. She had moved into the castle, bringing the widowed Corvina with her, thinking to give her son counsel and advice. He had welcomed her and showed her honor, but asked for her help less often than he asked the other Thanes. He was no longer his mother's bailiff, he was her Lord, and his sister's, as well.

Oliva could bear all that for the elevation of her line to royalty, but success sat heavily on her.

Now came this doubt. If Karol had left heirs, they weren't, Landry assured her, also his.

Which brought Thane Oliva to this dungeon, with this sacrifice.

Oliva spoke the sounds, in the sacred tongue Tarkastrus had learned from The Divine itself, to invoke the attention of Tortoise.

She put her cheesecloth packet into a cup of horn set in a base of jeweled silver filigree. She placed the cup on the floor at the head of the altar, at the corner which canted down over a drain. What liquids that altar and that drain had been constructed to dispose of, Oliva well knew. She fused the acts of policy done upon captured enemies in the past with what she did now. She reduced the poor peacock to a symbol, although there was nothing symbolic about the knife which slit his throat. The blood filling Oliva's horn cup, releasing the aroma of her tea and intermingling its own metallic smell, was also real.

When the tea was covered by blood, Oliva removed the cup. She held it, praising its warmth, its scent, its power. Then she added water from a goatskin bag and drank the mixture off. She plucked out the peacock's tail-feathers and cut off his crest, wrapping them all in a purple cloth. She tucked the cloth into her bodice, over her heart.

With drowsy words of thanks, Oliva sluiced the cup, the knife, and the altar. She untied the body of the bird and carried him, his lifeless head dangling, back to the kitchen. Thrifty and at peace with her God, Oliva gave the peacock to the cook as a gift for the servants' table and went early to her chambers.

The cook, who followed the unled Way if she did anything, clucked over the bird with pity and made it into a brewet for the Consort's supper. "She's *his* mother," she said. "Let *him* eat her filthy leavings."

In her rooms, Oliva sent her body servant down to the kitchen to fetch a pot of hot water, then dismissed the girl to a rare evening of freedom.

When she was ready to retire, Oliva put another packet of the tea she'd had below into a goblet and poured hot water over it. She consecrated it, uniting it with that other, richer, brew, and drank it.

Half-asleep already, Oliva tucked herself into her feather-bed, beneath down-lined quilts, behind four-poster curtains, under an indigo canopy woven with gold stars. She put the peacock's tail-feathers beneath her pillow, his crest upon her forehead. And she dreamed.

In Oliva's dream, Karol beren Ada and Landry faced each other; a child crouched on the ground between them. Landry hit Karol with his open hand. Although he struck her head, her arm began to bleed. As the blood fell, it turned to water. Karol dissolved in water, in a flood of water. The child became a fish, then many fish. Landry was swept under. He called to Oliva, and she was in the dream. She clutched his hand and he pulled her under, too. The waters drained away, the many fish became one fish, and then a child again; it sat upon the throne, at the table where her son now sat at dinner.

Oliva rose and dressed and hurried to the Hall.

Trestle tables were set up, one on a platform. Two more, perpendicular from either end of the head table, stood on the lower floor. Landed Thanes and their ladies sat at the upper ends of the parallel tables; unlanded Thanes, younger members of Houses, and un-Housed guests sat at the lower end. At the head table sat Landry, an empty chair to either side of him. Rhu beren Robia sat to Landry's right, beyond Karol's still-empty place, with Guthrie beren Melanell, the Chief Sword, at the left end. Corvina sat between Guthrie and the empty chair at Landry's left.

Oliva's was the place at her son's left hand. She sank into her chair, trembling, and called for wine. A villein filled her cup; another offered food, which she refused.

"You're late to dinner, Moder," said Landry. "– What's wrong?"

"Tortoise has sent a vision," she said. "The old Waymaster lied."

"He doesn't dare," said Landry.

"Yet he has."

"Then Karol isn't dead?" Landry spoke in tones too low for anyone to hear but Oliva. Even Corvina could only guess, and plan the words she'd use to draw it from her mother later.

"Karol is dead, but she left an heir. More than one, perhaps, but surely one, and that one will take your place someday."

"He wouldn't dare," Landry insisted. "Your dream spoke of that up-start silversmith from the southern district, the one I would have made an unwitting jester if he'd stayed. Your dream has confused itself with his."

"This was a vision from Tortoise. The meaning was plain." She told him all of it.

Landry was silent afterwards, signaling for song and music to cover his abstraction.

He spoke to Rhu beren Robia, then to Oliva.

"Tomorrow, we'll have the Waymaster up again. I think he didn't lie, but told the truth...cleverly. He said, remember, that Karol had left no heirs in any foster home. But she still might have a child or children under eight –"

"The baby farms! But would she, do you think? Wouldn't she leave them with trusted friends, who knew who they were? Wouldn't she guard against...against what did happen: A stronger hand seizing the power she wouldn't use?"

"She didn't," said Landry. "As the old man said, if Karol had an heir, and it was known, whoever held the child would say so, and prove it, and try to rouse the people in its name. No one has, so no one has charge of one – at least, no one who knows it. How old was the child in your dream?"

"I couldn't tell," said Oliva. "It was small, but that sort of detail can't be trusted. Still, you may be right. You *must* be right."

"I'll quiz the Waymaster tomorrow," said Landry. "He may See more than he told."

~*~

That night, Andrin dreamed himself in darkness, surrounded by the sound of wind or water or shallow breathing. His hands clutched little fingers; they slipped from his grasp like fish, cutting him with their fins.

Summoned the next day to the great hall, he walked slowly. He felt disaster coming though he couldn't See it, as a blind man senses an approaching storm. His dreams confused him now. His teas were always bitter, though not cleansing. Every sound jangled. Every line was skewed. Sometimes he caught a glimpse of clarity, and thought he might regain his balance, but the glimpses always shimmered and were gone.

When Wayfarers of the bailey came to him for help, he could only listen and mouth mechanical advice. They didn't know the difference. But Andrin did.

This time, when the old Waymaster approached Landry and his family, Corvina tossed him no pillow and Landry let him stand.

"Word has reached the court," said Landry, who had no compulsion for the truth, "that Karol beren Ada left a child. She placed it in one of the District baby farms, intending to guide its placement and its training as one of the people, planning to bring it to the court when it had come of age."

"She left no records?" asked Andrin.

"None have been found. If there were any, she must have had them with her when she disappeared. What do you know? What have you Seen?"

"I know nothing," said Andrin. "As for what I See.... Nothing is clear. Perhaps tomorrow.... Soon...."

He tried to meet Landry's eyes, but shame made him drop his gaze; not shame before the Consort, but shame before himself.

"I see," said Landry.

Andrin was afraid that Landry did.

The Consort dismissed him. He left as slowly as he had come, and returned to his comfortless, cold, and barren temple.

When the Waymaster was gone, Landry asked Guthrie beren Melanell to stroll the battlements with him.

The Chief Sword was tall and solid. His skin was pale, and it burned where the sun touched it. He wore a black and silver uniform and a wide-brimmed black leather hat. The backs of his hands were covered by black shields, such as hawkmasters wear. His hair, moustache, and sidewhiskers were of smooth red-gold. His eyes were the green of still pools where venomous creatures hide.

He was writing a history of warfare, based on Layounnan sources only, now that he had the leisure of his position.

He wished, as he often did, that he could gloat with his father over his rapid rise to power. His father, though, was as bitter a grudge-holder as Guthrie himself. When Guthrie had been fifteen, he and his father had pummeled one another bloody over a woman who owned her own cottage and loom. Guthrie left home and joined the militia as a career soldier. The Chief Sword's very success served as a constant crowing in his father's face.

Then there was his mother, who had declared herself sick of both of them. She had abandoned them and pronounced herself unmarried. Perhaps he'd run across her again someday. He liked to think he might have done so already, and sometimes lingered over his memories of female casualties of war, wondering if he detected some resemblance to himself.

When Landry, during one of Karol's long absences, had converted the Swords from an honor guard to an all-male private army, Guthrie had joined. Every benefit he gained, he shared with his supporters, a wise investment which sped his promotion to Chief Sword. Enemies? A strong man always has enemies; a clever man leaves them dead or disabled.

Landry was quick to recognize Guthrie's valuable qualities: deviousness, ruthlessness, a complete lack of scruples, brutality kept in check by ambition, and what Landry took to be blind loyalty. Landry had called upon those qualities when he decided the time was right for Karol to make way for a more attentive administrator.

Now the two men walked in silence for a while. The wind was strong and steady, bringing a touch of dampness with it, though Fiddlewood River flowed past some miles to the east.

"Suppose I had an enemy," said Landry. "And suppose my enemy had a child. Suppose he hid this child at a baby farm, and no one knew which one, or under what name he'd left it."

"Kill your enemy," said Guthrie, "and the child is lost."

"But suppose it's prophesied the child will not stay lost. Suppose the child is fated to be my downfall. What then? How can I protect myself from a child I can't find?"

"You can find it," said Guthrie. "You just can't identify it."

"Find it for me," said Landry.

"And when I have?"

"I don't forget. Not help or hindrance."

The Consort held out his hand. Guthrie clasped it, feeling that clasp raise him from hireling to friend, a feeling Landry's strength lay in stimulating.

"I'll give you a letter of empowerment," said Landry. "Do what you must, and do it soon."

Guthrie remained on the battlement when Landry left to compose his letter. What he must do was simple; how, would take some thought.

For Guthrie beren Melanell had dreams of his own. Not dreams of what he might do, but dreams of what he had done. He and his sword.

Guthrie drew his sword now, and held her across his knees. She caught the sun and flashed it into his eyes. She had been forged in Kozabir; Guthrie had taken her from a mercenary he killed in a border skirmish and had named her: Deya beren Blotha – Death, born of Blood.

They worked well together, he and Deya. They had served Layounna in the militia and now in Landry's Swords. She sang when he drew her in battle. She sang when he wielded her; even the cries of her victims held a note of awful song.

In the night, in Guthrie's dreams, she sang to him. The burden of the song was always death. Blood spattered his dreams. If he dreamed of flowers, they were red. If he dreamed of jewels, they were red. If he dreamed of earth, the clay was red. He dreamed of women, and he slew them. He dreamed of friends, and he slew them. Nothing he dreamed of lived, except himself – himself, and Deya's voice.

He could almost hear her when he was awake now. She whispered of the blood in living things. He could almost see it pumping, could almost hear it buzzing in veins. He almost thirsted for it, but nearly choked with his dreams' surfeit.

How to kill, and not kill? he asked himself. How to satisfy the Consort, satisfy himself, and keep it from his dreams? For he must keep these children from his dreams. He'd spilled the blood of children before in border skirmishes and the occasional ethnic rebellion in a District. The dreams that had followed had been most dreadful. That blood had clung to him, and it had burned like acid.

Guthrie rode out alone that afternoon. He carried Landry's letter of empowerment, but didn't plan to use it, yet. First he must reconnoiter.

He went to each District's farm; went to view it, rather. He sat in the taverns of the nearby towns and took the public measure of various officials. Within a week, his plans were made and laid. He sent picked men to the farms in the South, the West, the North, the Central Districts. He, himself, went East.

Bahari and its baby farm lay in the Eastern District, where the Inland Sea – and Layounna's navy – pushed the Kozabirian border northward.

Bahari was where the plan would end. Guthrie was there to feed it to that end. Guthrie was there, because that house's Moder just might be a problem.

Of the Moders of the other houses, three were old; these had welcomed a pension, even with relocation. Their replacements might be puzzled to come to empty houses, but orphans were never in short supply for long, and the houses would soon be filled.

The fourth Moder was slightly younger, and was happy in her work. She had grown fat on the crown's allowance, while her charges had grown thin. She had contracted to absent herself on a certain night, and to ask no questions the next morning.

The fifth... The fifth was Masheva beren Moder, of Bahari. Too young to retire, too honest to be bought, she would have to be dealt with when the time came, and Guthrie trusted no one but himself to do so.

The night of the "campaign" came. At each baby farm, armed men entered with quiet steps. They opened bottles and poured the contents onto cloths. They laid the cloths on sleeping children's faces; then, when the children's breathing changed, they tied the cloths securely. The children were stripped, leaving them more anonymous than even orphans. They were sealed into barrels Guthrie had bought in Kudasad and his men had brought for this, strong barrels, but not watertight.

The Swords knew only that the children were to be moved in secret. They crated them, loaded them, drove them with bruising haste. Each group of Swords left its captain with the cart; when he was alone, he opened the containers and made sure the children still slept, adding liquid to the cloths on their faces if necessary. Then each captain passed his cart-load to another, under orders not to exchange a word. These secondaries knew only that they had loaded carts to drive to a certain place in the Eastern District.

The four carts reached that point at different times, unloading into a wagon to which was hitched a horse bred to pull such loads. The four groups went their ways, not seeing or suspecting one another.

Guthrie beren Melanell drove the wagon, his own horse tethered behind. He drove it to the baby farm outside Bahari, arriving by night, stopping before his arrival could be heard. His three most trusted men, he placed outside the house.

Then he walked in.

Masheva beren Moder woke – and died – to Deya's singing.

Guthrie drove the wagon to the Bahari road into a stand of trees. He left a man to guard it and rode his own horse back to the town.

He knocked on the door of the District Roll-Keeper; a man, Guthrie had learned, of more ambition than ability. The door was opened by the man, himself.

"It's time to make yourself useful, Darcy Aminta," Guthrie said. "Come prove your worth."

Darcy Aminta hesitated as if something might hold him back from coming.

Guthrie showed him the letter of empowerment from Landry Oliva.

Darcy stepped inside, got his cloak, and said a soft word to someone in the house.

An unintelligible cry was cut off when Darcy came out and shut the door.

Darcy saddled his horse quickly, and Guthrie led the way to the wagon.

"There's cargo in the back," Guthrie said. "Drive it to Lands End Point and throw it over. Keep the cart and horse. You'll need them, when your transfer comes through."

"Transfer?"

"Your promotion, I should say. Landry Oliva forgets no one, neither friend nor enemy."

"I will do it."

"His Grace expects no less."

Guthrie turned his horse and rode away. The man he had left to guard the wagon followed and watched until he saw Darcy begin his task; then he, too, rode away.

Guthrie journeyed without sleeping, stopping only to eat and rest his horse.

He washed and shaved and presented himself in the Hall.

Landry was there. Rhu beren Robia was there, showing him some papers. Corvina was there, watching them both like some beautiful bird of scavenge.

Landry saw Guthrie approach and dismissed the other two.

"What news?" he asked.

"My Lord," said Guthrie, "your fears were unfounded. It seems there are no children at the baby farms."

"None?"

"No, My Lord."

"Does anyone know what's happened to them?"

"No, My Lord. They've vanished from the earth. They've even vanished from the Roll-Books at the farms."

"What promises or threats did you need to make?"

"Threats: None; I don't make threats. Promises: A few sacks of copper and your good will. And a promotion and transfer for the Roll-Keeper who unwittingly did the magic. He's a man of no spirit, little wit, and high hopes. A man who may prove useful later, and no threat in the meantime."

Landry rose, and took Guthrie's hand again. "Tomorrow," he said, "there is one throne in Layounna: Mine. And you shall sit at my right."

Later, Guthrie slept, and Deya beren Blotha sang. She lay before him, shining like the sea. The sun rose, and she was a sea of blood. He fell into the sea and the sea sang in his ears and broke upon the sand with the sound of children's cries.

chapter 7
SALALI

Fala Salali was a woman of more than forty years. She was petite, hair frizzy and grizzled, face smooth and brown and tough, like tanned leather. Her deep-set black eyes looked at the world with a gaze both bright and impenetrable. She wore studs and baubs in her ears and nose, bracelets on her wrists and ankles, and layers of whole cloth upon her body, wrapped and tucked and pinned.

Salali made small toys, trinkets, charms, and the cheaper sort of jewelry out of feathers and beads, wire, string, shells, stones, anything she found or could buy for next to nothing. She carried her goods folded up in a blanket with handles stitched onto it, and she traveled – by charity, if she could find it, by foot, if she could not – from Kozabir to Sule to Layounna to Istok to her native Nishi in the north west.

She was a woman alone, and had been so, for as long as anyone remembered.

Salali, herself, couldn't remember a time when she had not felt alone, even as a child. She came from a warm and demonstrative family in the southern sector of Nishi, both parents kind and attentive, three elder siblings pompously indulgent, two younger siblings grudgingly deferential, all tumbled together in an apartment just big enough to hold them. Yet there had always been an empty space of uncertain shape and size in her life. She had accepted the hollow ache as normal until adolescent heart-to-hearts with friends had revealed otherwise. Something was missing – something vital – something she couldn't define, since no one else felt such a lack, nor could anyone identify anything they possessed or understood or felt that she did not. She had family, she had friends, she had a place in her society…yet she was profoundly alone.

Sometimes, in the middle of the night, she would awake from a dream in which she looked into a mirror and saw another form, reached out to it, twined her arms around it and was gathered to its heart. Then, waking, she would weep for what she had never known.

When she confessed the dream to a friend, she was assured that her longing was for a sweetheart. The young Salali was graceful and lovely; she had no trouble attracting admirers. Some warmed her heart, some warmed her bed, but none banished her solitary sorrow. She remained unwed. She left the security of Nishi's border fortress and wandered the world, seeking an answer to which she did not know the question.

"Have you heard…?" "Have you heard…?" Everywhere she went, she was asked about the troubles in Layounna. She knew nothing of Layounna's troubles; all countries were alike to her, empty wastes where she sold her wares and searched in vain. Her ignorance was more welcome than any news, as it turned her questioner into someone with superior knowledge, who could tell her something she didn't know.

"A man came forward to claim the throne. Claims he's the old Kinninger's son, the missing Kinninger's brother. They say he ought to be Kinninger by right, but that other one, that Landry, harried him out of the country. His name is Kinnan. That even sounds like 'Kinninger,' doesn't it?"

She was told the story so often, she began to take an interest in it. Kinnan had been seen here, had ridden with raiders there, frequented this tavern or that outlaws' roost. It was just as easy for her to go one place as another, so she went where he was said to be.

She succeeded where Landry's Swords continued to fail. One evening in the southern land of Sule, she walked into a brightly-painted canvas pavilion, greeted the lady who reclined in the place of Ownership, and unwrapped her wares. The lady and her maids, perhaps mistakenly supposing she didn't understand their language, fingered the trinkets, exclaiming at the cleverness of their make and laughing at the cheapness of their makings. Meanwhile, she looked around at the other recipients of the lady's desert hospitality.

Her heart lurched and thudded at the sight of one group, even before her ear separated the sense of their speech from the tangle of accents and tongues around her.

One man, a Sulian, was the focus of the others. He was tall, a little plump, rather pale, with yellow hair and beard, sparkling blue eyes, and a small pointed nose. He was leaning forward, elbows on knees, his regard fixed on a man with his back to her.

"Kinnan!" the plump man said, and laughed. His voice carried the name into her soul and fitted it into the void there.

"Farukh!" replied the man he had addressed. "Now, how do you like *your* name shouted aloud in the Tents of the Open Plain?"

"I like my name shouted anywhere, Master, except by the bailiffs. What storyteller doesn't?"

"And what rebel does?"

The other men laughed.

Salali caught her breath as the storyteller saw her interest and pointed her out to the rebel, Kinnan. Her mouth went dry. Kinnan seemed to turn slowly, slender form pivoting on his cushion, gold-brown curls revealing a profile, then a face. Not a beautiful face, but a striking one, with clear gray eyes, a large nose, and a cynical quirk to his mouth.

Just before his gaze met Salali's, the pavilion's lady tapped her on the hand to bargain for a selection of ear-baubs and hair-bangles.

She did not dare look toward him again, but she was aware of him and of the storyteller, knew where they were without looking, and knew they had left the Tents when she woke the next morning.

~*~

In Nishi, it was customary for a young man to take a much older woman for his first wife. She had been in the world long enough to know that the custom, though not rejected in Layounna, was not common there. So she followed the young man her heart yearned after, sometimes crossing his path, sometimes even speaking to him. The figure in her dream mirror was now his, often with Farukh standing behind him, holding out a hand to her, as if inviting her to step through the mirror and meet her destiny. Awake, she conversed with both men in commonplaces, and waited for her love to either abate or master her. If it did not wear away with time, she knew she would show how she felt and accept what happiness or humiliation might come. She feared facing Kinnan with her hopes – feared it more than anything she could imagine – more than anything except the prospect of not seeing him again.

His claim to the throne, she believed absolutely. She sought out the storyteller Farukh when she could and delighted in his company, because

he had been with Kinnan when she had first seen him. She heard the claim
debated in mercenary camps around the border of Layounna and she listened to the gossip in the marketplaces, especially in Layounna's Eastern
District, where Kinnan's brother died and his sister disappeared.

She believed in the young rebel and she longed to be of service, to
help him to his rightful place and see him content.

One morning in Kozabir's capital city of Granitz she saw a way, and
the way involved Farukh.

This happened on the storyteller's sixth day in the capital. As usual, he
made his entrance after the marketplace was full and lively, but the first rush
of urgent business had ended. From where he took his stand, Salali had a
view of his face and the faces of most of his listeners, though she couldn't
hear what he said – his words were gauged to carry only as far as his power
to extract payment.

One of his listeners, Salali noticed, was a little girl, about five years
old. She was a tiny thing, thin as a new-hatched bird, skin a milky brown
toned with the gray of poor food and not much of that. Her cropped hair
was reddish-brown; her eyes, deep blue – bluer than Farukh's. She was
liberally decorated with bruises – red and purple and blue and yellow. They
shimmered like the bodies of hummingbirds.

Salali had noticed her before: She listened to pieces of stories every
day, obviously stopping only as long as she dared on someone else's errands. Farukh always had a smile for her, but had never coaxed a smile in
return.

On this day, his gaze locked with that of the bruised child, and he
smiled encouragingly. He beckoned her closer with a motion of his head.

She took a wavering step toward him, then she seemed to catch herself. With a swift glance around at the cobbles, as if looking for something
she feared to find, she ducked her head and hurried away.

It was at that moment, when she saw the power of Farukh's tales over
a child who was clearly forbidden to stop and listen, that Salali made her
plan. It was the plan of a woman who knew the swiftness of time and the
dullness of unfulfilled longing.

Neither could say later who had approached whom, but the storyteller and the trinket-woman left the plaza together. She poured forth her
plan, or he drew it from her, but it passed from one mind to the other and
was quickly agreed to.

"He'll be at The Serpent's Tooth," Salali said. "He usually drinks there, then sleeps where he can find a dry spot."

Farukh did not ask how she knew this.

They went to the tavern together.

The owner was not welcoming. "Get out, the pair of you! Does this look like the marketplace?"

"No," Farukh answered. "In the marketplace, the people tend the pigs; here, a pig tends the people."

Amid laughter so general the tavern keeper thought it best to seem to join in, Salali and Farukh slid into a booth across a scarred and dirty table from Kinnan.

"Respects and greetings, Master," Farukh said.

"I'm not your master."

"I choose to call you so," said the storyteller. He looked at Salali. "Do you call him so, as well?"

She shook her head. "No man is my master," she said, with dignity.

Kinnan laughed, and looked surprised, as if he hadn't laughed for a very long time.

"Good for you!" he said to her.

Her eyes shone, but she made no sign of how his approval fed her spirit.

"Master or not," she said, "I put myself in your service. We both do."

"What service is that? And why?"

"My why is my own. I speak for no one else."

Farukh only grinned and came to the point: "Master, you will never buy an army with words."

"I know."

"But I can." He touched his tunic with the fingers of one long thin hand.

"You? How?"

"If you could raise an army to march against your country, they would face not only the Swords and militia but resistance from the common folk, who would rather be slaves of countrymen than be freed by foreigners. Am I right?"

Kinnan frowned, and picked a splinter from the table before him.

Farukh went on, "But, if the people of Layounna would rise –"

"If they had done that," said Kinnan, "I wouldn't be here now."

"That is not a closed door," said Salali. "It's a drawn curtain, at worst. They can be made to rise, or be made ready to rise. It will take time. Not months, but years. A generation, or half a generation. Eight years. Ten years. Can you wait that long?"

"Do I have a choice? I can't fight an army alone, with every hand turned against me – or, at best, turned *from* me. What can you do?"

"I can do what I do," said Farukh, spreading his hands, palms up, fingers curled, as if they held wonders. "I can tell stories. Stories with hidden meanings that will creep into the people's minds and spirits. Stories whose meanings become more clear with time and thought and plainer speaking. Stories that grow from tales to legends to myths to truths to precedents and justifications." His fists thumped against the table, real and incontestable.

Salali nodded eagerly and said, "And I can do what I do. I can listen. I can overhear gossip in the marketplace and in the kitchens where I sometimes sell my goods. I can gather information and bring it back to you."

"Why?" Kinnan asked again.

"When Farukh has prepared the ground," Salali said, "and I've done my part, I'll come back and tell you why. The work Farukh does will be useless without the information, and the information will have a price. If my price is too high, find your help elsewhere. If my price is paid, I'll count the years cheap."

Kinnan toyed with the splinter he'd pulled from the table. "I ought to think it over," he said.

"Think all you like," the storyteller said. "You'll have the time for it."

"Suppose I say, 'Don't do it.'"

Salali took her own hand, to keep herself from taking his. "As I said, you're not my master. I leave tomorrow. I return when I return."

"And I stand with Salali," said the storyteller. "She's offered me a chance to overturn a throne with the mere sound of my voice. How could I resist?"

A small shadow sidled up to their table. A hand like a flower trodden into the mud touched Farukh's arm.

It was the child who hungered for smiles, whose bruises shimmered like the bodies of hummingbirds.

"What is it, child?" Farukh asked.

"Go out the back," said the girl. "Two men in black armor are in the front, and two more are at the side."

"Swords!" said Kinnan.

The child nodded. "And knives, too. I saw them and I knew you were in here –" her eyes never left Farukh's face, "– so I came to warn you."

"Landry Oliva's arm is long," said Farukh, "and his power is greater than I knew. I *will* enjoy this."

"You're a good girl," said Kinnan. "*Is* there a back?"

The child nodded again. "It's boarded up, but it opens, if you know how. Sometimes I sleep there, when they lock me out at home. Hurry."

The men and the woman followed, trusting her good will and honesty. She led them to safety in an alley.

"That way," she said, pointing. "That takes you around and into another part of the city."

"Thank you," said Kinnan.

"Bless you, child," said Salali.

Kinnan reached into his money pouch. "I haven't much, but…this is for you."

The girl held Kinnan's coin in her palm as if she saw with new eyes. "They won't let me keep it." She closed her grubby fist and touched her knuckles to a fresh bruise on her cheekbone.

Farukh laid a gentle hand on her matted hair. "I'm leaving town. Come with me."

"Or with me," said Salali. "I can teach you to make such pretty things…."

"No!" the girl cried. "He'd bite your heads off. They told me he'd bite the heads off anybody who tried to take me away from them!"

"Who would?"

"Tortoise."

Farukh stifled a snort. "My dear child –"

The girl melted into the shadows and was gone.

Sounds of rumpus and upset came from the public house behind them. Kinnan and his supporters took the way the girl had pointed, following the alley's twists in silence. When they were far enough away to separate on a well-lit cross-street, Salali spoke to Kinnan:

"What will you do, now?"

"I've been offered refuge, if I ever needed it, in a smithy in Vatra."

"I'll seek you there. If you move on, leave me word."

"I will. Until we meet again…."

The three clasped hands and parted, Kinnan to seek sanctuary in Vatra, Farukh and Salali to raise a rebellion one mind at a time.

chapter 8
death of a stranger

Farukh and Salali left Granitz that evening, mingling with a troupe of traveling players bound for Istok. Salali did a brisk business in trinkets that looked rich from the stage. Farukh spun tales easy to perform and full of dramatic intensity.

Half a day's journey into the heavily forested Istok, their crude dirt-and-cinder track abruptly turned into one of the Old Roads that cut through the country.

A lavender dove shot into the sky above the treetops and arrowed southeast before them. Within five minutes, they lumbered past a Dragon's Eye – a watcher's hut and dovecote. The hut was empty, of course; no one sees a Dragon's Eye on duty. He or she had sent the dove ahead; around its leg was a string knotted in a code that told the next Dragon's Eye all about them.

By the time their wagons reached Bought for Three Goats – the first cluster of huts along their route – the central common was filled with an eager audience. There were many hands to help unpack the sketchy stage, the faded costumes, the battered props.

The troupe conferred and decided to give a time-honored comedy. It was well-received and was paid for with hospitality and supplies.

After three days' travel and two evenings' rehearsal, the troupe performed one of Farukh's plays.

It was a pantomime, of course. The old plays, the ones audiences had seen all their lives, could be done in any language available. Each player could speak in a different tongue and it wouldn't matter; everyone knew what was being said and what would happen next. A new play, though, was best done wordlessly, producing its own dialogue as a plant produces seed.

Farukh called his play "Death of a Stranger", which translated in Istok to "Dragon Guest Sinks to Paradise."

The play opened with a family group pulling a wagon from one side of the stage to the other. Their clothing marked them as Kozabiri. In a dance-like series of movements, they indicated they stood in a high, lonely, open place. Piles of unused props draped with blankets indicated rocks. A boy, his head and arms sticking out of a sack, hung from the stage's back arch. The audience ignored the boy, waiting for their cue to see him.

The family struck at the stage boards with tools and lifted pieces of white-painted wood, lifted them as if they were heavy as stone. The audience understood the value of stone in a landscape where stone was rare.

Mother, father, and the two boys stopped work. The boys, one smaller than the other, shoved and quarreled and clowned. The audience laughed and clapped along to the spirited music of the troupe's pipes and drums. The mother took a bundle from the cart and opened it, handing food to everyone, drinking from a jar and passing it to her husband.

Another woman entered, dressed as a Layounnan. She carried a bundle of her own, and clearly wanted to join the group. They agreed. She undid her burden, revealing a cooking pot; she drew food from it and shared it, and the family shared their jar with her.

The smaller boy wandered away from the group. He poked among the rocks, moving upstage until he was almost beneath the boy in the sack. The suspended actor moved his hands; one of the musicians shook a tambourine; the boy on stage jumped back. A snake fashioned from a bit of rope rose to striking position, lifted with a string manipulated by the boy above.

The audience gasped in fear for the story's character and in admiration for the ingenious simplicity of the effect.

The threatened boy moved; the serpent lunged. It was clear that the serpent would attack – successfully – if the boy tried to run.

The family and the stranger hurried to his aid, but stopped when they saw his danger. A step too close and the serpent swayed and darted its head toward the nearest target: the small boy.

The father picked up a stone but was obviously afraid that using it would trigger an attack on his son. The mother, distracted with terror and despair, clutched her other boy.

The Layounnan woman eased away to the site of the meal and retrieved the cloth which had wrapped her bundle. She wound the thick fabric around her left fore-arm, making a shield. In her right hand, she held a knife. She moved directly behind the snake and kicked a stone. The viper swiveled toward her. She brandished her knife and stepped closer. The villagers, accustomed to the ways of reptiles, knew that the knife was only a symbol. The creature could neither see it nor understand its use, but displaying it gave the woman courage in her perilous rescue. The snake, completely distracted from the boy, swayed and dodged toward this new focus.

The father ran to his son and snatched him away.

The Layounnan woman eased back from the serpent now that the boy was out of danger, but the viper struck. For the space of five heartbeats, the action held in tableau, then the woman's knife swooped and knocked her attacker away. To an irregular chorus of percussion, the snake and the woman did battle, strike and strike. At last she dropped her knife and shield, held the poisonous limp body aloft, and dashed it to the rocks.

The grateful family rushed to her with celebration in their gestures, until she showed them her wounds. To their horror, she collapsed into their arms.

A frenzy of grief showed the audience the Layounnan was dead.

In the silence, the mother's voice started small and grew; she was joined by the father, then by the small boy, then by the older boy, then by the company, and then by the audience. They sang an Istok war song of blended sorrow and triumph, a song which had a counterpart in every land in the civilized world.

chapter 9
The waymaster's grandmother

When Andrin beren Tooli woke, the late morning sun shone through the temple's shutters, laddering the floor with gold.

His dreaming had been no more informed and meaningful than his waking had become. What he knew, he knew without proof, but with utter certainty: He had lost his Sight for nothing. The children he had tried to save by denying his Vision of them, he had lost. His own action in lying had lost them, leaving his hands empty of everything but blood.

Andrin rose and put his sleeping mat away, stirred the fire, and did his exercises. He washed and shaved and dressed, performing all these familiar activities as if they were odd and alien, their purposes unclear. He put no herbs in his temple pot; his center of balance gone, any choice he made would be random and useless. He felt sluggish and bloated, like a toad in a sudden frost. His mind was cloudy. His spirit was obstructed. His inner being which, until so lately, had seemed to him like transparent patterned silk, now seemed like sandpaper twisted to rub against itself.

He suddenly saw himself as if he sat across the room. He saw an old man, his face sharpened by discontent, his still-strong and supple body slumped.

But this was not himself. This man's hair fell thick and white to below his shoulders.

Out of sorts, Old Man? Andrin heard a voice with laughter in it say.

The man was his grandfather; the voice, his grandmother's.

This was a memory, but as clear as any vision. His grandfather, a village elder, grumbling with ill-temper over some administrative detail. His grandmother, leader of the Council of Women who chose and advised the elders, gently amused, ready to lift him over his obstacle as a mother lifts a baffled child out of a little maze.

Andrin's paternal grandparents had raised him after his parents' deaths by disease. They were the only family he had ever known. Now he looked at them again with the eyes of memory joined to the mind of knowledge.

His grandfather had been clever. The wealth he accumulated hired the best teachers in the Eastern District for young Andrin. His endowment assured Andrin a place in an already well-endowed Waystation, beginning as a scribe, by-passing the grinding manual labor usually given to novices.

Verrina beren Unna, his grandmother, had been wise. Andrin remembered her as an old woman, a broad hat shading her face, hoeing the garden, a visiting Adept of the Way working beside her.

Andrin's grandfather had died when Andrin was still a Waystation priest. Andrin's grandmother….

Not long after Andrin had returned from Grandfather's funeral, a friend of the family wrote to him, saying that Verrina beren Unna had one day dressed as if for a feast, and spread her arms and leapt into the river. Her body had never been recovered.

It sorrowed Andrin that Grandmoder, touchstone of balance in his life, in the village, and beyond, became unbalanced in her mind at the last. He tried not to think of her on that final day, but as she had been until then.

Andrin thought, *How had Grandmoder helped Grandfather? How would she have helped me, now?* Andrin let his memory do for him what he could no longer do for himself.

A flash of yellow. A flash of yellow, struck off a bottle by the sun.

Dandelion wine. She would have opened a bottle of dandelion wine, called it a "tonic," placed it before him, and left him alone. Some time later, she would have come back in and helped him talk out his own answer.

Andrin had a bottle somewhere; the kitchen maid Biddi had given him one last Winter Solstice. He had never opened it; he didn't need – he hadn't needed – wine, which dulled the mind. Now that his mind had turned to mud, wine could only enliven it.

Andrin found the wine in the back of a cabinet. Scrupulous cleanliness being part of his discipline, the bottle shone as if it had been on display. How odd, he thought, that he had polished this bottle every day for months, and yet had forgotten where it was and what it was.

He poured some of the wine into his drinking bowl, lifted it to his grandmother's memory, and drank.

By and by, he was hungry. He went out to his garden, picked some peas and dandelions and took them inside, washed them and ate them. He made up a song about them but when he had finished it he couldn't remember how it began.

This was the state he was in when a Sword knocked at the temple door, telling him that His Grace demanded Andrin's presence in the Great Hall of the tower.

"Stay, brother!" Andrin shouted. "Walk along with me!"

When he found his feet and arranged them beneath himself, elevated himself above them and opened the temple door, he was disappointed to find the Sword had gone.

Andrin sighed and arranged the folds of his silken yellow robe. A rich material, but it struck him now that he had never cared for the feel of it against his skin. Some said it felt like water, but Andrin thought it felt like oil. Most unpleasant.

Which reminded him that he was wanted in the tower.

On the way up the boardwalk (a very long and very steep boardwalk; he wished he had gone up the other one, then realized there was no other one), he tried unsuccessfully to imagine what Landry Oliva could possibly want with him today.

He entered the hall, then stopped. Something was wrong. Something was different.

The banner on the back wall, to begin with. The blue field, the serrated green leaves, the pink-and-white flowers – the banner of the House of Onagros – was gone. In its place was the blood-red field, the rampant golden lion with his unnatural blue tongue and claws, his head strained furtively to look behind him, of the House of Sarpa.

Landry sat in Karol's outsized chair. His consort's chair was gone. The Chief Sword sat at his right hand, the Chamberlain on his feet behind the throne.

Only the Chief Sword seemed pleased. The Chamberlain looked sour. Corvina looked sourer still. Thane Oliva's mouth was pursed, as if she smelled mice in the pantry. Landry frowned, drumming the fingers of one hand on the arm of the throne.

Andrin walked slowly and carefully across the floor.

"My mother, Thane Oliva," Landry said, "requested your presence. As the afternoon's business was concluded, and as she is my mother, I indulge her in this. Moder, put your questions."

Andrin looked at the Thane.

"Where are Karol's children?" she asked, in a voice that told him she knew the answer, and was only asking to hear what he would say.

Andrin's dandelion mood turned black.

"Where are Karol's children?" Oliva repeated.

"Dead, My Lady," he said.

Landry and the Chief Sword, Guthrie, grew very still.

"By whose hand?" said Oliva.

"Mine."

Corvina gave a puff of laughter, but quieted herself.

"And Karol?"

"Dead, also."

"Also by your hand?"

Andrin said nothing. His eyes strayed from Oliva to Rhu, the Chamberlain. The man met Andrin's look; his plain, open, craggy face as out of place as a cow in a law court.

Oliva turned to her son. "You see?" she said. "The man is a liar and a fool. He's battened on the crown long enough, filling the villeins' heads with his disconnected twaddle."

"He's harmless," said Landry. "If he's made himself a fool, he's more harmless, still. His presence keeps the villeins happy. They wouldn't honor Tarkastrus, even if this man were sent away."

"His temple is an abomination. His presence is an insult to me, and to Tarkastrus."

"But not to the Divinities," Andrin said. "Not to the perfection of the unled Way. That abomination lies elsewhere."

Landry scowled at him. "Be careful, old man," he said. "I'm inclined to tolerate you, but I will not tolerate disrespect toward the crown or the royal House."

"The royal House is gone," said Andrin. "Ada, and Karol – Sorcha as good as dead – and the one who called himself Kinnan beren Ada – disappeared to who knows where…. Oh, you mean *your* House? Sarpa's time is coming, too, My Lord, and soon."

Andrin was surprised at himself. Lying to protect the innocent was bad enough; lying for the sheer joy of stating desire as fact was shocking. Andrin's shock fed his anger, and his anger clenched his teeth behind the lie and refused to take it back.

"You had better be silent. Go now," said Landry, "before I forget your age and usefulness."

"He's spoken treason!" said Oliva. "Have him arrested!"

"Have me arrested!" Andrin shouted. "Have me executed! I'll only be a little before you! You, My Lady –" he pointed to Oliva and her children – "and you and you! Your House is doomed!"

Oliva and Landry both opened their mouths to speak; Oliva to her son and Landry to his Chief Sword. Neither spoke, for Corvina broke into harsh laughter.

Andrin's anger left as quickly as it had come. Sullenly, he waited for Landry's order.

When it came, it wasn't the order he had expected.

"Gather your things and go," Landry said. "Ask what you want from the castle stores. Rhu, give him a cart, but not a horse. Let him take whatever he can pull. Guthrie, see that he's gone by sunset. Will that content you, Moder?"

"He should be arrested."

"Should I begin my reign by executing a man the people see as holy? Would I show strength by pitting the power of the crown against the angry words of a fool?" He spoke to Rhu again. "Take that silk robe from him and give him a villein's tunic. Paint 'Liar' on the back. Let him go in that."

"Well thought of," said Oliva. "Yes, that will do."

Rhu led Andrin downstairs to the storerooms. At the foot of the steps, the Chamberlain spoke, his powerful baritone muted to a murmur. "Was it true? What you said to Thane Oliva about her House being doomed?"

Andrin looked away. His earlier falsehoods had been told for the sake of others; surely the damage they had done to him could have been repaired. But this....

Andrin felt sick at heart. He wanted to go to sleep. He wanted to dance himself senseless.

"I've been with Thane Oliva's household all my life," said the Chamberlain. "They're not evil people."

"Neither were Karol and her babies. Besides, what does evil have to do with doom?"

"To curse them, like that...."

"I didn't curse anybody," said Andrin. "I haven't the power to curse.

I never did. What I said was a prediction." Andrin waved a hand, as if to erase his last words. "What I said was a lie. Landry was right. It was a lie."

Rhu didn't ask the reason for the lie. One question, one comment, and one aborted protest seemed to be all the liberty he would allow himself. Instead, he asked, "Would you like me to get a cart first? After you've seen it and tested its weight, you can decide what to take."

Andrin nodded. "Thank you."

"Will you come with me? Or would you rather stay here; see what stores are available to you?"

"I think I'll stay here, please." The sun was bright outside, and villeins went about their business, talking and laughing; this cool, silent room, layered with smells both sweet and pungent, seemed a haven.

Rhu nodded. "I won't be long," he said, and left.

There was a well in the center of the storeroom floor. It occurred to Andrin, although he had no intention of putting the plan into action, that some opportunity for revenge lay in his power. If he drowned himself in the castle's well he would be out of his misery, and he would create a nuisance or a health hazard, depending on how long it took them to discover his body.

Andrin went to the well. He leaned over. He could see his silhouette in the well's depths, his features and shaven head picked out feebly by the window's light.

It was cooler over the well. Andrin put one hand below the rim; it was cooler still. The water would be cold – a most refreshing drink.

He leaned further over, as if he could gulp directly from that pool so far below. The wine he had drunk seemed to sweep into his head, full of air and fire now; his brain fizzed with it.

A voice whispered from the depths, "Careful…."

Andrin pulled back, then leaned over again. His silhouette wavered and broke to bits, replaced by another face, larger than his and bluish-green. Its muzzle was long and rounded; its mouth opened to show a double row of sharp white teeth. Its eyes were large and dark. The creature glowed, faintly, but enough in the black pit of the well to show itself to the Waymaster.

The head rose above the surface of the water, then the long, slim neck, then the front legs, scaled and clawed, and the body came and continued coming, as Andrin scuffled back to give it leeway.

At last the creature was in the storeroom with him. It was three times as long as he was tall including its fluked tail, but no more than twice his thickness at its broadest part. It had four legs, each ending in five claws. It was covered with scales, some smooth and some rough, ranging in color from yellow-green to violet-blue. As Andrin watched, it dried in the storeroom's air, and its rough scales feathered out until it bore a soft ruff around its head just behind the eyes and a soft crest down its back to the tip of its tail. It held its neck and head erect, at about his eye level.

"You aren't ready for that, yet," said the water dragon, in the whispery voice Andrin had heard from the well.

"Ready for what?"

"Translation," said the dragon.

"Translation...." One of the beliefs of the lay Wayfarers – considered contemptible superstition by the scholars – was that of Translation. They said that a Waymaster could achieve such a level of spiritual transcendence that he or she could convert a mortal body to an immortal one, or could take on another level of being altogether.

"You mock me, Creature," said Andrin. "You're something of Oliva beren Audre's, fabricated by her and placed before me to ridicule my philosophy and to jeer at my failure. I deny your existence and I defy her who sent you!"

Andrin's head still fizzed; he heard himself speak as if from far off, and he thought his words sounded extremely fine.

The dragon spread its lips and gurgled softly. It narrowed its eyes, and tilted its head to one side and, in all this, Andrin recognized gentle laughter.

The fizzy fuzziness snapped out of Andrin's mind. This was no illusion. This was no bottle-dream. Before him stood a creature revered as a symbol by the scholars, documented as actual by the peasants, and...!

"I... know... that... laugh...."

"No one fabricated me," the dragon said, "unless it was myself. No one placed me before you, unless it was you. I've been keeping an eye on you all along, but pride kept your eye from me. Not my pride, you understand, but yours. Today, you're humble. Today, you see me. I've missed you, my Little Plum."

That laugh.... That sweet, silly name.... That clear, breathy voice....

"Grandmoder?"

"You haven't forgotten me, then?"

"I could never forget you." Andrin moved closer to the creature, afraid she would melt into thin reality at his touch. He reached out, tentatively. He brushed a finger against her feathery scales. They tickled. She was real.

He slipped his arms about her neck. She embraced him in return, scratching his back with her claws, in the spot where he had always felt itchiest as a boy.

Andrin's grandmother felt warm, warmer than the room. "Can you breathe fire?"

"Of course."

"Can I see?"

"Later, perhaps. Now, we have business to discuss."

"Business?"

"Your business. The business of your survival. What to take with you and where to go. Are you listening?"

"Yes, Grandmoder." Andrin stopped playing with the dragon's feathery scales and moved away from her so that she could see his paying-attention face.

"When Landry's man comes back, ask only to take a hen. One hen, Andrin, any one. From your temple, take your casting pebbles, your books, your herbs, your sleeping gear, and your kettle. Go west, to the bank of the Fiddlewood River. I'll meet you there."

"Is that where you live? In Fiddlewood River?"

"Yes, no, and sometimes."

"I don't understand."

The dragon caressed Andrin's face with a talon. "Those are words I have never before heard you use. I'm proud of you."

The hardware on the storeroom's outer door rattled. Rhu had returned.

The flukes of the dragon's tail flipped over the well rim as Rhu stood and blinked away the sun's brightness.

"Will you come see the cart?" the Chamberlain asked.

"…Yes."

Andrin felt light again, young again, as he followed Rhu into the keep's courtyard. He was no longer an old man who had lost his way, but a bemused wanderer with a sure guide. Verrina beren Unna had returned to take care of him, and she was proud of him. Precisely why, he didn't know and couldn't imagine.

The cart Rhu had chosen was the lightest in the castle compound. Its floor was two feet by two and made of thin boards. Its sides were made of wattle and its wheels were spoked instead of the much heavier solid ones. It had only two wheels: its rear rested on the ground, its whiffletree canted in the air, breastband dangling.

"Try it," said Rhu. "Then you can gauge how much to take."

"All I want from the castle is a hen. Let Biddi choose her for me. Any one will do. I want some things from my temple."

Rhu drew breath, paused, then spoke, as if he had nearly said something else. "I'll have the cart taken down. Biddi can follow with the hen. I'll bring your... your change of clothes myself."

Change of clothes? Andrin had forgotten about the change of clothes. A villein's tunic, with "Liar" painted on the back.

He could envision himself. Himself – Andrin beren Tooli, Crown Waymaster – in that garment of shame. He turned from Rhu to hide a grin.

What a pompous old ass he had become! What a pretentious young dolt he had been! What a waste his life had been! What a fraud!

He ran over Grandmoder's list of movables in his mind and stumbled at the first one: the kettle. The kettle would be full of simmering water by now. How was he supposed to...?

The Waymaster opened the temple door onto darkness. The central fire had gone out, gone completely out, as it had never done in the thirty years he had been Royal Waymaster. The coals were not fitfully smoldering or slowly going to ash, they were dead cold. Andrin lit a candle and by its light emptied the kettle's tepid water into the garden sluice.

He dried the kettle with a rag and spread the rag over the fire pit. Flames blazed up, consuming the sodden cloth as if it were tinder – or a lifetime's reputation.

"You *can* breathe fire," he whispered.

Andrin gathered the rest of the items his grandmother had listed. He approached each object with a reverence his studies had told him he should feel always toward everything, but which he had only felt in his imagination, and only when he studied the texts charging him to do so in reality.

The goods made a very small pile: kettle, sleeping pallet rolled into a cylinder around the contents of his herb cabinet, ten large thin books with parchment leaves and soft leather bindings, and his ebony box of casting pebbles.

Shouts and rattles announced the approach of his cart. The Waymaster ran a hand over his head, scratching at the stubble already growing there.

He grinned. "You forgot something," he said, and added his razor to the pile. He would hate to leave it: it had been one of Karol's gifts to him. The blue steel blade was engraved with the inscription "Ever true" in the high Kozabirian script. The blade folded into a silver steel case etched with a sprig of sage, the device of Onagros.

There was a small thud on the temple door, accompanied by a burst of clucking that sounded like a demand for entrance.

Andrin opened the door and Biddi stalked in with a burning glance over her shoulder and a fat black-and-white hen under her arm.

"I picked the best layer," she said. Her freckles were all but lost in the flush of her face, and her pale blue eyes were bright. Her chin thrust forward like a siege machine. "It's all over the castle, about your cursing the Sarpans, and about how Landry was afraid to arrest you."

"That isn't what happened," said the Waymaster.

"And about how you're leaving and taking your protection from them. And about how you're going out dressed like one of us, with the word 'Liar' on your back to tell everyone what His so-called Grace really is."

"That isn't what's happening."

"It serves them right."

Rhu beren Robia stooped through the still-open door.

Biddi raised a defiant face and turned her back on him so pointedly her auburn braid thumped against her spine.

Andrin saw the Chamberlain's thin lips twitch in amusement controlled by courtesy.

"What will you take from here?" Rhu asked.

"Only this," Andrin said.

"Only *this*?" Rhu inscribed a circle in the air with his forefinger, unable to believe, without such definition, that Andrin was taking these things, and these few things alone.

"Nothing else."

"Perhaps I should take back the cart and give you a handbasket," said Rhu, as close to open humor as he ever came.

"He knows what he's doing," Biddi said, into the temple air.

"I suppose he does." Rhu called the two villeins who had brought the cart. Between them, they gathered up Andrin's little lot and arranged it, with a respect they wouldn't have shown for masses of goods, in the bottom of the tumbrel.

Rhu handed the Waymaster an undyed cotton blouse, loose in the sleeves, with rawhide laces at the wrists, a coarse brown tunic, sleeveless and knee-length, and a pair of stiff leather boots high enough to cover the old man's bare ankles.

Biddi looked everything over. "Those boots will hurt his feet."

"They'll protect his feet from stones," said Rhu, gently, "and they'll keep more water out than slippers would."

"You could give him boots of soft leather. And wooden clogs to protect him from pebbles and damp."

"And weigh down his every step."

"You could—"

"Biddi," said Andrin, and Biddi was silent. "He's done what he could. Can't you see that?"

"I'll tie the hen to the cart," Biddi said, not answering, and not looking at either man as she left.

"I can send the villeins back to the storeroom for more supplies," said Rhu.

"I have all I want."

"I can send them after you, in secret, if you don't want to be seen accepting Landry's generosity."

"Landry's generosity? Generosity comes easy when it means other people's goods and other people's effort. But I do thank you. You're a better man than your master, Rhu beren Robia."

Rhu scowled, his brow and cheekbones seeming more prominent even than usual, his mouth a grim line across his walnut-colored face. "Everything I am, I owe to Landry Oliva beren Ada. I am his vassal, and content in my post."

"Perhaps you know best," said Andrin, with a smile that was meant to pacify.

The Chamberlain nodded curtly toward the clothes Andrin held and left the temple. Andrin heard him ordering the villeins away from the cart, sending them about their business.

"I'm tying down the hen," he heard Biddi say. "The knots won't come right."

Andrin chuckled, knowing that the knots would continue to rebel until Biddi was ready for them to conform.

The Waymaster dressed in his new garb, leaving his silk robe folded on the low table, his red leather slippers on the floor beneath.

The boots were inflexible and pressed his feet and ankles in places that promised discomfort in the future. The short tunic was drafty. Still, Andrin couldn't shake the feeling that he was off on a tremendous lark. His earlier visions of doom, failure, death, and waste seemed – not less real – merely *less*; as the candle's light seemed less when he opened the door to the greater light of day.

The old Waymaster stepped into the afternoon, thankful for his devotion to exercises which had kept his dusky body strong and shapely. Many names might be called out after him as he passed through the streets, but "Shamble-shanks" would not be one of them. An inner Self who still wore a silk robe and followed the Way by the scholar's book reproached him for vanity. Andrin's new inner Self, who wore poor men's castoffs and followed only the public way, laughed.

The Chief Sword, Guthrie beren Melanell, strode out of a barrack near the outer gate, a half-dozen Swords behind him.

Biddi finally secured the hen and watched the Swords' approach.

"He's afraid of you," she said to Andrin. "Six, besides himself."

"It isn't him he's afraid of," Rhu said. His plain face was bland but his eyes were not.

"What's he afraid of, then?"

"Look around you."

Villeins stood about, singly and in groups, casually watching, casually holding thick sticks or casually stooping to pick up the odd stone.

With her doll's mouth spread in a very un-doll-like grin, Biddi raked the near ground with her glance.

"No," said Andrin. He took Biddi by the arm and made her face him. "If the villeins attack, the Swords will cut them to pieces. Who would that please? Who would it help? Run around to them all, Biddi, and tell them to let me go. I want to go. I… I have something to do outside. Hurry now, before it's too late."

"But where will you go? To the Waystation?"

"To the river. Hurry."

Biddi wadded her knobby fists into her apron to keep them empty and trotted to the nearest knot of watchers.

"Well done," Rhu murmured. "Though I doubt any one of them would have had the courage to strike first – anyone but Biddi, that is."

"Tell her I said to be careful –"

Guthrie and his men formed a line between the Waymaster and the temple door.

Andrin didn't wait to be told or forced, but went to the front of the little cart. Grasping the dangling breastband, he tipped the wagon level, to the outrage of the tethered hen. He took up the band's slack in loops around his arms.

Before Andrin could take his first step, Guthrie told one of the Swords, "Give him a push."

The Sword pushed so hard Andrin scrambled to avoid being run over by his own conveyance.

Guthrie and his men laughed.

Andrin laughed too, and louder than they; the cart was much heavier than he'd expected, and easier to keep moving than it would have been to start. The gate lay open. He was free, for the first time since he had… for the first time since… for the first time. And so he laughed, reveling in the play of muscles he normally used only for the discipline of his exercises and the keeping of his garden.

~*~

He found pulling a small cart through Kudasad's emptying streets more difficult than he would have thought. Turns were tricky, and every time he stopped – and he had to stop often – he strained harder to start again.

At last he was out of the city on Fiddlewood River Road which curved, like a roundabout blessing, around gentle rises in the plain.

The cart still dragged at him. His boots rubbed the hairs off his ankles in spots and patches, then went to work rubbing up blisters they could later pop. The lark became a challenge, then a grim burden.

Shadows of the plain's undulations deepened and overlapped as the sun sank lower. The crests of the land shone with a golden light; even the indigo shade seemed to glow.

Andrin had thought to reach the river long before now. He hadn't expected the little cart to hold him back. He hadn't expected to suffer.

His mouth was dry. When he realized he had brought no water, the dryness ran down his throat and out to his fingertips.

Although he knew his strength would not start the wagon again that night, he stopped walking. The cart didn't give him so much as a free quarter-inch, but ceased to roll the instant he ceased to tug against its weight.

With a groan, he let the traces fall. He rubbed his arms, feeling what the dusk would not let him see: the bruising marks of the breastband.

He hoped the hen might have laid an egg he could swallow for its moisture but she had gone to sleep, her daily task undone or done before her transfer.

The cart tipped forward so slowly nothing shifted, not even the sleeping hen.

Andrin sat, his back against a wheel. One hand touched the roadside grass and felt moisture. The evening dew. Eagerly, the former Waymaster rubbed his hands along the grass and licked them. The water was dusty but sweet.

The dew grew more plentiful as Andrin gathered it. Soon he could bring his cupped hands together and raise them, brimming with water, to splash against his face.

It was after he rubbed that water out of his eyes that he noticed the shadow which continued to glow, though the rest had disappeared into darkness.

"Grandmoder," he said. "Thank you."

"You're a long time coming."

"The cart must be made of lead. I can pull it no more tonight."

"What did you bring?"

Andrin repeated the list she had given him.

"And what else?"

For a moment, Andrin honestly couldn't think of anything else. Then he felt himself flush in the darkness. "And a razor. But that could hardly make a difference."

"It couldn't?"

"A little thing like that – how could it?"

"That would be impossible, wouldn't it?"

Was this a test? "…Yes."

"Andrin," said his grandmother's whispery voice, "you are talking to a dragon."

After a moment, Andrin stood. "I can't see."

Flames unfurled from the dragon's nostrils, faint and blue but strong enough for Andrin to find his kettle and the unauthorized baggage inside.

"What do I do with it?"

"Let it fall."

"But my… my hair will grow." The Waymaster rubbed his scalp, already beginning to itch.

"If you *will* take what you don't need, don't complain of the weight."

Andrin opened the hand which held Karol's gift. There was a tiny rustle as it passed into the grass of the roadside.

"Now to the river," the dragon said. "Follow my light until the moon is up."

Refreshed by the dew and the presence of Verrina beren Unna, Andrin took up the breastband once more. He leaned into his burden and felt none. The cart and its contents might have been weightless. His boots even felt softer. His blisters melted away painlessly; his reserves of strength grew with every step.

"Grandmoder," he called softly.

"Yes?" the dragon's voice floated back to him.

"I'm a fool."

"Yes," said the voice. But there was a sugar plum in it.

The moon whitened everything it touched, and the moon touched everything. Andrin beren Tooli followed his silver grandmother; when she melted in the moonlight, he followed the tinsel road. He felt no raising and lowering of his legs, no shock, however mild, of foot against ground. He might have been sliding on ice, or levitating.

I'm asleep on my feet. Am I really walking, or am I lying in the ditch, dreaming it? He was fairly certain that he was really walking, but cuddled to himself the warm assurance that if he should wake in the ditch after all he wouldn't be surprised.

A girl appeared around a bend in the road. The leaden light, which blanched out subtle detail, and her own odd manner – eager but cautious, uncertain but deliberate – made her age impossible to pinpoint. She was small and rail-thin, the knobs of her shoulders holding her ragged gown like the uprights of a chair. She made no sound.

The voice of Andrin's grandmother whispered to him, "Give her good day."

"Good *night*, you mean."

The breath in Andrin's ear became stronger, hotter, and a whiff of sulfur drifted to his nose.

"Good day, child," Andrin said.

The girl stepped off the road, away from the old man. She lifted her near shoulder warily, as if a blow were the natural sequel to being addressed.

"Tell her you dropped a razor in the ditch on this side of the road two turns back. Tell her to find it and put it in her pocket."

Andrin repeated his grandmother's words.

"Tell her to ask for Biddi, and to say that the hen lays well."

Andrin told her.

The girl inched past, keeping her eyes fixed on him as if she expected him to pick up his cart and fling it at her.

"She must think I'm mad," Andrin said, aloud.

The girl walked more quickly.

"Two turns back, mind," Andrin called. "And ask for Biddi."

The girl was gone, even her feet making no slap upon the roadway.

"Now," Andrin said, "what was that all about, please?"

Mist rising from the river crept over the road. A faint blue glow warmed within the deeper mist off the path, and Verrina beren Unna's blue-green face rose above it. "This way. That was about the downfall of the House of Sarpa."

Andrin left the roadway and followed, still feeling as if he were gliding a dust-mote above the ground. "The downfall.... So soon?"

"What is soon? An hour? A thousand years? Suppose I told you that you had been speaking to a shadow, or that the girl had? That she hasn't been born yet, or that she passed and did as you told her before the Districts were unified? There have been women named Biddi before, and will be more again."

"Time and place are illusion," said Andrin, dutifully.

"The words are meaningless in the mouth," said the dragon. "Stop here."

Andrin stopped and dropped the breastband.

"Unload the cart. Put the kettle here, the box of stones here. Put the books on the ground, here and here."

Andrin placed everything as she told him, the books forming a rough semi-circle around the empty cart and at some distance from it.

"Now turn the cart over. Put it up against the stones with the kettle just inside it."

Andrin found the cart as easy to up-end as it had been to pull – under his grandmother's eye.

"Now you can rest."

Andrin sat. The drowsy hen snuggled in a nest of weeds nearby.

I'll wake in the ditch just outside of Kudasad and have to finish the journey all over. I wonder how much of what I'm dreaming will happen again by day.

But when he woke, although the mist was gone and the sun was shining, he wasn't just outside of Kudasad and he had nothing to do again. He was out of sight of Fiddlewood River Road, on the bank of Fiddlewood River. Behind him was a semi-circular grove of ten trees – willow and fruit. Before him was a small cottage of wattle-and-daub with a stone chimney up one side.

"My books. My casting pebbles. The cart."

With a grassy shushing, the water dragon came around the corner of the house. Her feathery ruff and spine-crest riffled in the faint breeze. "Are you hungry, Little Plum?"

"Yes."

The cottage chimney began to smoke, and the odor of roasted bacon brought tears to Andrin's eyes.

Biddi's hen called attention to herself by leaping up and clucking a chicken-shout to the morning. Having announced the entrance of an egg with such triumphal fanfare, she lost her own interest and pecked about the tree roots.

"Bring it inside," said the dragon.

Andrin picked up the egg. It was uncomfortably warm. He wondered what kept eggs from cooking themselves in the shell, being so hot when fresh. He took his bedroll under his arm and ducked through the low door after his grandmother.

The inside of the cottage was small and bare except for a low table near the fireplace. The table was of solid ebony.

"My pebble-box."

His kettle had grown a lid, and sat on its three legs over a charcoal fire.

The one-room cottage was windowless, lit by the fire and by rush candles set in holders all around the wall.

Safe, was the word that came to Andrin's mind.

"Now, my dear," said Andrin's grandmother, "would you rather have an egg or a broom?"

"I beg your pardon, Grandmoder?"

"Would you rather have an egg or a broom?"

Andrin looked around at the near-empty room. Charcoal ash had already crept out onto the floor.

"If that bacon I smell is for my breakfast, I suppose I have more need of a broom."

"Break the egg. Break it anywhere. On the table will do."

Andrin cracked the egg and somehow, without his seeing quite how it happened, egg and eggshell came alive in his hands and stiffened again as a broom.

Andrin swept the hearth and stood the wonderful broom respectfully against the wall. He felt quite grateful to it for the honor of using it. He nearly told it so.

"Your breakfast is ready," said Verrina beren Unna.

"Perhaps I should wash first."

"A river runs just outside."

Andrin thought with longing of the warm and scented water in his temple, but he went without protest.

Fiddlewood River was chill but not unbearable. He contemplated his reflection in the water, rubbing at the silver fuzz on his face and head as if he were dog and master at the same time. Hair – a symbol of worldly vanity and illusion, requiring to be washed and combed, available for braiding or cutting in thus-or-such a style, or ornamented.... Andrin felt his holiness compromised, his spirituality stained. Again he reminded himself that he had compromised and stained his own soul, hair or no hair, when he had set himself above the Way. That sacred life was over and he had best accustom himself to the fact.

Andrin rinsed out his clothes and laid them on the grass to dry while he performed his morning exercises.

How long had it been since he had breathed air untainted with the bailey's odors, with or without the additional scent of boiled herbs? How long, since his eyes had been tickled into dancing by the play of light on flowing water, or the wind in wild growth? How long, since he had felt the sun on his naked body, grass beneath his feet – yes, and hair upon his head? Forty years and more.

Andrin, hungry as he was, was sorry when his exercises ended and he found his clothes were dry.

He went, barefoot, back into the cottage, where a block of roasted bacon lay upon a plate made of corn-meal bread.

"Perhaps tomorrow," he said, "Chandler will lay my plate."

"Do you plan to hire a servant, then?"

"I've decided to call the hen Chandler." Andrin sat cross-legged on the floor before the table. "A chandler provides small articles and necessaries, and the hen provided me with an excellent broom this morning. Perhaps tomorrow she'll lay an egg, and you'll ask me if I would rather have an egg or a plate, and I'll say 'a plate.'"

Andrin's grandmother chuckled. "A joke, Little Plum? I have hope of you."

"I begin to have hope of myself. Will you share my breakfast, please, Grandmoder?"

"No, although I thank you for asking. I only stayed to see you settled."

"You aren't leaving? When will you be back? What am I to do? I have so many questions."

"I have no answers. – Would you like to hear a story while you eat?"

"I would rather…." Andrin bit his lips – *Who are you, to "rather"?* – and bowed. "Yes, Grandmoder, if you please."

"Well, then," said the dragon….

~*~

Once, many years ago – or perhaps it occurs as I speak it, or hasn't happened yet – there was or is or will be (let us say "there was") a smith in Kozabir.

He was burly and bald (whether nature denied him hair or the danger of catching fire discouraged it from growing, I couldn't say, but he was bald, and he did not shave). His eyebrows were sparse and the hair on his arms, though thick and black, was as soft as a baby's. His jaw was always dark, as if a savage beard, heavily armed with curl, were about to spring from ambush, but none ever did, not so much as one scout or patrol or lookout. His skin was the color of baled straw. His clear brown eyes were narrow and his nose was broad and his voice, while tenor in tone, had a rumble to it, like thunder when it has safely passed.

This smith was named Trahern birn Lona, and he lived on the outskirts of the village of Vatra, just over the border from a country called Layounna. Trahern birn Lona had little business from the village, for his forge stood on the fringe of Geiskeflor, "the haunted wood"– Fiddlewood, they called it in Layounna, for the forest ran through both countries. Vatrans preferred to travel farther than Trahern's forge for their iron goods, so long as they traveled in another direction.

So Trahern eked out a living doing piecework for another, more wholesomely situated blacksmith, making and delivering bespoke work in cookware and ornamental wrought iron, and spending the balance of his time making objects in various metals to please his own fancy.

From time to time he would take some of these objects, muffled in cloth like so many men with identities to protect, to the Great Market in Granitz, the capital of Kozabir. There he would sell to mercenaries, travelers, and sometimes to the Emir himself. His prices matched his moods and he always went home with fewer coins than he might have had.

One day at the Market, a young man wandered up to the stall. He was twenty-five or so, of average height, slender and well-muscled, with short, dark blond, curly hair, gray eyes, and a nose that was rather more than less. His arms were bare except for a wristlet of bronze and old scars that spoke of steel and skill more clearly than did the sword at his side.

His interest in Trahern's wares was casual at first. He picked up, turned over, and put down lanterns, bells, bridle bits, brooches, and toast racks. He ran his finger over the lines of money chests, candle boxes, kettles, and tea pots.

"You do fine work," the young man said.

"As you should know, Master – you wear it on your wrist."

"This, you mean?" He touched the bronze bracelet patterned with long-tailed birds. "But this is quite old."

"Not so old as I am," said Trahern, with a grin, "for I made it myself. Inside is written, 'I am here when you need me.' I sold it in this very bazaar to the Emir's procurator."

"And I was given it by my sister when I was very young. She said it came from Kozabir. The inscription…. If you put it there…. If she didn't inscribe it so, for me…. What is its purpose? What is its meaning?"

Trahern shrugged. "What is the meaning or purpose of the birds? Of the metal I chose? Of the thickness of it? I made it that way because… because I made it that way."

The young man nodded. "I understand. I was trained as a silversmith, myself. I grew up in a silvershop. My father and my brother…both dead…." The young man stopped. "My name is Kinnan birn Matka – 'beren Moder' in our language."

~*~

"Kinnan!" said the Waymaster.

"So the story goes. Do you know someone by that name?"

"If you've kept an eye on me, you know I do."

"How clever you are. Shall I go on?"

"Yes, please," said Andrin, in a small voice.

Later, the young man was driven from town by enemies. He had no horse, he had no cart, and he had no goods. He sold his leather armor for travel-money and got little enough for it. His sword, an old companion, and his bracelet, fit for an Emir, he kept.

The sun went down on his walking and as it went a mist rose up – an unwholesome mist, a miasma, smelling of old cucumbers and damp almonds. Kinnan could see no farther than his waist; when he extended his arms to feel before him, he couldn't see his hands. The sun was hidden before it even set, and darkness closed around.

Kinnan stopped. Among other things no longer visible was the road. He was just about to crouch and crawl, keeping the road by touch, when a light cut through the gloom.

A light, when the sun itself was powerless.

The light was silver gray, like moonlight on grass. It did more than pierce the mist, it punched a man-sized hole in it. From where he stood to where the light's source flared too brightly to be seen, Kinnan's way was clear.

He stepped into the path of the light, leaving the road as he did so.

~*~

"That was a mistake," said Andrin. "It might have been a trick."

"But Kinnan wasn't old and wise, as you are," said the dragon.

~*~

He walked through the corridor of light. It shrank to a beam, until he saw it came from a lantern – a simple tin lantern with small holes punched into it forming a pattern of moons in various phases. When Kinnan looked back, the corridor was gone and so was the mist. There was only a tin oil-lamp sitting on a porch.

He picked up the lantern and held it high. To his left was a large building with wide double doors and shuttered windows. About it hung a smell of fire and iron – in short, it was a smithy. Behind the porch was a snug little house with a whitewashed door and whitewashed shutters, both closed.

One of the shutters hung somewhat awry. Kinnan stepped softly up and over to it and peeped in.

Trahern birn Lona scratched himself, beginning with his head and ending with his thighs. Then he sat before his empty hearth and scratched his legs down to the tops of his slippers. His face and hands shone red with recent scrubbing.

Kinnan heard a thin growl, and feared a guard dog, but Trahern patted his stomach and said, "By and by. Sit easy."

The lid of his cooking pot rattled with the bubbling of something that smelled wonderful. This, above no fire. Kinnan knocked at the window before his own inner rumbling gave him away.

"Come in," said Trahern, turning to face the door.

Kinnan entered, bringing the lantern with him. "Should I leave this outside?"

"No. It was for you."

"…You expected me?"

Trahern shrugged.

"How did you know I'd need the light?"

"I didn't. I put the lantern out…. I don't know why. Things move in me. Not in my mind, but *in me*, somewhere."

~*~

"He sounds like Biddi," Andrin said. "She 'knows' things."

The dragon nodded.

~*~

"Some of the things I make…," Trahern went on, "there's something to them. *I* don't put it there but there it is, and it comes from me somehow. That bracelet, of my making…. It's found its way to you and it's stayed by you, and something brought you to my stand the other day. My lantern – also of my making – lit you to me. I don't know who you are or anything about your doings, but something wants you with me."

Kinnan waved the wrist wrapped in the bracelet. "Is that what this means? You're here when I need you?"

"You know as much as I," said the smith.

~*~

"And did he? Need him?"

"Perhaps he did. Or does. Or will do. The story says that Kinnan stayed in Vatra for some years. He worked in the forge, and he worked in soft metals. But he never made a thing that was more than it seemed, and

Trahern birn Lona never made any finer stuff through benefit of Kinnan's teaching."

"Where did Kinnan go, after that?"

"The story says he walked into the Geiskeflor one day, and was gone."

"Then the villagers were right," said Andrin, sorrowing again for Onagros. "The Geiskeflor is haunted by evil spirits. They sent the mist to baffle him. When that didn't work, they drew him away and destroyed him."

"Andrin," said the dragon, not unkindly, "don't be such a child. Good and evil haunt only human hearts. Spirits aren't good and evil; spirits *are*. I *am*. The Way *is*."

"Then he's alive?"

Verrina beren Unna stirred, gathering her legs and tail in readiness to leave.

"Don't go," said Andrin.

"I'll come again."

"I'll think about your story. I know instruction when I hear it. By and by, I'll learn its lesson."

"Do you know fact when you hear it, Little Plum?"

"…I think so."

"Put the lid on the kettle when you want hot food. Put the lid on upside down when you want something cold."

"But, if you aren't here…."

"It will work, just the same. The power isn't mine; it's in the pot."

Andrin beren Tooli turned to look at his kettle. It was familiar, ordinary; a gift from Ada beren Cinnie, mother and predecessor of the late Kinninger Karol.

"She said it had been given to her, brimming with precious stones," Andrin said. He turned again, but his grandmother had gone. "She said it came from Kozabir."

chapter 10
martyrs to the crown

When Landry ascended Karol's throne, he did not expect his rule to be popular. Profitable rule is seldom popular, and the love of the people was not one of Landry's objects. Their obedience, however, was, and obedience depends only partly on fear. To a far greater extent, it depends on respect.

The people did not respect him, Landry knew – not the ones who gave any thought to who ruled them. They saw Landry as a jumped-up Chamberlain, as Oliva's vassals would have viewed Rhu beren Robia had he suddenly claimed her Thanehold.

Landry sought the advice, not of his own Chamberlain, but of his new favored advisor – Guthrie beren Melanell. He called him to his private sitting room.

"The respect of a swarm of cottars and villeins?" said Guthrie, as if he had not risen, himself, and recently, from that same swarm. "Fear, and fear, and more fear: That's what the grumblers need. Single out a few and make examples of them."

Before Landry could complete a gesture dismissing the advice, Guthrie hurried on. "I mean for good, as well as ill. Let me find some who speak for you and some who speak against you. Reward each according to his merit. You'll soon find more to sing your praise and fewer to… do less."

Landry considered this. "Turning the people against each other would serve nobody – except, possibly, the Emir of Kozabir." The Kinninger shook his head. His eyes were downcast; he didn't see how Guthrie's hand grasped the pommel of his sword as a man might grasp his lover's wrist to signal silence. "Giving with one hand and taking with the other makes the people ignore both hands or want to cut them off. I've seen Thaneholds go to shambles through that method. I need to rally the people to me, somehow."

"Declare a war. Uncover a secret society of evil within some small ethnic group – detect a conspiracy."

The Kinninger's eyes were on his Chief Sword, now, but Guthrie was looking past the room, past the bailey grounds, and into a crimson mist. Landry couldn't feel the Sword's heart thudding; he couldn't hear the monstrous symphony of clash and shriek and breakage the Sword heard. He only saw and listened to a man who was onto something. "Go on."

"My Lord, there are rumors among the Swords that the men who killed Her Grace's heart-husband were not mere renegades. Some of my loyal men are whispering that there is a ring of traitors, in the pay of the Emir. They were ordered to kill Karol before she could invest more power in you, because they feared your discernment. They thought that Karol's death would pass the throne to Sorcha beren Ada, who would not have been able to keep control."

"They would have disrupted Layounna, if I had not taken it in charge!"

"The foundation of the country rests only on your shoulders, My Lord. The spies, themselves, will say so, in their confessions."

"You know these spies' identities?"

"Most of them, My Lord. Some of them might slip our net and turn up behind more mischief later. But most of them, we can arrest momentarily."

"Suppose you were to gather the final proof some night while most of the ring met secretly. Suppose you were to bring it to me that same night."

Guthrie considered this and added a touch – and a test – of his own. "Suppose, Your Grace, you rushed against them, with only myself beside you, to avenge your Liege-Lady and the country."

To his admiring surprise, Landry didn't flinch at the prospect. Instead, he nodded and said, "Some must survive to make confessions."

"Some will survive to confess, My Lord, however grievous their wounds."

"Again, you say this can be done on short notice? You know the men you seek?"

"I rode with them, not long ago, My Lord, on the night the new Deputy Roll-Keeper was promised his promotion."

"The night…. You don't mean these same traitors robbed us of Karol's heirs?"

"Does Your Grace tell me such a thing has happened?"

"If such a dark deed ever came to light, I mean, these men would have been the ones responsible?"

Guthrie wanted, very badly, to laugh. What a fool and weakling, after all, to rule the realm! Landry deceived no-one – himself included – telling his lies, even in private, as if they were the truth. Did he really think his hands were clean of blood if he persisted in saying so? It made discussion difficult, although the memory of one's evasions could be amusing.

"Of course, My Lord."

The Kinninger was quiet except for his fingers, drumming on the low table by his side.

"We will speak more of this, soon."

~*~

"Be seated, Thane Guthrie," said Landry Oliva.

They were once more in Landry's private sitting room. This time, Thane Oliva beren Audre was present.

Thane Oliva's face was expressionless, as it had become when Landry had first seated Guthrie beside his throne.

The Chief Sword bowed to his Lord, then bowed even lower to his Lord's mother.

"With My Lady's permission….," he said.

"My mother grants her permission," said Landry, impatiently.

Guthrie backed toward his chair, still in a bow, his eyes raised to Oliva's. As the backs of his legs bumped the seat, Oliva gave a nearly invisible smile and a nearly imperceptible nod. Guthrie sat.

"I've discussed these terrible rumors you told me of with my mother," said Landry. "She agrees with me that final proof is essential. It should be clear, damning, and inflammatory. How soon can it be obtained?"

"How soon can Your Grace provide me with bits of jewelry and small portable property – items such as Karol used to carry? A surprise inspection might turn up such items in the suspects' bunks and bags."

"I'll see to that," said Oliva. "Anything else?"

"It seems to me, My Lady," Guthrie said, "that, shortly after the rumors first came to my attention, you told me of a dream about Swords and Her Grace –"

"Or was it a vision?" said Oliva.

"Yes, My Lady, a vision is what you called it. It troubled me, at the time, but I didn't understand it, so I don't remember it at all. Perhaps when

I tell you the rumors and show you the things I find hidden, you'll tell it to me again, and I'll see how it all hangs together."

Oliva nodded, then spoke to her son. "Is there any need to wait?"

"Tonight?"

"Why not tonight?"

"The suspects are all off-duty," Guthrie said. "They're all stationed in the bailey. None are out on leave. I took the liberty, after our last discussion, to speak with each man privately and arrange a secret signal. When the signal comes, each man will slip away to the old temple. They expect to be given another opportunity to serve the crown."

"And so they will," said Oliva.

"When they've gathered," Guthrie said, "I can search the barracks. Witnesses can testify as to who was missing at the search, and what was found. I'll look around, stumble upon the meeting and spy a moment, then report to you. You'll recognize the jewelry. Thane Oliva will repeat her vision...."

"And so on," said Oliva. "Let it be tonight. Delay in no way serves you, My Lord."

Landry nodded. "Go with Guthrie. That silver trash Karol had from her lover should do the trick, don't you think?"

Oliva rose and put a hand on Landry's shoulder.

"One thing more." Landry stood, his mother's hand sliding off and away as he rose past her reach. "These men were not traitors. Misplaced patriotism made them the innocent dupes of a foreign government. No use in alienating their families and friends. In fact, let them refuse to betray the government which enticed them. Their honor as Layounnans won't permit it. Besides, we have trade agreements underway with all our neighbors. Let each of them offer us additional concessions in token of their guiltlessness."

The Thanes bowed and left the Kinninger, who sat, forgetful of them, before they had closed the door.

In the hall, Thane Oliva spoke. She did not look at the Sword, but her tone was as direct as a glare. "Let us understand one another. Tortoise will not be mocked."

"My Lady, I mean no mockery. Since you command plain speaking, I say to you, as I would never say to His Grace: This charge is a lie. So the vision which 'supports' it is a lie. If the charge were true, Tortoise would have sent a vision of it, truly."

"Do you believe this, or do you only say it?"

"I'm a man of no religion, My Lady. Let it be enough that I believe *you* believe it, and that I honor your belief."

"You have no faith in dreams, then?"

Guthrie took a moment to speak. "Dreams…. Dreams are another thing. Dreams are not holy."

Oliva stopped, and took the Chief Sword by the arm. "They are," she said earnestly. "They can be visions. They can be sendings. You say you don't believe that, but I tell you it is so. Somehow, I think you know it."

Oliva's fingertips registered his response.

Guthrie's chin went up and the corners of his mouth went down. "She isn't a god."

"Tell me about her."

Guthrie tried, but found he could not speak. He had never spoken of Deya, not even when deep in drink.

Thane Oliva pulled him along and into Karol's room.

"You're in the power of a demon." She spoke in a harsh whisper, her eyes aglow. "I know the signs – Trust me, I know all about it. You think she's in your power, but you lack the strength to turn her to your will. She turns you to hers, and you let her, because you like it. She makes you think she's worth it, while she drains you."

Guthrie could scarcely hear her over the sound of his own pulse.

"It isn't too late to be free. Say the word. Ask for my help. I am an Adept."

Guthrie said nothing. At length, he shook his head. "I don't know what you're talking about. You misunderstand me. I spoke of a soldier's nightmares, nothing more."

"And 'she'?"

"My mistress, Lady."

"That," said Oliva, "I do believe." She began to pick through Karol's treasures.

Landry's berserk retaliation for Karol's death spread screams and torchlight throughout the castle grounds. Wards on the gate shouted the story down to watchmen in the street, and the city was awake long before morning.

The Kinninger-hero heard a confession or two in company with his

Chief Sword, issued a statement through his stunned Chamberlain, and retired to his rooms to mourn afresh. He emerged long enough to plead in memory of the dead men, and see that they were cremated properly, which won even their mothers to his defense. When a week had passed, he resumed official business, his tailor having delivered a wardrobe of somber color and rich material.

The people were sick with adulation for Landry Oliva – most of them.

Then began the course of reward-and-punishment Guthrie beren Melanell had recommended. Along with it came policies Karol had refused to approve; policies which made, Landry thought, reasonable demands on the populace; policies which brought, Landry maintained, deserved recompense to the crown.

As months passed into a year, then two, Landry's common supporters began to fall away but, by that time, he was secure. His partisans had been raised and his detractors had been brought low, and he had no fear of the powerless.

A handful of neighboring freeman farmers revolted against Landry's new taxes and forfeited their land. Landry bundled the deeds together and made Guthrie a landed Thane.

Another year passed, then another; the people learned that their only safe course was to speak fair of the crown and report anyone who did otherwise. The divisiveness Landry had spoken against he now saw as his ally, for he drove it as a wagoner drives a horse.

No one was safe; outspoken old Roll-Keeper of the Realm, due to retire in less than a year, had information laid against him anonymously. He admitted his words and refused to recant them, and so gave his life to the crown and his place to his Deputy, Darcy Aminta beren Valda.

~*~

Oliva beren Audre kept cold silence as her son crossed her private sitting room and took the chair she reserved for his particular use. It had been his favorite at the Thanehold: outsized and overstuffed, perfect for lounging in odd positions.

But Landry no longer lounged in odd positions. Landry now sat with regal dignity, even alone with his mother. If His Grace ever sprawled or lolled or folded himself in ways which looked uncomfortable but were not, his mother never saw it.

His mother seldom saw him privately at all, these days. Despite her best efforts, Oliva was finding herself – and Corvina was finding herself, in a separate campaign – blocked from the font of royal power, and blocked by the font himself.

Tonight, for example, Oliva had waited the Kinninger's pleasure to grant her an interview, waited until long past midnight. In fact, the Thane suspected her son had gone to bed and had only come to her when he woke in the night and couldn't sleep again.

He said nothing now, but waited for her to speak.

Oliva decided she had forced her last smile. "My Lord," she said, not bothering, either, to cloak her voice's chill with maternal softness, "your attendance honors me."

Landry smiled a little, and inclined his head. He had waited long to hear such words in such a tone from her.

"My advice may be unwelcome," Oliva went on, "or it may be unnecessary, but as I am no longer in your closest confidence, I cannot know. May I speak?"

Landry inclined his head again.

"It is time you remarried, My Lord. Ten years have passed since Karol's murder was discovered, eight since you 'avenged' her. Layounna needs an heir. Or are you grooming Guthrie beren Melanell for that?"

Landry laughed. "My Chief Sword is my tool, and a very useful one, but hardly Kinninger material, and hardly fit to follow me."

"Exactly so," said Oliva, although she had been, and would continue to be, at pains to reward the Chief Sword's courtesy. He might prove useful to others besides Landry. "And so you need an heir."

"But an heir presupposes a wife, and I have no time for courting. I have no time for searching or for choosing, and I have no will to it."

"Let me serve you in this, My Lord. I've given it much thought. If I may ask a blunt question: You want not only an heir, but an heir in your keeping and control, do you not?"

"Yes."

"Then your wife must be in your keeping and control."

"What woman would stand for that? A mental incompetent? What sort of mother to my heir is that?"

"She needn't *like* it. She need only have no choice."

"'Refusal would be treason'? Is that the idea?"

"I had youth and inexperience in mind. Compliant parents, custody made luxurious and called protective, with Karol's death and lack of heirs to justify it."

Landry thought, then nodded. "That would do. Have you anyone in mind?"

"I would look for girls of fourteen to sixteen, who have not been much in society. The parents must be unimportant, subservient, and without power or powerful friends, yet they must be just well-bred enough to be worthy of connection to our line."

Landry smiled again, then laughed. "I know the very woman you've described. Her father presented her to me last honors day as having come of age. Rather nondescript, but not ill-favored. The daughter of the Roll-Keeper. Darcy, his name is. Her mother is a public scribe and copyist."

Oliva pulled a face. "Not so high as I would have looked."

"But, oh, such compliant parents!" said Landry, with another laugh. "There'll be no trouble from that quarter. Yes, young Whatever-her-name-is will do nicely."

Landry rose and for the first time in years willingly kissed his mother's cheek.

Oliva saw him out, not entirely pleased with the interview, but not entirely displeased, either. Landry had held her firmly in the place he had relegated to her. He had taken her advice, though he had plucked the project from her hands and dealt with it himself.

Landry was no longer swayed by his mother's counsel. Oliva was content to see if his tender wife might not be swayed by her mother-in-law's, and his heirs by their grandmother's.

The Kinninger's mother dreamt that night – dreamt of placing a crown on the head of a faceless child. The crown settled over the child's head, onto its shoulders, and tightened into a collar. The crown stifled the child, but Oliva held the other end of an invisible leash and she made the body move to suit her purpose. No one but Oliva knew the child who wore the crown was dead.

Chapter 11
Royal Honors

Not long before the Waymaster was exiled, Landry Oliva instructed his Chamberlain to purchase and prepare a house outside the bailey grounds for the new Deputy Roll-Keeper of the Realm of Layounna. The post was new, and would have seemed a natural creation if it were to be filled by one of the current Roll-Keeper's assistants and not by the Eastern District Roll-Keeper. Darcy Aminta beren Valda had never attracted any previous official notice. Where had the name come from? Who had supplied it?

Chamberlain Rhu beren Robia had his suspicions, based on the way Guthrie cut his eyes at His Grace when the order was given, the way he pressed his lips together as if to crush a smile. But what service could the man have done the Chief Sword? And why should His Grace reward him for it?

Despite all questions and misgivings, the Chamberlain performed his duties. A small manor house was soon found, at the near edge of town. Behind it ran Wall Street and then, beyond the town wall, the royal hayfields, the rolling floodplain, and Fiddlewood River.

Rhu had orders to meet the new Deputy and his family when they arrived and see them made comfortable. He hired local servants, laid in a season's supply of staples and stores, and had a boy waiting on the stoop to run for perishables the instant the cart should draw up.

In the early afternoon, the new official came, driving a one-horse wagon. Both horse and wagon Rhu recognized; they had been commandeered from the castle livery stable, commandeered by Guthrie beren Melanell.

The wagon turned into the manor courtyard and stopped. Darcy, his wife, and their daughter stepped down and into the Chamberlain's life.

Darcy Aminta beren Valda was a pale man, his long hair and drooping moustache white-blonde, his eyes an icy blue-gray.

The Deputy's wife was altogether different: Devona beren Valda was petite, bespectacled, solid, and brown. Her hair, her eyes, her skin were all in colors of the hearts of so many woods. Like wood, one sensed the life in her – and then one sensed the latent fire.

But it was the third member of the family…. It was the third of these who struck him to his very soul.

Elsie beren Devona was somewhere between four and five when Rhu first saw her. Her hair was darker than her father's even then, and fell in ripples to her shoulders. It was constantly wafting into her eyes, and her mother was continually tucking it behind the little ears. Her eyes were round and of the clear brown of a polished gemstone. Her hands were so tiny. Her feet were so small. The Chamberlain lost his heart, but not to the child. For the child, he felt only a bachelor's half-charmed indifference. He lost his heart to the woman she would be.

At twenty-six, Rhu was long past the age at which men were usually married. No one had ever asked him. At his age, he doubted anyone ever would. Even if that miracle should happen, the thought of requesting permission from the court, as a court vassal was bound to do….

But this child, whose future self had so touched his heart, might be his hope. In the years it would take her to grow to marriageability, a man might become more secure in his place, or even rise. He might propose the match to the girl's mother, when the time neared, and Devona might speak a word in his behalf.

Meanwhile, Rhu determined to make himself useful to the family and pleasant to the girl – but not *too* pleasant. He knew of more than one May-December match that had been spoiled by the elder man or woman becoming a playfellow or a foster parent.

Darcy Aminta beren Valda was officially installed on the next Honors Day. On the same day, Guthrie beren Melanell was made a landless Thane.

~*~

Days passed, then weeks. The Deputy Roll-Keeper slipped into his place as if he had been greased.

The Chamberlain visited the little manor at the edge of town twice in the time, assuring himself the household would be run smoothly and that all members of the family treated one another well. Darcy Aminta flattered himself the attention was on his account, then began to worry for the same reason.

Rhu beren Robia sensed Darcy's unease and supposed the Roll-Keeper feared losing his wife's interest. Rhu couldn't imagine such a man as Darcy ever having such a woman's interest in the first place.

To be thought enamored of the mother of the girl he hoped to wed repelled the Chamberlain, yet he was not ready to declare for a future bride so young. She was, after all, little more than a baby. Tentative vows had been made on behalf of those younger than Elsie, it was true, but Rhu found this distasteful. Rhu ceased his visits.

After the Crown Roll-Keeper's arrest, Darcy was officially installed in his stead with the small pomp his status merited. Devona beren Valda and eight-year-old Elsie beren Devona attended the ceremony.

Rhu beren Robia also attended. His face had grown less open in the four years since his master's heroic night avenging Karol's death. His most common expression was none at all; his second most common was a sardonic lengthening of one side of his mouth, the corner turned neither up nor down.

The first precious flowering of feeling he had had for Elsie had dried in the bloom. He was decades older, now, than he had been four years ago, and Elsie was only eight. He was scarcely aware of her at the ceremony, and attended the rather meager buffet spread in a lesser hall only because his duty required it.

As he entered the hall, a small figure moved toward him so deliberately she seemed to glide, concentrating so fiercely on not spilling the food and drink she carried her eyes were slightly crossed.

Elsie beren Devona handed the Chamberlain her offerings and dropped a deep curtsey. Behind her, at the table, her father beamed and nodded.

Rhu beren Robia nodded in return and put the overloaded plate on a nearby cabinet.

Elsie rose from her curtsey but still stood before him, her head cocked and her eyes narrowed. Her baby face had lengthened. Her chin was tapered but her broad jaw provided all the strength the narrow chin might lack. Her hair was a little darker, a little longer, but it still rippled, and still escaped from its fastenings.

Suddenly, she smiled."I know you. You're The Tall Man. You used to come and visit me when I was little."

How had she known it was she he had been visiting, when he had been so careful to mask his interest? Then Rhu realized the child spoke only from the self-importance of youth, that she probably supposed the wind blew for her alone. He was disconcerted, nonetheless.

"Why did you stop coming?" she asked. "I missed you."

"You did?" The Chamberlain's grim face relaxed a degree or two; the iron line of his lips warmed and softened.

"You didn't treat me like a baby. Everybody treats me like a baby, and I'm not."

Indeed, she looked like a woman in miniature in her yellow cotte and her blue surcote, a tiny blue hat awry on her head, slipping more awry the longer she tilted her head up to meet "The Tall Man"'s eyes.

"You are still very young," said the Chamberlain, gently.

"I'm eight. Nearly nine. In a little over five years I'll be married. Five years isn't long."

Rhu's face stiffened again, though only he knew it had begun to yield. "Married to whom?"

"Oh, I don't know." Elsie looked around at the thin crowd, as if they had assembled for her choosing. "Someone nice. I wish I could be courted now. Other girls are, but Moder doesn't like it so it can't be done."

Moder wouldn't allow her child to have her future settled by unripened affections – Rhu looked up to find Devona beren Valda watching him with her large eyes, made larger by her spectacles. He considered raising his winecup to her, but remembered the old rumors and refrained.

"Your mother is quite right. You may be a very clever girl, but an older man could fool you and a younger man could grow to disappoint you. Better to wait. My own mother didn't marry until she was nearly sixteen, and my father was both husband and heart-husband to her all his life."

He had lost Elsie's ear, now. She curtsied again and touched his hand with her own, her fingers covering barely half his.

"Come back and visit me again," she said. "I have a cat."

She ran to her father, to be praised for showing such winning manners.

~*~

Rhu beren Robia was surprised when His Grace proposed Elsie beren Devona as his Consort-wife. The family was respectable, but not of the best blood. The misgivings Rhu had had about the Roll-Keeper when he

had first arrived returned. There was something between Darcy Aminta, the
Kinninger, and Guthrie, but Rhu would take oath Darcy Aminta was not an
intentional member of the conspiracy. Whatever amused His Grace and his
Chief Sword when Darcy Aminta was mentioned seemed to be more to his
discredit than his honor. Yet he had been singled out repeatedly – for his
post at the castle, and now this.

As for Elsie, Rhu had no regret nor sense of loss. He had visited the
family on several occasions in the five years since Elsie's artless invitation
and had been happy he had never spoken for her.

Darcy seemed determined his daughter should reflect well on him and
that she should adore him unquestioningly. Devona insisted on teaching her
daughter household arts, the scrivening business, and common sense, and
had thinly veiled scorn as her reward. Elsie's high-handed treatment of her
mother's Kozabirian apprentice added to her disfavorable impression.

Elsie had become as vain and pampered and self-indulgent as she
could manage to be over her mother's protests. Rhu thought that marriage
to Landry would suit her.

Perhaps, he thought, with her vanity satisfied, her sweetness would
return. Perhaps she would remember "The Tall Man" and her old tenderness for him. Some men were not made to be married, Rhu told himself, but
friendship and even intimacy of a sort might not be beyond his scope.

Then he was given his instructions to prepare for the bridal. Elsie was
to be kept immured in a sumptuous suite. She would see no man but her
husband.

His Grace gave his reasons. The Chamberlain bowed to them, hoping
they would only hold until the crown had been presented with a short string
of heirs.

Rhu wondered if Devona knew of the arrangements, or Elsie, if they
would see or state objections if they knew. He began to haunt the Roll-
Keeper, listening for a clue or for an opening. One day, he kept Darcy at
work until the sun was nearly set, but nothing was said on either side.

The bridal morning came and Darcy brought Elsie. His Grace was too
absorbed in the affairs of state to greet his bride and Rhu was told to do it.

She arrived dressed in black. Her eyes were direct and impish, as
they had not been for many years. Rhu remembered the hope he'd had of
the woman Elsie could have been, and he knew that, whatever orders His
Grace might give, however long those orders might be meant to hold, he,

Rhu beren Robia, would win that woman's heart. Against the will of the crown, against the woman's inclination, he would win it. She would be under lock, but he was the Lord High Chamberlain. Nothing would keep her from him.

Nothing.

chapter 12
the roll-keeper's wife

Devona beren Valda had been the youngest of four children. She was bound, at seven, to a family of stationers in Bahari. The family was an established firm who made their own unique paper (a family secret that Devona was not to learn).

The young apprentice suffered under the slights of her pompous patrons and under the unkindnesses of their children. The only member of the household who treated her with any respect was Darcy beren Aminta, the second oldest child, a boy two years her senior.

Darcy grew to be good with figures and good at sales, but pulp would not come to paper for him. Although the family had a taste and a tradition for local political intrigue, Darcy seemed unable to grasp the subtleties of pulling official strings. He believed he couldn't make paper because he was meant for higher things, and that he failed at working the officials because of his greater loyalty to the offices in the abstract. He told this to Devona, turning to her for sympathy when his family's barbs had pricked him once too often.

When, at fourteen, Devona came out of her indentures, Darcy offered himself to her as a partner and as a mate. Devona accepted him. They opened their own small stationer's shop in a poor and inexpensive section of Bahari, selling paper purchased from various makers. Devona began scrivening for unlettered neighbors. She invested some of the shop's profits in calligraphy and bookbinding lessons and expanded the business.

Darcy's taste for dabbling in public affairs and his blind loyalty attracted the attention of the town tax-collector. He had Darcy appointed to the Roll-Keeper's office and Devona was left to run the shop alone. Darcy confessed to his wife that he had felt sullied by commerce. He was doing what he had been born to do: Serve the crown.

Devona was able to smile and nod and listen with apparent interest when he chattered about services he had rendered to this or that near-nobody. It was the times he came home silent, with guarded face and words, that she hated.

By and by, they were blessed with a child. They named her Elsie, and she was the treasure of her mother's heart. Her father hardly seemed to recognize her existence except that she annoyed him, interrupting his speeches with demands for food or other attentions. She didn't climb into his lap with muddy legs or clutch at him with sticky fingers; familiarity was reserved for Devona. Devona punished and rewarded and gave to her limit. Moder was a god; Father was a graven image.

Then, one morning in her fourth year, Elsie didn't wake. She burned with fever. Devona forgot her shop. Darcy sent word to his office.

Poultices, cold baths, herbal infusions – nothing helped. A physician was called. She bled the child and said that these things happen, they often cured themselves, she had done what she could.

Elsie died in her mother's arms.

Devona and Darcy sat for hours while the flesh grew cold and the limbs grew stiff, then pliant again. At last, Darcy took the corpse and laid it on the settle.

Perhaps they slept as they watched beside the body, but the night was some way advanced when a knock came at the door.

Darcy answered.

Devona heard a man's voice speak briefly. Darcy looked back into the room, at her, at the clay that had been a child.

The voice spoke again. Darcy took something, read it, handed it back.

He stepped in for his cloak and said, "I'm needed." He pressed the hand Devona put out to keep him, then worked himself free of her. "There's nothing I can do here now."

"Stay with me," Devona cried, but he was gone, closing a door between them he could never unlatch again.

The sun wasn't fully risen when a cart rattled up to the door. Darcy came in, carrying something wrapped in his cloak. He bolted the door one-handed. He brought the bundle to her.

It was a child – a living child – a little girl of Elsie's age. Devona heard Darcy say that she must ask no questions. He said that the wanderings of the Way had brought this child to them. Devona could not accept Elsie's death? Here was a meaning for it. Here was a chance to save a life in place of a life that had been lost. Darcy said that they must bury their own baby – bury her in the dirt – with no ceremony and in secret. He said that they must call this child "Elsie" and keep her out of sight for a week or two. He spoke of a promotion which would involve a move to another District, where this child would be accepted as their own.

Devona heard, and translated the story into one she could believe. Not that she doubted the sincerity of Darcy's plea, nor that she rejected it, but she knew Darcy as a man who could always find noble motives for looking after himself. Darcy, Devona told herself, had agreed to foster another man's child. A Thane's, perhaps – someone in power. Darcy would do such a thing only for someone in power, never for a friend. She supposed the mother had died. The someone at the door had come to claim the District Roll-Keeper's official help in keeping the child from the baby farm. This promotion and transfer was his payment, or a way to bring the child closer to the father who wasn't yet willing to claim her.

Devona held the child, feeling her warmth, listening to her breathing, watching the fluttering of her eyelashes. Filled with such bitter cynicism toward her husband, Devona felt only gratitude toward the little girl in her arms.

Elsie had gone to the heart of the Way; she was at peace, but her mother was not. Elsie's flight to freedom had left Devona's heart distended with emotions too deep and mixed to be ranged and given names. This child was not Elsie, but she was so much the dearer for taking Elsie's place in a world of chill and disappointments, while Elsie escaped to the safety of untouchable death.

The love and care and guidance Devona would have given the child she had borne, she would give ungrudgingly to the child she now cradled. That and more, in recognition that she held her in trust from another woman, also now at peace.

~*~

Darcy's nightmares began soon after the new Elsie's coming.

Devona was wakened by his groans. She thought he was suffering on the true Elsie's account and was overcome with tearful fondness for him. She stroked his face and called his name.

Darcy raised himself on his elbows, his eyes still clouded with sleep.

"Where is she?" he asked, sounding fuddled.

"Dead, my dear," Devona said, as gently as she could.

He lay back with a smile of relief. "I thought I saved her," he said, and went back to sleep.

The next morning, he remembered nothing of dreaming or waking in the night. When Devona mentioned it, he grasped her tightly by the upper arms.

"Did I speak? What did I say?"

Devona broke his hold. "Nothing. You only moaned and tossed a bit. But touch me with roughness again, my man, and I'll give you more than enough to say."

"I'm sorry. I didn't mean…. My position isn't one with many secrets but there are some confidential matters…."

Devona had laughed at that. She wished, later, she hadn't. She wished she had been more devious and deceptive. She wished she had made her husband believe she admired him and would defer to him. It would have been better for Elsie if Devona had been honored with some truths.

Darcy pampered the sad, confused child as he had never done his own. He spoiled her, made alliance with her against Devona's discipline. He reveled in the child's single-minded adoration of him. But love her? As before, Moder was a god, but now Father was a golden idol.

~*~

She disliked the new manor house in Kudasad on sight. Oh, it was nicely situated: At its front ran Broad Street, which was crossed, not far from the manor, by East Gate Way; business could find the shop with no trouble. At the manor's back was narrow old Wall Street, seldom used in this quarter since Broad Street had been cut through the ruins of a neighborhood fire.

But the house was imposing and grim. The two stories of dull gray stone sat nearly flush with the street, walls extended like threatening wings to either side, an archway in the wall to the left leading to the courtyard and stables. She later learned that the blank walls concealed gardens, that the rear of the stony house held hives full of honey and sweet wax and life, but now she saw only the stone.

The Broad Street entrance would do for her business, she thought, and the family could use the courtyard door. She could have storerooms – buy up bargains when prices were low and wait out times when prices were high. She could have a room just for copying, where a project could be left out to dry under cheesecloth, not blotted before the ink was properly set for fear of smearing.

The place was too big for the three of them even with the business taking up part of it. She could take an apprentice, as she had been apprenticed to Darcy's family. They could each have a room, instead of sleeping all in one, as most people of their station had to do. Perhaps the house would serve, after all.

Their cart (which Darcy had brought home, along with Elsie, and which also must remain unquestioned) passed into the courtyard and drew up beside the house. A door opened and a man came out.

He was as grim and imposing as the house. He neither smiled nor frowned, but dipped his head in the briefest bow.

His blue-black hair was straight and fell to the middle of his back. His high cheekbones and large-knuckled hands looked carved of chestnut-colored rock.

The man introduced himself as Lord High Chamberlain, Rhu beren Robia, and he eyed Devona's husband with as much distaste and suspicion as she used on him herself. Rhu beren Robia bowed to Devona.

Why would the Lord High Chamberlain interest himself in us? Because he was ordered to? Because he knows who Elsie really is?

Then Elsie clambered down from the cart.

One corner of the Chamberlain's mouth curled up at the corner, and Devona's image of him as stony was forever gone.

Elsie could look like her mother, and he sees it. He looks at the child with tenderness.

She thought herself wrong, when Rhu stopped visiting. She thought herself right again when she saw him with Elsie at Darcy's installation as Roll-Keeper of the Realm.

Darcy set her straight about that, though. He pumped Elsie afterward about what the Chamberlain had said, and if the Chamberlain had mentioned Father. Elsie repeated Rhu's support of Devona's protective control, and Darcy laughed at him for supporting something Elsie didn't like. If Rhu were the man Darcy feared and lived to please, Darcy wouldn't laugh; he would change his own opinion and tie himself in knots trying to maneuver Elsie into changing hers.

Yet the Chamberlain was fond of Elsie. Of that, Devona was certain.

His very disdain of the girl's behavior as Darcy's work bore fruit echoed Devona's own disdain, and Devona's was born of love. Could it be love, then? A prospective suitor's love?

Elsie could do worse – much worse, Devona thought – than marry a man whose integrity shone from his skin like candlelight through parchment. In opposition, marriage to the Chamberlain would take Elsie into the castle itself, and Devona did not share Darcy's desire to crawl into the royal pocket.

~*~

The nightmares persisted. Darcy woke himself sometimes with cries and moans. He took to sleeping in a separate room. Devona took to creeping into it from time to time to listen.

She gathered that Elsie had not been simply fetched from a hut somewhere. Death was in it, as Devona had supposed, but some sort of dreadful death. Perhaps a disease, and Darcy dreamed he'd brought it into his home with the girl?

Later, she decided this was not it. Someone had done something, and Darcy was a witness, and no one knew. The only words Devona ever heard him speak clearly in his sleep were, "No, My Lord! I didn't look, I swear! It was dark…."

Perhaps the girl knew he had looked. Perhaps she knew what he had seen. He wanted her not to remember; in the event she did remember, he wanted her to seal her own lips for love of him.

Gradually, the nightmares faded. Then Elsie reached marriageable age. His Grace, Kinninger Landry Oliva beren Ada, claimed Elsie as a Consort, and the dreams returned full force.

Devona considered going to the Chamberlain. If he knew something…. If he were truly concerned for Elsie…. She did not dare. She was terrified for the girl. Fear and power flapped about Elsie's head like invisible birds of prey.

Darcy preened himself by day, and whimpered by night. Devona knew him too well to think she could predict what he would do if terror got the better of his pride.

One day, he rode off to Pazni on an errand his Deputy could have handled. Devona spent the days he was away on pins. She blotted everything she tried to write. She couldn't remember the prices of items she'd stocked for years. She snapped at Brady birn Ilka, her Kozabirian apprentice, every time he spoke, and called him sullen when he didn't speak. She left the house three times, determined to seek an interview with the Chamberlain. She returned three times, having gone no farther than the street.

Darcy came home at sunset. He hardly spoke to her. He hardly spoke to Elsie. He strode through the courtyard and into the herb garden like a man late for an appointment.

Elsie and Devona exchanged looks, but Devona knew better than to be the first to find fault with anything Darcy did.

Elsie tried to tease an explanation from him at supper, but he put her off, claiming that he had been performing a Tarkastrian rite he had just learned. He said he was offering thanks for Elsie's glorious future.

That night, Elsie sought her mother. They sat side by side in the windowseat overlooking the back garden.

"Father's lying to me," Elsie said.

"I think you may be putting it too harshly." The years had taught her that Elsie would speak against her father only if she were sure Devona would defend him.

"Do you believe that, about Tarkastrian rites?"

"It's possible. What does it matter?"

Elsie shrugged. Her face soured into a pout, then tears came, then sobs. She put her arms around Devona's waist and wept on her shoulder. Devona held her and stroked her hair.

"You're frightened," she said.

"He was right. Rhu was right, the time he said I should wait to be married until I was older. I'm not ready. I'm afraid of it."

Devona didn't point out that she had said the same thing. That was just as well, for Elsie went on.

"If I had been courted when I was younger, like other girls, it wouldn't seem so strange and frightening."

"My fault."

Elsie patted her on the back. "You meant it for the best. I know that. And, if it hadn't been for you, I might be betrothed to someone else now, and I would have missed my chance."

"I hadn't thought of it that way." Devona wished she had been more lax. Whatever Darcy might feel about this "honor," Devona detested it. She knew nothing of the new royal family, had only seen them on official occasions, and from a distance, but she loathed their smug arrogance. Landry had shown how little he valued women; what mother would gladly see her daughter marry such a man?

"It's just…." Elsie plucked at the trim on her sleeve. "I don't like…. I don't like the manner of it. A man doesn't write a directive to a woman's father. He applies to the woman. Surely, even the Kinninger should do that."

"One doesn't say such things nowadays. But I agree."

Elsie looked out over the garden, over the field, to the floodplain and the mist rising from the river beyond. "Do you think it's because…. Do you think it's because he knows I'm not really your daughter, yours and Father's?"

Devona gaped. "Who… Who says that?"

Elsie looked at her foster mother with a frown. "Am I still not to know, now that I'm a woman? Now that I'm to be a wife – the Kinninger's Consort? What is so terrible about me it has to be hidden, even from me?"

"What makes you think –"

Still frowning, Elsie said, "I was told I had 'dreamt' so many people, so many little things I knew I recalled. Did you think I forgot those things? I only stopped talking about them, because it was so clear I mustn't. What is the truth? Who am I? Where do I come from?"

"I don't know." Devona took Elsie's hands in hers. "I know very little more than you do. Enough to know that the less you know the better for you. Say nothing to Darcy."

"Does he know?"

"I think he knows more than I."

"Don't you ever speak to each other? Really speak?"

"Not anymore." *The girl's right to be frightened of marriage. She sees how it can be when two people bury themselves alive with a dead commitment.*

"I'm going to ask him," Elsie said.

"No! Please, you mustn't. Say nothing to anyone."

"Does this marriage depend on my keeping quiet?"

"I don't know…. I don't know what depends on it." Devona stroked Elsie's hair, touched the dear face. "Probably nothing. Darcy probably wants you to forget the past to save yourself the pain of some loss. Your mother's death from illness, I used to think."

"Yes…." Elsie smiled a little, and kissed Devona's palm. "Do you think the Kinninger knows? Don't you think he should?"

"Suppose I ask your father. I'll tell you what I learn and we'll decide together what you should do."

Elsie considered this, and agreed.

But Devona was afraid to ask. She sat by Darcy's bed most of the night, hoping to catch a word that would make all clear without his knowledge. She caught no such word.

The next evening, Darcy came home just at sunset and all but ran to the garden. Next evening, he went again.

The fourth evening after Darcy's return from his mysterious ride, Elsie was sent to spend the night at the house of a friend. Devona dismissed the servants, wrapped herself in a dark cloak, and settled down to wait in the deepest shadows between the kitchen garden and the herbery, right up against the wall.

The sun was half-way set when she heard Darcy crunching the gravel path. Then she heard his tale. When he said that the man who had taken him away that night had been one of Landry's Swords with Landry's letter of empowerment, she covered her mouth to keep from crying out.

Darcy's story continued. The cart. The unsound barrels. The dead boy, the living girl.

And Darcy had saved her. Here, in what he took to be bare solitude, Darcy need tell nothing but the truth. He said he had saved the girl because…. He didn't know the reason. He said he had searched for one these past days but he could think of none. He could remember none. He had done it, and reasons had suggested themselves later.

Devona, silent tears running down her face, her nose stopped with them, her mouth open to breathe and to prevent a betraying sob, knew what the reason was. *You did it because you're a man and not a weasel. The man you could be moved the man you are and did something admirable. The man I married won out for a moment over the man I'm married to.*

Darcy went in, finally.

Wiping her face with her cloak, Devona ran around and in the front door with a tale of an afternoon when everything went wrong. She tried to draw her husband out, but he felt no need to confide in her.

She couldn't sleep that night. Something had to be done. Elsie could not marry Landry Oliva. He had hated one or both of her parents enough to want to kill their children – if Darcy had, indeed, thrown thirty-six infants into the sea, Landry had either hated more than one couple or had been willing to sacrifice the inoffensive to be sure he destroyed his intended victims.

Elsie could not marry him.

~*~

The Kinninger's summons came before Devona could devise a plan, before she could make up her mind to speak to Darcy, before she could decide what, if anything, to tell Elsie of what she'd heard. In less than a week, Elsie would be taken to the castle.

Devona took the summons from Darcy's hand and carried it to the girl's room.

"What is it, Moder?" Elsie asked, as Devona bolted the door behind her. The girl's eyes went to the paper her mother held. Color flooded her cheeks, and she sighed. "He's released me. He chose a high-born lady, after all."

"No. He directs Darcy to bring you to him."

Devona sat the girl beside her on a long stool.

"Your true parents might be – or might have been – great threats to Landry Oliva."

"To Landry?"

Devona repeated Darcy's story – or most of it. She couldn't bring herself to speak of the dead boy or of her own dead child.

Elsie nodded.She read the summons again. "Does he know who he's marrying?"

"I don't think so. I don't see how he could. He might. If he does, he hasn't told Darcy."

"Yet my father…. Yet Darcy would marry me to him, and *he* knows."

"Perhaps he thinks the safest place to hide you is under the Kinninger's own nose." Devona would have liked to believe that of Darcy: That he did as he did out of love for Elsie and not for himself.

Elsie let the paper fall to the floor. Deliberately, she put her foot upon it. "I'll never marry such a man."

Whether she meant such a man as Landry or such a man as Darcy was unclear. Devona didn't ask.

chapter 13
tale from a wine shop

In a wine shop on the waterfront of a small sea-side village in Kozabir, the talk turned to shape-changing – or variance, as they also called it. The shop was no better than a lean-to, built of cast-off lumber and shingles. The tables and chairs were sturdy but worn, as scarred and battered as the shop's clientele. The most truculent customers were by this time – the small hours of the morning – passed out, knocked out, or thrown out, so the conversation was spirited but not violent.

"There's no such thing as variance," one man stated flatly. "It's all a fraud."

"It's not!" another man declared. "I've seen it happen, myself."

"You only think you saw it. It was some kind of trick. It's a story they tell the children."

A woman – a sailor, by her clothes – said, "It used to be real. Those stories mean something. Once, the people of Kozabir knew how to change their shapes. That's why the other countries don't trust us. The Mother of Life gave us the ability, but we fell away from worship and she took back her gift…."

She trailed off as one of the customers coughed with laughter. Since this customer was a large and brawny fisherman, the others tended to listen to what he had to say. He was over six feet tall and weighed more than three hundred pounds, all of it muscle and dirty hair. His table was covered with spilled wine and the remains of meat pies. As he pounded the table in his mirth, more wine slopped out of his wooden tumbler.

When he had stopped laughing, the sailor said, "You don't believe in shape-changing, or you don't believe in the Mother?"

"I'll tell you a story about shape-changing," the fisherman said. "A true story. Anybody who doesn't want to hear it can leave."

Nobody left.

~*~

There was a woman (the fisherman said) named Devona, who owned a stationary shop in a large town in Layounna. One day, a customer – a wealthy woman, by her dress, although she bought only a single miserly sheet and envelope – advised her to hire a clerk.

"My daughter is learning the business," Devona said. "She's nearly eleven, and a willing enough worker."

"You need older help. Someone to do heavy lifting. I have a young man working for me, Brady birn Ilka…." They say "beren" in Layounna, so the merchant had to explain this name to the woman. Then the merchant said, "He writes a good hand, good with money, honest, reliable…but he has one fault. He's prone to homesickness. Every ten-to-eighteen months, he's off to Kozabir. Gone for two weeks."

"Some of my suppliers are near the border," Devona said. "If he were content to go home on my schedule, he could go with my blessing and a purse for his expenses. – He is honest, you say?"

"I would trust him with everything I own."

The young man showed up that afternoon, bearing an introduction from "Alfea beren Hulda, Merchant," written on the very paper and in the very envelope the merchant had purchased from Devona. A nice touch, Devona thought.

~*~

The fisherman signaled for more wine. "And another meat pie," he demanded.

"They make those out of cats, you know," the sailor told him.

The fisherman showed a row of stained, blocky teeth and said, "I like cats." When he had been served, he took a long gulp of wine and said, "Back to the story."

~*~

Brady told Devona he was seventeen, and he looked it: Although he was below-average in height, he was rawboned and gangly, like a bundle of sticks tied together with elbows. His flat black hair was long, and held at the base of the neck with bright ribbon. His eyes were black, too, as shiny as glass beads. His skin was dark, his smile was wide and winning.

On the basis of the merchant's recommendation, and because the lad did, indeed, write a good hand, Devona took Brady into her service.

She found him everything the merchant claimed – excepting honest – and he was certainly very good with money.

He charmed the customers, he was quick and efficient and always cheerful. When no one was in the shop and he had swept and dusted and checked the inventory, he sat on the stoop and sang a song of his own device extolling Devona's stock and services. Sometimes he accompanied himself on the Kozabirian "bird's tail" pipes, sucking a few notes to set the tempo and tune, then singing, playing, singing. His pilfering was minuscule and never grew, and Devona overlooked it, counting it as a rise in salary – a rise he deserved, after all.

She expected his first trip at her expense to be his last; that she would see no more of Brady nor of the money she sent with him for purchases. Still, she sent him, hoping he would fulfill his trust.

He did.

~*~

The listeners laughed. "He did *that* time," one of them said. "The boy is already stealing from her. Now he wins her trust, and he'll have the chance later to steal more."

The fisherman favored the speaker with an unlovely smile and continued.

~*~

Darcy – Devona's husband – used the boy with haughty contempt. Their daughter, Elsie, would have followed his example, but Devona forbade it. So Elsie treated Brady with a grudging courtesy when Devona was present and mocked him with her father in Devona's absence.

Devona grew fond of him, light fingers and all. And he seemed fond of her, with the patronizing affection of the young adult for a favored elder.

One night, Devona woke with a start. She was sure she heard something. A sound so slight, it could only have been made by someone hoping to make none. Someone was in the shop. Doing mischief? Stealing goods?

The gilt?

As a copyist and book-binder, Devona often worked with gold leaf. She had recently been engaged to provide a set of heavily-gilded books. The bindings would be traced in pale red gold, and every page was to be illuminated in various alloys of gold.

Accordingly, Devona had ordered, on the Thane's credit, a full ounce of beaten gold of the thicker sort: 750 leaves to the ounce. Thirty books of twenty-five leaves each, three books apiece of each of the ten available colors. And all were downstairs, locked in the house, locked in the copyroom closet, locked in a trunk, locked in the oaken case in which they had been delivered.

There was another sound from below.

It's probably Trenel, Devona thought. *Elsie's cat.* Trenel was an uncommonly good-looking cat, and a rarity – a male tortoiseshell. A thump at the bedroom door and a muffled meow told her that it wasn't Trenel making stealthy noises below.

Darcy slept in another room, and Devona was accustomed to dealing with her own troubles. It never occurred to her to go to him for help. She put on her spectacles, slipped her night-gown over her shift and crept downstairs. Trenel led the way, flowing like lantern-light down the staircase.

The copyroom door stood ajar. The closet was open. A man crouched before the open trunk, a candle on the floor beside him.

Devona moved to defend her client's property, plucking a metal straight-edge from its place on the wall as she went.

The thief heard her and whipped around. He rose, and knocked her wrist aside.

It was Darcy.

"What is the meaning of this?" he said.

"What is the meaning of this, indeed," said Devona. "How dare you sneak into my shop? How dare you touch my things without my permission? What do you think you're doing in here?"

Darcy looked down his nose at his little wife, his mouth hard beneath his drooping moustache. "I will not be spoken to in such a tone," he said.

"Will you not? Adjust my tone, then, if you don't like it."

The fisherman was a wonderful mimic. The other patrons rocked with laughter at his recreation of the argument, which he made sound very like a traditional Kozabirian puppet-show routine.

Darcy's cold blue eyes flashed. "Go back to bed," he said. "Any explanation I choose to give, I'll give when I choose to give it."

Devona gasped.

"Woman," Darcy said, "I gave you an order."

"The man's gone mad," Devona said. "Do you speak so to me?" She said the next three words with all the authority of a mother, wife, and employer. "Leave these rooms."

Darcy's face registered irritated boredom. "Must I deal with you now? Will you make me carry you out?"

"Carry me, will you? Deal with me, will you?" Devona cried. She stepped back and rained so many blows with her steel ruler the man could neither duck nor dodge nor catch her wrist to stop her.

She stopped herself, as the shape, the size, the coloring and clothes of the man before her altered with the suddenness of a kaleidoscope view.

Brady birn Ilka stood, hunching himself away from her whackings.

"Brady?" said Devona. "*Brady?*"

~*~

"It isn't a fraud!" the believing patron crowed. "I told you I'd seen it myself! He says this is a true story! It happens!"

The fisherman scowled savagely at the interruption, and the triumphant patron subsided.

~*~

The young man took his arms from over his head.

Devona looked at the length of steel in her hand, the touch of which had returned Brady to his true form. "Varier!" she said.

"Mistress, I swear, I didn't intend to plunder you." The fisherman made the boy wail. "I wanted a leaf, no more, just to see if I could take it without its being missed."

"As you've taken pennies and scraps of goods from me for these five years, and thought none of that was ever missed?"

The dismay in Brady's face disarmed his mistress almost altogether. "You knew?"

"Of course I knew. Do you think I don't know my own business?"

"And you didn't have me taken up for it? And you kept me on?"

"I've known shopkeepers and their clerks and apprentices from my early days," Devona said. "I've known many worse than you, and many even more indulgent than I have been. But this...."

Brady fell to his knees. "Believe me, Mistress. One leaf, I swear it!"

"Why should I believe you? If I had known you were a varier, I never would have hired you."

"'Who would learn to alter form but a thief,' is that it?" said Brady.

"Well, are you not?"

"No, Mistress. At least, not on the whole. Please, Mistress, don't dismiss me."

"Dismiss you? Why shouldn't I have you put in irons? Change your way out of *them*, if you can."

"Iron…? Yes! That's it! Don't you see?" Brady stood. "A brad. A steel stud, or a loop." He pulled at his ear. "Fastened here. I couldn't change my shape. You would know you could trust me for that. As for my thievery…. Could I take an oath? Would you accept my sworn word?"

"Of what value is your sworn word? Honest, indeed! Oh, if I could find that merchant again…."

"What merchant?"

"The one who told me of you. The one you worked for –"

Brady turned his lips inward and bit them.

"You…. You came here, in the guise of a merchant…of a woman…. You recommended yourself…. That letter of introduction – you wrote it…." Devona glared in blank outrage. Then she laughed. "You scoundrel! Why should I let you go free? Why should I keep you on here? Why should I trust you?"

"That, I couldn't say," said Brady. "But will you?"

For the sake of that laugh, because she had a maternal weakness for the boy, because Darcy would not have approved, Devona agreed.

~*~

In a tone of intense disgust, the fisherman concluded, "The boy never stole another farthing, not so much as a pen-wiper. At least, not from Devona."

chapter 14
the kinninger's bridal

Devona stood watching the hired chair bearing Darcy and Elsie to the palace. She watched one of the chair's occupants, at any rate: She pored over the figure of her daughter as if she were proofreading her, or as if the girl would vanish if her mother's attention wavered.

The chair turned a corner. Devona beren Valda scuttled into the manor house and climbed to its upper-most window. From there, she could catch glimpses of the vehicle and its four husky bearers as it passed through the streets.

Darcy was taking the long way, down Broad Street to East Gate Plaza and back up High Street – which was reasonable, she supposed. The streets of the short way were narrow; the conveyance would have taken up more than its share of room. Of course, it wasn't in Darcy to think of things like that; he took the long way so more people could see him taking his daughter to the Kinninger. She could just imagine him, fingering that rat-tail moustache he wore as if he had invented facial hair, barely restraining himself from waving to The People.

She wondered that a man with so little courage could have so much brass-faced gall. It was all surface, of course, and as thin as ten-sheets-a-penny parchment.

The chair crossed the drawbridge and entered the bailey grounds. Someone met it at the foot of the tower motte – not the bridegroom. Though distant and obscured by the sharpened tops of the palisade, the man was clearly tall, broad-shouldered, dark: Rhu beren Robia, the Lord High Chamberlain.

Devona watched Rhu lead Darcy and the little figure in black into the keep.

A noise from below brought her thoughts back to her business. The shop was shut for the day, of course. She was in no condition to tend to sales, and Brady birn Ilka, her clerk, was running a most important errand.

She hurried down the stairs. In the kitchen, she filled skin bottles with water, and sacks with bread, cheese, and dried meat. The trip to Kozabir would take days, perhaps more than a week keeping to the back roads and moving with caution. She added a purse of coppers to buy food and shelter far enough from Kudasad for safety. A purse of silver to start a new life in Kozabir.

Boots clattered on the stairs.

Devona looked up to see Elsie, dressed as a young man on a journey: baggy leggings, thick-soled boots, a short tunic with the hood drawn up, and a heavy cloak. *At this very moment, an "Elsie" is climbing the steps of the castle tower. Or perhaps she's already "vanished."* The audacity of the scheme made her head swim.

"Are you ready?" Devona asked, and received a breathless, "Yes," in response.

Devona and Elsie picked up the sacks and bottles and carried them into the back garden. Devona unlatched the gate to Wall Street.

"Start now," she said. "If the plan should miscarry – may fortune forbid it – at least you'll have a chance."

There was a shout from the house. A Sword burst through the court's archway and pelted toward them. He threw himself over the kitchen garden's low wall and dissolved, at their feet, into breathless laughter. He caught sight of the figure in traveling clothes, and laughed the harder.

Elsie, frowning, threw back her hood as the Sword's armor became black leggings and a gray tunic, and the Sword became Brady.

"Get up, you fool," she said. "We haven't the time for antics."

Brady rose, brushing himself off, still chuckling. "*You* haven't the time, you mean. *I'm* safe enough. If I'm caught with you, I'll just turn back into a Sword and arrest you." He rubbed tears from his cheeks and told Devona, "I volunteered to come to her home and search for her."

Devona embraced the boy. "You had no trouble, then?"

"None, Mistress. The Chamberlain even complimented me on my sweetness and beauty." Brady cocked his head, and batted his eyelashes.

Elsie's frown deepened.

"What then?" Devona handed her daughter and her clerk the sacks and bags and purses she had prepared, giving the coppers to Brady and the silver to Elsie.

"Some Swords escorted me up a spiral staircase. Clever of you to realize there would be Swords around. Dressing 'Elsie' in black and silver made the change that much faster." Brady looked down at his black boots and leggings and his mouse-gray tunic. "And I got a new suit of clothes, into the bargain."

"No one saw you change?" Devona asked.

"An unimpeachable witness."

"A witness!"

"Listen: I took some of the stairs two at a time, to get a bit ahead, changed, turned, and met the guards as I came down."

He put a hand over his eyes. "'In the name of Tarkastrus! I'm nearly blinded! One moment, I'm stepping aside for a girl to pass me. The next – poof!' The Chief Sword said it was sorcery, but that was just for want of anything intelligent to say. It was the Chamberlain who had enough wit to order a search of the tower – and to forbid the Swords to take part in it."

"But you said –"

"I volunteered. They couldn't seem to decide if 'Elsie' was still in the castle or spirited far away. But the Chamberlain didn't seem to mind letting one of Guthrie's men go off on a fool's errand."

"No doubt he recognized your quality on sight," said Elsie.

"He knew beauty and sweetness when he saw it." Brady fluttered his eyelids again.

"Enough!" said Devona. "Off with you." She embraced each of them.

"I'll be back, when I've got her across the border," Brady said. "She'll be safe with me." He gave Elsie a dismissive look. "In every way."

Elsie turned her nose up.

The apprentice fingered his empty earlobe. "Funny, but I miss your steel ring as much as I've missed altering my form these past two years."

"You shall have a gold one, when you return," said Devona. "And you can change and pilfer to your heart's content."

"You take the fun out of it, Mistress!"

Devona kissed her foster daughter for what she thought was probably the last time. She let the young people out into Wall Street and watched them until a turn of the way hid them from her sight. She locked the gate and leaned against it.

Light hid her eyes behind spectacles like twin full moons as she whispered, "So ends His Grace's bridal."

CHAPTER 15
TORTOISE BITE

Nerissa birn Matka was the name she came with.

She grew up knowing she was a slave, knowing her name had been sold along with her person. Black-market purchase, cut-rate price, her greatest value to her bottom-feeding owners was her status, more base even than their own.

Her earliest memory was of Isa birn Isa carrying her out begging. She remembered being pinched whenever she laughed or cried aloud, and came to understand that people did not give money to a woman with a happy baby or a noisy one.

When she was big enough to go out on her own, she was sent out early and told not to come back until late. Sometimes she was beaten. Sometimes she was locked out –"to teach her a lesson," although the only lesson she ever learned from it was how to find a hole to crawl into for shelter.

Sometimes she was mocked with her origin.

"Know where you got your name, girl?" Barand Tara birn Isa might say it with a growl or a grin.

She was always supposed to ask, "Where?"

"Means you came from the sea. Slaver said he bought you from an Inland Sea fisherman who claimed you washed up in a barrel. That's what they do with bad luck, sailors. They throw it overboard." Or he might say, "Means 'out of the sea.' A sea turtle climbed on shore and vomited you up."

But sometimes, in her cups, if Barand were away, Isa would tenderly work the tangles out of Nerissa's hair and call her "my little Merchild." That was the worst mockery of all.

As for moral instruction, the birn Isa's were very strict – on one point.

"Honesty. Everything you beg or find or earn or steal belongs to us, just like you do. Keep anything back from us or 'forget' to come home at least once a day and you'll be sorry."

Once, in a defiant moment, she asked, "What would happen?"

Her owners looked at each other, then Isa said, darkly, "Tortoise."

"Tortoise? What's that?"

"Not what, slave-girl, who. The Mother of Life created him when the earth was new, him and… Unicorn and…um…Dragon and…."

"Bird," said Barand.

"Bird. – No, Phoenix."

"That's a kind of bird."

"Is it? Phoenix, then. But Tortoise was made on purpose to punish the wicked."

"Tortoise is good?" A good creature, Nerissa thought, wouldn't harm her.

"Good? Oh, no, not him! Tortoise is evil – horrible!"

Barand nodded, supporting his wife. "He's so bad he wants all the evil for himself and he hates people who try to use some of it. He lives in the water. He hears everything and sees everything and knows everything. Whenever somebody's been wicked – some slave-girl steals from her owners or disobeys – Tortoise creeps up at night and bites pieces out of her, one piece for every bit of wickedness she's done."

Nerissa never forgot the chill this gave her.

"Sometimes he bites your eyes out or your nose off, sometimes your hand or your leg – that's where all the crippled beggars come from. Sometimes he bites your head off and you die. Sometimes he eats you up and you're never seen again."

So Nerissa dealt honestly with her owners – for the most part – and obeyed them in letter if not in spirit.

She learned, on her own, that she could make more money running errands than begging, besides keeping warmer and being given kitchen scraps and the occasional sweet. True, she was sometimes thrashed and accused of getting the message wrong. Even at that, the treatment was no worse than she had at "home."

In all her young life, there were only two traces of warmth. She kept them secret, like sparks in damp tinder, jealously guarded from winds that would love to blow them out.

One was the market square when Farukh, the storyteller, was in it. The wondrous words Nerissa overheard in passing, the disconnected images she built from various moments when she had time to linger, wove themselves into a tapestry more colorful and strange than any single story would have been. She invented a story about herself: She was the Sea King's daughter, exiled to land for a time; one day she would cast herself back into the sea and return to her rightful place.

The scraps she gathered from Farukh made the child's life bearable. Besides, Farukh smiled at her. Not towards her – at her. Farukh was her friend, the only one she had.

Sometimes her path would cross his outside the marketplace. Then, if she wasn't on an errand, she would follow him. She wouldn't speak to him or let herself be seen, but she would follow just to be near her friend, just to be watching over him.

Nerissa was glad of her vigilance the night the men in black surrounded the tavern Farukh had entered. She was five then, nearly six. She warned him and his friends. And ran when they offered rescue in return.

Perhaps it was the pitiless light of her misery that showed her how she had cheated herself. She understood soon after, but too late, that Isa's Tortoise was only a story to frighten children, that she could have broken free that night.

She also saw that her owners didn't strike her in punishment for "misdeeds" learned of through dark and mysterious means. That was just how they dealt with things – by knocking them about.

The only other spark in Nerissa's life was the city's animals, hardly more feral than the girl herself: cats, dogs, rats, mice, birds – creatures that scavenged their livings in alleys and the gardens of empty houses. Many times Nerissa followed such a creature to its lair, shared with it what scraps of food she had, and found a night of peace.

She saw how the animals lay in wait for what they wanted, and how they stored part of what they found against a time when they might find nothing.

Nerissa worked harder, for she had begun to work for herself. She hid some of what she earned beneath a flagstone in the back walk of an abandoned house. How much would she need to get away? How far was "away?" Did the birn Isas have the right to send official Hunters after her, or did her black-market origin safeguard her against that?

Only in dreams and daydreams did Nerissa think of claiming the storyteller's help so long after it was offered. Gratitude was short, and no one did anything for nothing. Enough money would take the place of gratitude, perhaps. Meanwhile, whenever the storyteller came to town, Nerissa ignored him, not trusting herself – not trusting her only friend. She was horribly afraid she'd make her plea before she'd saved enough and that the disappointment would give her away to her Master and Mistress. More than that, she was afraid the smile she remembered as hers would be reserved for someone else.

As she turned eight, nine, ten, she cursed the old threat which had balked her escape and which still held a childhood power to affright. At the same time, she made the threat her own. Though she took every bruise and curse with her customary sullen silence or with ritualized pleas and protests, in her heart she accepted none as her due, but marked down each abuse for retribution. She comforted herself by staring through aching nights at the birn Isa's sprawled limbs, seeing them bloom with wounds inflicted by the bites of a spiteful Tortoise.

CHAPTER 16
QUEEN OF THE DRAGONS

Where Kudasad Bridge Road met West Bank Way, a large common, paved with squares of slate, had been laid. Some merchants didn't bother going into the capital; carts lined the edges of the square.

One small space was taken by a puppet booth. A sign above the curtained stage was painted with the stylized figure of a crowned dragon, blue on a green background. Children tugged at parents' sleeves and begged to linger, in hope of a show.

The aroma of sage-and-corn cakes infused the air as an old woman in red and yellow wound through the crowd with her basket. "Must have a sage cake for the performance," she coaxed cheerily. "The Dragon Queen and sage cakes go together like milk and honey."

Biddi beren Anna forgot her irritation. Janet, the castle's chief cook, always sent her out here for lettuces, as if anything Biddi walked a mile to fetch were fresher than anything a farmer drove a mile to bring. The show made up for it. This booth wasn't always here, and it was a play Biddi had loved since she first saw it some years past.

By and by, someone inside the booth struck a gong and wove a wordless song through the ringing echoes. When a large enough crowd had gathered, the song ceased.

The miniature curtain slid aside, revealing a family of four in Istok peasant dress. They seemed to pull and push a cart of logs. The puppeteer was skillful: under his mastery, the strings of the marionettes vanished and the wooden limbs became warm and supple. The nonsense syllables that represented dialogue were nearly intelligible to the charmed watchers.

Mother and father froze in place while the crowd's favorite part played out. The two boys jabbered and cackled at each other, pinching and kicking surprised bottoms, whacking one another with slap-sticks, sending the audience into guffaws with their contention and bizarre hoots of protest.

Too soon to suit the crowd, the puppet boys delivered a final mutual whack and stumbled apart, each holding his head.

Biddi enjoyed that part, but she liked the rest better.

The parents came to life and were joined by a woman dressed in purple and green and carrying a sprig of fresh sage.

That's meant to be Onagros, Biddi said to herself.

The puppeteer made her sing a tune of supplication; he had her dance hunger and dignified entreaty. Mother and father welcomed her to sit and share their meal.

With a discordant crash, a realistic viper – life-size, disproportionate to the other puppets – rose and threatened one of the boys.

And that's Sarpa.

Murmurs of anticipation burst from the crowd as the beggar-woman took one huge, deliberate step toward the snake. She took another step, then a third, shaking her sprig of sage. With every step, a chorus of a hundred tiny bells tinkled, a strangely menacing beauty.

The beggar flew up out of sight and was replaced by a sapphire and emerald dragon, crowned in gold and wielding a golden lance. A roaring cheer greeted her appearance; she turned to her partisans and bowed graciously, then faced her foe again.

Biddi wasn't sure what that represented. *That boy, Kinnan, maybe?* The people, themselves?

Bells clashed with cymbals as the snake and the dragon fought. Even adults shouted encouragement to the Dragon Queen, rejoicing when she struck her enemy, groaning when she took a blow.

The fight ended, as it always did, with the viper skewered on the dragon's golden spear. The applause was muted, though, for the next part was equally inevitable. The dragon staggered and shook. Her silver bells tinkled more and more feebly. With a final shudder, she rolled onto her back and slid from view.

The more easily moved sniffled and at least one child broke into sobs. The puppet family drew together in a slow dance of mourning, while the puppeteer crooned a lament.

Biddi held her breath, waiting for the best part.

As the last note of the dirge died away, one silver bell clinked brightly.

Mother, Father, and the boys looked at each other. They looked all around.

"Look down! Down!" the crowd shouted.

The puppets looked down, and tiny bells jingled – quietly, then merrily – as a sprig of sage appeared to grow. It disappeared and was replaced by a dancing beggar in green and blue.

The curtain closed.

No one applauded with more gusto than the chief maid in the House of Sarpa's kitchen.

chapter 17
VARIANCE

"Can't we stop and rest now?" Elsie asked.

"We've barely started." Brady gave her a contemptuous glance.

"I'm not used to walking so long. I'm tired." She fisted her hands and locked her knees.

There were few things Brady wanted less than a scene in the middle of Fiddlewood Road with a woman dressed as a man. He considered it a good omen that he and Elsie had met no one between the Roll-Keeper's manor and the East Gate of Kudasad. At the East Gate, the city's busiest portal, they had slipped unnoticed into the muddle. More people were coming in at this hour than going out, but there were enough leaving that these two "young men" were only two more.

They had only been walking an hour, they were only at the paved common near Kudasad Bridge.

His companion was flushed, and not only from temper. Her face was a fierce, mottled red, compounded of exertion and nerves.

"All right," he said, grudgingly, "we'll stop a bit. Not long."

After another moment's consideration, Brady and Elsie threaded through a crowd watching a puppet show, off the road, and around a grassy rise. He saw the tops of some trees a little farther on and led the way to them. He and Elsie stepped into the hanging shelter of a willow. Somewhere nearer to the river, a hen crooned a soft monologue. The air was still, and rich with the smell of living wood. Bees hummed around their dappled sanctuary, reminding Brady of the skeps at the back of Devona's manor, of the beeswax candles in the scrivenry and their smell of caramelized honey as they burned.

"I'm hungry," said Elsie.

"I could eat a little something."

Elsie unpacked bread, cheese, and water, took some, and left Brady to help himself.

"Oh, very nice, girl," Brady sneered, enjoying the luxury of speaking out instead of biting back his words. "'Risk your life for me. Don't expect me to thank you, of course – '"

Elsie snapped, "Don't call me 'girl!'"

"Well, I won't call you 'Mistress Elsie' anymore. And I won't call your father 'Master' – until I see him again." Brady poked at his anger, trying to make it blaze. He was disappointed to find that, once unbanked, it was no more than irritation. "Your mother is my Mistress. You other two are only nuisances –"

"And you're a work-for-hire man!"

"With your life in my hands."

Elsie's face drained of color. To Brady's shock, she began to cry: not a poor-me snivel or a give-me-my-way wail or a lovely-when-I-weep single teardrop, but ugly, wracking sobs.

At a loss, he watched until she pressed her hands to her temples, took a series of shuddering breaths, and grew quiet.

She kept her head lowered as she said, "I didn't mean to cry. I don't want your pity. You can't know – The kind of life you've lived – I think you *like* what's happened. You *like* running away with danger at our heels."

Brady had to admit, provided the danger was unlikely to catch him, he enjoyed the chase.

As if she read his thoughts, Elsie said, "I don't. A month ago, I was happy. My life was secure. I knew who I was, and I could be fairly certain of who I would become. Now...." She took a quick, deep breath. "I'm terrified. But I'm so tired. I can't bear to stop but I couldn't go on. Every second, I think I'll hear Landry's men, but I couldn't.... And now you threaten me–"

Brady forgot that Elsie was a woman's age, and only remembered that she was six years younger than he – a baby. He scolded her as an older brother would have: "Oh, don't! Why would I help you escape if I didn't intend to finish the job?"

"Finish?"

"Take you to Kozabir. Get you settled there. Safe. I promised your mother, didn't I? Just watch how you talk to me, that's all I'm saying. You owe me some courtesy."

"I suppose I do." Elsie wiped her face on the sleeves of her shirt. Brady nearly smiled, seeing the fastidious Mistress Elsie with her face smeared and blotchy. It added to her disguise; she looked even less like the Kinninger's runaway bride and more like a grubby schoolboy. She snuffled once more then, with recovered dignity, said, "When I told you to stop calling me 'girl,' I only meant that I'm not supposed to be a girl. I wish I were the one who could change my shape."

"Did I ever tell you about the time I joined a troupe of traveling players? Men played women's parts, women played men; it depended on what was needed. We –"

A hen cackled nearby. The sound grew louder, followed by a voice saying, "What is it? I'm coming."

Elsie froze.

The dangling stems of the willow parted and a head poked through. It was the head of a man – an old man with roughly-trimmed silver hair and beard. His purple-black eyes were bright, even in the willow's green shade, and his full lips spread in a smile.

"Company!" he said. "This is a rare treat!"

"We can't stop to visit," said Brady. He hoped the man wouldn't insist; he didn't want to show their hurry, but he did want to be well away from the city by nightfall. Besides, he wasn't convinced of Elsie's ability to carry off her charade at any length, especially in her present state of mind.

"No, I was sure you couldn't stay." The old man plucked a string bag from the rag that served him as a belt. "This morning, when she gave me this, I said to myself, 'Something's to be carried somewhere.' You need this, don't you, my young gentlemen?" He leaned forward, to get a better look at Elsie, and said, "Why, boy, you've been crying!"

"He's homesick," Brady said. "I'm taking him back to his family."

The old man raised a finger in the air and shook it, saying, "Fruit! You're traveling. You need fruit. I'll be right back."

As soon as he had withdrawn, Elsie repacked their provisions.

"We're not going anywhere until that old man comes back," said Brady. "We're not in any position to turn down anybody's help. Besides, we don't want to do anything to make us stand out. If he says, 'I gave two young men a bag of fruit,' nobody will think much of it. If he says, 'I offered two young men a bag of fruit, but they ran away before I came back with it'...."

The willow branches parted again and the old man returned, the string bag bulging with globes of different sizes and colors.

"Here you are. May it give you strength and bring you luck." He chuckled in delight.

"Many thanks," said Brady.

Elsie said nothing.

~*~

They didn't cross by the Kudasad Bridge, but kept to the little-traveled western bank.

After another hour or two of travel, Elsie begged another stop.

"Let's have some of this fruit," Brady said, as they sat in the roadside grass. He held up the bag, looking through the netting at his choices. Then, slowly, he lowered the bag. He took out a piece of the fruit, examined it, and set it down. He took out several more and set them beside the first. "Look." He pointed to each one. "Fresh-picked."

"Of course. We knew that."

"But look! Peach. Apple. Plum. Apricot. Orange."

"Orange? Oranges don't grow this far north."

"And the others don't come ripe at the same time. Yet they're fresh."

Brady, of course, was no stranger to the wonderful. He picked up a peach, stroked it, and bit into it.

"Don't!" cried Elsie, putting a restraining hand, too late, on Brady's wrist.

"Why not?" he mumbled. He wiped his chin with his sleeve and leaned over the grass to eat. "Delicious! The best I ever ate!"

Elsie looked on with horror and envy. When Brady finished the peach and leaned back onto his elbows, beaming with satisfaction, she picked up a plum. She only held it until Brady laughed at her, then she bit in and laughed back at him, plum juice dripping over her hand.

"Save the pit," she said. "Maybe we can grow our own."

"There was no pit. Does yours have one?"

"…No." She raised her eyes from the plum to Brady. "How is that possible?"

"Maybe it's a new variety. Maybe that old man was magic. Maybe we're both crazy. But the first thing I do when I get back is raid that orchard."

~*~

They didn't stop again until sundown. They slept in a barn, dining on fresh milk and breakfasting on raw eggs. Elsie insisted on leaving some coppers in payment, much to Brady's disgust.

"We'll spend enough on things we can't get on the hook," he said. "Why waste pence on things no one will miss?"

Elsie took both purses into her own keeping. Brady permitted this, trusting himself to extract whatever he wanted from them whenever he might want it.

The second day of walking was harder, for they were both footsore from the first.

"Why don't you turn yourself into a horse and let me ride?" Elsie asked, as she shook a pebble from one of her boots.

"And go to bed with four sore feet instead of two, and an aching back, as well? No, thank you. I ask you, Elsie beren Devona: Do you ever think of anyone but yourself?"

Elsie blushed and stomped onto the other side of the road.

They went slowly, and rested often, keeping near the river and the convenient overhang of its bank, where Elsie could hide if Swords rode into sight.

No Swords did ride into sight, however, and every hour found the two more certain that they were unpursued. Even so, Elsie was afraid to lower her hood or unlace her tunic, and she prickled with the heat. Brady prickled, too, with the heat of her disposition.

When they stopped for lunch they took off their boots, rolled up their leggings, and waded in the shallows.

"Aahh! that's good…." Brady sighed as he plopped his feet into the water. The river was narrow here, and swift; even in the shallows, the current was fast. Miniature breakers tinkled against the banks, and miniature waterfalls poured over shelves a child could climb. Brady sat on a shelf the water didn't reach and let the current play about his ankles.

"Why don't you make use of your one talent and catch us a fish?" Elsie asked. "You could turn into a bear and knock one onto the bank."

"I could turn into a bear and knock *you* onto the bank. Listen, you silly twit: I change my shape, not my nature. Brady the bear could no more catch a fish unaided than Brady the man. That takes instinct, or practice, anyway. If you want a fish, why don't you spear one with your sharp tongue? That's *your* one talent."

Elsie sloshed around a spit where Brady couldn't see her and surreptitiously tried to catch a fish barehanded.

Brady propped himself against a twisted tree. He took out his bird's-tail pipes and pulled a gentle tune. As the sun warmed him, his playing ceased and he closed his eyes. He breathed deeply and tried to identify smells. Old dead fish, of course. Drying mud. Himself. Something minty.... He drowsed.

Something buzzed nearby – a bee or a hummingbird. The humming grew louder, and modulated into an old Kozabirian folk tune. Brady opened his eyes and saw the reflection of a woman rippling on the surface of the river.

Her hair was roan red. It was pulled back and showed itself as a large soft bun behind her neck. Her face was broad at the brow and narrow at the chin. She wore a short-sleeved white chemise and was draped in an embroidered linen palla, a rectangular shawl worn by Kozabirian women. Her lips parted in a tender smile, the tenderness reflected in her dark blue eyes.

"Careful," she said. "Don't fall in."

Brady's first thought was that Elsie had been carrying these clothes with her and had changed into them to be cooler. The smile, he took as mockery.

"And just how far do you expect to walk, dressed like that?" he shouted.

Elsie sloshed back into view, hotter and more vexed than ever from her vain pursuit.

"I don't expect to walk any distance dressed like this. I'll be dry and have my boots on before you're ready to move, you lump."

Seeing Elsie, Brady leapt up and scrambled onto the verge of the road, leaving his pipes teetering on the edge of his rocky seat.

There was no one. Nothing.

"I thought I saw someone. A woman. She was beautiful. She smiled at me."

"You *were* dreaming."

"I must have been: She was beautiful, and I still thought it was you."

Both preserved dignified silence for most of the afternoon.

Neither apologized, but shared suffering forged a sort of truce between them. By the time they took shelter for the night in a riverside fishing hut, they were speaking again.

They found a pole and a line in the hut. Brady baited the hook with a knot of pressed bread. "Now you'll see Brady catch a fish. I'm surprised you didn't suggest I turn into a worm. Of course, the steel of the hook would have changed me back, but I'm still surprised you didn't ask me to try."

Elsie looked up from wood-gathering, a scowl at the ready, but Brady's wide smile took the sting out of the insult.

"But then the fish would have eaten you," Elsie cooed. "I couldn't bear the thought of that."

"Why, Elsie! A kind word for me?"

"It's just that I was taught never to eat fish that feed on foul things...." Grinning wickedly, she pretended to dodge a blow.

Elsie laid a small pile of dry twigs in a careful criss-cross, as Brady had instructed. She searched the four corners of the shanty and looked on and under the table while he cleaned and filleted the fish in the river.

"I don't suppose you could change yourself into a tinderbox," she said darkly, as he came in.

"A tinderbox is not a human or an animal, so I can't. But it just so happens I have a tinderbox. In my pack." Elsie opened the rough brown sack. "It's tin, enameled in blue. No steel in it, of course."

"How do you strike a spark off the flint without steel? Another Kozabirian wonder?"

"This." The knife he'd been using on the fish was still wet from its washing. Its handle was of gleaming black wood, and its blade was bright and unscathed by any use it had seen.

Soon, flames whooshed, all but smokeless, up the chimney. Brady stuck the fillets on forked sticks and crisped them, before the quick little fire burned itself to ash.

"Those are beautiful things," Elsie said, as they ate. She nodded at the tinderbox and the ebony-handled knife.

"They *are* mine. I didn't steal them. She wouldn't have minded me having them, I know. There was a pot, too, but of course we sent that with her."

"With who?"

"This old woman. She seemed old to me, anyway."

"Tell me," Elsie coaxed.

Brady took a bite of fish and ate it slowly. At length he said, "You know that story about the beggar woman who turns into a dragon and saves a boy from a snake?"

"I don't think so. Wait – Yes, I do! Mathilde, one of my friends when I was younger, loved that story. She used to act out all the parts. The dragon dies, doesn't it?"

"Sometimes. There are a lot of versions of the story. They say Farukh created it, but you know how his stories sort of re-tell themselves when they get passed around."

"In Mathilde's version, the dragon dies. It makes a long, pathetic, noble speech, and then it dies. Gracefully and dramatically, of course."

Brady didn't mirror Elsie's smirk. He handled the knife and tinderbox, withdrawn into memory. "Something very like that tale truly happened to me when I was a boy. I used to talk about it, but people thought I was parroting the tale, trying to be clever and failing. The acting troupe I traveled with performed it sometimes. I wouldn't. Wouldn't even provide the music. Nights they did that story, I went somewhere else and got drunk."

Elsie's voice was quiet, and the smirk was gone. "Tell me."

"One time, when I was ten or so, my father and mother and brother and I were on our way back to Kozabir. We used to come over onto the Great Chalk Moor, north of Bahari, and carry back chalk to sell."

"That's *our* chalk! Layounna's!"

"Tell Landry to send me a bill, next time you see him. Do you want to hear this, or don't you?"

"Yes."

"Well, we were on our way back, and we'd made camp. I was gathering dry moss for the fire when I nearly put my hand onto a snake. A viper."

Elsie shuddered. "What did you do?"

"I froze and screamed."

"Couldn't you change into something that kills snakes?"

"I wasn't a varier, then. We aren't born, you know. Most people in Kozabir don't even believe in it – they think it's a child's tale."

"Never mind that. What happened with the snake?"

"This old woman came up. She had long brown braids streaked with gray; a Layounnan, by her dress, although I didn't see that until later. Just then, I didn't see anything but that snake. She pulled out this knife and went after the snake with it."

"With a *knife*?"

"With this very knife. My father snatched me away. The viper bit her. But, by the Mother of Life, she killed it."

"And she died, too?"

"And she died, too. We've talked it over so many times…. We think she only meant to distract it but it was fast – you can't believe how fast it was. She died within minutes, and all she said was, 'So.'"

"'So'? What did that mean?"

Brady held up his palms, empty of answers. "She had a pack made out of a woven rug. There was food in it and this tinderbox and knife and a little cooking pot and a waterskin and…." Brady shrugged. "We stuffed as much food as we could into the pot and wrapped the rug around her shoulders. There was a bog not far away. We put her into it, with the pot in her hands, and sang her to the Safe Haven."

"That isn't how we do things."

"Don't I know that? But that's how *we* do things, and we thought she deserved the best honor *we* could show her. Were we wrong?"

"No," said Elsie. "You were perfectly right."

She sucked the fish off her fingers and picked up the knife. Its ebony handle was carved in the likeness of a leaping horse. "And you were right to keep these things, too."

"My father said she must have been mad. My mother said she was sent by the Mother of Life."

"What do you think she was?"

He was still for a moment, visiting the past. Then he said, "My parents are both dead now. The Gray Sickness."

"I'm sorry," Elsie said, and Brady saw she meant it.

He took the knife and put both it and the tinderbox into his pack. "I owe her a life. If I could ever find out who she was, I'd pay her back somehow. That's one reason I carry her things: Maybe somebody will recognize them someday. Your mother didn't."

"Did my father… Did Darcy?"

"I didn't ask him."

Elsie nearly told Brady about her own kidnapping, near-drowning, and rescue. She opened her mouth twice to begin but, in the end, said nothing of it. She felt a dread of speaking about it while still in Layounna, as if to do so would be like a hare dancing before a hound.

She did say, "Why are you doing this for me? You walked right in among the Swords. Where there are Swords, there's sure to be steel. You might have been discovered any time. Why did you run the risk?"

"I didn't do it for you. Don't get all snappish again, but has your treatment of the work-for-hire man been anything to inspire heroics?"

"No. And I'm sorry."

"You're sorry for your treatment because I helped you. Wouldn't it be nice if you were sorry because you knew you had been wrong?"

"I am! How do you know why I'm sorry?" But she knew, to her shame, that Brady was right. "You haven't answered my question."

"Well, then, I did it for my Mistress, to pay back a great debt of kindness. And to tweak Landry's nose – None of you seem to like him very much but nobody ever does anything about him. And to spite Master Whey-face, your father. And to see if I could. For the fun of it."

"Dangerous fun."

"When I'm too old for danger, I'll settle for being wise."

~*~

That night, as they wrapped themselves in their cloaks, Elsie suddenly asked, "How *did* you become a varier? And why?"

"It was because of that snake. And because of a tortoise."

"A tortoise?"

Brady laughed, remembering. "When I came of age – men come of age at twelve, in Kozabir. For women, it's sixteen. Did you know that?"

"No," said Elsie, her tone adding that she didn't care.

"Well, that's how it is. Men aren't considered worth much, on the whole, until they're married. So my father and mother gave me a bride-price to take to the bridal fair. Do you know about them?"

"No. Does it have anything to do with the story?"

"Mmmm…No, not really. Just that it wasn't a very large bride-price, and the only skill I had was with the pipes, so I probably wouldn't have attracted much interest anyway. But before I got to the fair I saw this huge old tortoise being hauled to the market. He had four holes drilled in his shell, filled with four brass rings; that meant he had been caught four times and released four times."

"Why catch him, if you're going to let him go?"

Brady sighed and gathered his patience. "People catch tortoises to sell. The meat is good, if you cook it low and slow. Apothecaries make arthritis jelly from the plastron, and seers heat the shell until it cracks, and claim they see the future in the pattern the cracks make."

Both young people laughed derisively.

"Anyway, here was this poor old tortoise – oh, I was saying, sometimes people buy one of these tortoises and punch a hole in its shell and put a ring in the hole and release it. It's supposed to be good luck. So here was this old fellow, on his way to be turned into dinner and jelly and hogwash and I…I had to buy him. I had to. You understand?" He hoped she did, for he couldn't have explained the compulsion he had felt.

"I know what it's like to want something so much you feel like you'll go up in flames if you don't have it. Rich cloth and jewels –" As Brady made a contemptuous sound, she spoke louder and said, "And the time Fa – Darcy said I couldn't keep Trenel."

"Well," Brady conceded, "a cat is closer to what I mean. So I bought the tortoise. It took almost all of my bride-price. So I didn't go to the bridal fair. I bought another ring for his shell and took my tortoise all the way to the Inland Sea and released him."

"What did your parents say?" Elsie asked, with a companionable giggle.

"Well, after I let the tortoise go, I met this man, a fisherman named Tartarus. Huge man. So dirty he was greenish-gray. He invited me to stay with him for a few days in return for cleaning his shack, and I didn't have the nerve to go straight home with no money and no wife. He told me he was a sorcerer and he offered to teach me variance."

Brady shifted uncomfortably. "And that's where the snake comes in: I never got over that snake. I never got over the feeling of being helpless, looking my death in the face. And I never got over thinking that, if I could have done something to save myself, that woman would still be alive. So when I got this chance, and I thought how I could have turned into a bird and flown away…into a wild ass, and cut it to pieces with my hooves…I had to learn."

"Of course you did."

"That's when I went home, to see if my parents would give me the money to pay Tartarus' fee. They wouldn't, of course. They were furious with me for 'wasting' my bride-price, and my elder brother, Josse, all but kicked me out of camp."

"So you started stealing?"

"Yes."

"Did Tartarus know where you got his fee?"

"He thought it was funny."

"He doesn't sound like a very nice man."

"He wasn't a very nice man."

There was a moment's silence, then Elsie asked, "What's it like? Variance?"

Brady raised himself on his elbow and said, "After I gave him his first payment, he stood me against the cliff, facing the Inland Sea, and put a piece of tortoiseshell in the end of a hollow reed and blew it at me." He put a hand over his chest. "I felt it go in. It felt sharp and hot, like a splinter. My heart knotted up; I thought it would stop. I thought I would die, right there. Then I sort of relaxed all over, and...."

"And what?"

"I could see things and hear things...."

"Things that weren't there?" When Brady didn't answer, Elsie said, "Things you couldn't see and hear before?"

"Something like that, but different. It's like, there's another world behind this one, and sometimes they come together. Like – You look out a window in the summer, and you see what's there. You look out in the winter, and it's different, right?"

"Right."

"Well, what if you looked out and you saw both at the same time? The way things really are and a different way, both at the same time, and you know one of them is what everybody else sees and one of them is something else, but they're both the same view, really?"

Elsie was silent so long, Brady was sure she had fallen asleep. Then she said, "I don't understand that."

Brady laughed. "Neither do I. I ignore it, most of the time. Anyway, after that, I could vary. Tartarus guided me – it takes practice, too, you know. Then one day he was gone. Just gone."

"So you came here."

"I nursed my family through the Gray Death first," Brady said, jaw tight at the memory. "My mother died. My father recovered, but he wasn't strong. He died soon after. My brother, Josse.... Well, we never did get along, even after I brought him through it. That's when I came to Kudasad."

"And found my – And found Devona."

"And found Devona."

"Why her? Why did you foist yourself on us, of all the families in

Kudasad?" Elsie reached over and jiggled Brady's foot on the word "foist" so he would know she meant no harm.

"I met an old woman – I mean a *very* old woman – at a cookshop. The place was cheap and crowded; we shared a table. Frankly, I had my eye on this necklace she was wearing, with a pendant shaped like a dragon – looked like it was made of gold. I told her I was looking for work."

"Probably a lie."

"Oh, unquestionably a lie, but I had to make small talk while I came up with a plan for separating her from her jewel."

Elsie's silence was chill.

"I've reformed since then. I really have. And I didn't rob her, and I did come looking for a job."

"Go on." Elsie thawed a degree. "How did she escape your clutches?"

"Well, she told me Devona, a scribe in Kudasad of Layounna, needed help but didn't know she needed it, that it would take more trick than talent to get a place with her."

"I imagine that appealed to you."

Brady's chuckle came through the darkness. "It did. Not as much as the old woman's necklace, but she slipped me, somehow, after we left the cookhouse. So I joined the Festival Players and worked my way to Kudasad and tried my luck with your mother. And she turned me honest. … Well, mostly."

After that their talk was of Kozabir, and what Elsie might do once safely within its borders.

"I think we should go up through the Fiddlewood," Brady said. "The border's closer that way. The Fiddlewood runs right up into Kozabir. We'll cross the border and not even know it until we come out of the woods. It's the back of beyond, where we'd come out, too; even supposing Landry got the Emir to let him send Swords after you, no one would think of looking in that backwater." He chuckled. "Don't tell anybody in Kozabir you came out of the Fiddlewood, though. They think it's haunted. That's our name for it: Geiskeflor. Means 'Haunted Wood,' in our language."

"Do you believe it's 'haunted'?"

"Do I strike you as being superstitious? Spirits are anchored to the body in life and go to the Safe Haven after death. I'm not saying there's nothing in Geiskeflor; I'm only saying there's nothing there that doesn't belong there."

"They say the Unicorn lives in the Fiddlewood. But I suppose you don't believe in it."

"I believe if there *is* a unicorn, it probably has better things to do than trouble itself with people." Brady said something scornful in Kozabirian.

"I suppose I'll have to learn your language."

"It isn't strictly necessary. We're used to ignorant Layounnans who can only speak their own dog-yap."

This was meant as a pleasantry, and was taken as such.

~*~

The next day they ate the last of their food. The Fiddlewood closed in upon the river to their right and cut in front of them, the river running into it.

"How much longer to Kozabir?" Elsie asked.

"I don't know, really."

"…You don't know?"

"I always go east, around the tip of the Inland Sea, and up through Bahari. I've never been this way before. Maybe three or four days?"

Elsie's eyes narrowed, her lips compressed as if she were about to sound "charge" on a war-trumpet. "You brought me a way you've never been before? What were you thinking of? Or is 'thinking' the word to use, regarding you?"

"I was thinking of getting you out of Layounna by the safest route, in consideration for your mother. Or is 'consideration' a term you would understand?"

"You don't know how far we have to go. You don't know what dangers or obstacles might be in those woods. Can we even find enough to eat in there?"

"Maybe. The Fiddlewood River goes nearly to the border." Brady patted his sack. "I brought along that fishing line we found back at the hut."

"But I didn't pay for it!"

Brady reached into the bag. "Here, you'd better return it, then."

Elsie ignored this. "You'll have to find a village and buy some supplies."

"*I* will?"

"It isn't safe for me to go. They may be looking for me."

"Looking for you? Nobody's looking for you. Landry's probably sacrificed a barnyard full of animals in gratitude for having lost you."

Elsie took up her pack again and headed for the woods.

"Where do you think you're going?" Brady called after her.

She walked on.

Brady collected his own sack and water bottle and caught up with her. "Where do you think you're going?"

"Why don't you just go back to Kudasad and be Moder's little pet? I'm no more likely to get lost than you are, since you don't know where you're going, either."

"I have some idea, at least. And I'm nobody's 'little pet.' Anyway, I can't go back until I see you to safety. I promised."

"Nobody expects a Kozabirian varier to keep his promises."

Brady grabbed Elsie by the arm. She struck him a rather feeble blow with her free hand.

"Don't hit me," he said.

"Don't clutch me."

Brady let her go. "You win. I'll go find a village or a farmhouse or something and buy us some food."

"*Buy* it."

"I need some money." Brady reached for the sack Elsie was carrying.

"I'll get it." Elsie pulled out a purse and opened it. She counted out several coppers and put the purse away.

"That won't be enough." Brady stuck his hand into Elsie's sack, but she twitched it off and out of his reach.

"That will be more than enough," she said. "We don't need much. We won't want to carry much."

"Have it your own way, then, Mistress I-Know-Best. You go on. I'll meet you at the edge of the Fiddlewood, right by the river. If I'm not back by nightfall, you'll know something happened and you go on alone."

"Nothing is going to happen unless you thieve and get caught at it."

"Listen. I'm not going to thieve and I don't think anything's going to happen, either. But if it does – just in case it does – listen. Follow the river until it curves to the east. That's your right as you'll be going."

"I know which way is east."

"Keep heading north. If you know which way is east, I can only assume you know which way is north."

Elsie threw out an arm, full-length, and pointed.

"Very good. If I do get into trouble, I'll get out of it again, and catch up with you along the way. Do we understand one another?"

Elsie nodded. "Go on. The sooner you go, the sooner you'll be back."

Brady left Elsie and struck off away from the river. When he was out of her line of sight, he dropped the handful of coppers she'd given him into the purse he'd palmed from her sack. *How does she know what prices are around here?*

He thought it would be best to change himself a bit, just in case Elsie was right and there really was a hunt out for them. He would still be a traveler on his way to Kozabir; it was the simplest explanation for his need. He mustn't look too prosperous, though. Travelers were generally charged outrageous prices, anyway, since they had no choice but to pay; the more the traveler looked able to afford, the higher the price. The purse of coppers he'd taken from Elsie wasn't bottomless, after all.

When Brady stepped into sight of the farm buildings, he was tall and robust, bronze, blue-eyed and blonde. He wore clothes of brown homespun.

A man came out of a low-roofed thatched cottage, holding a bit of bread. He popped the bread into his mouth as Brady approached and folded his arms across a chest like a hairy barrel.

A woman peered out between the slats of an unglazed window, then came to lean over the top of the divided door. Another man, a gray-haired version of the first, came around the house from the back.

"What can we do for you, son?" he asked. "Holiday up the river, and couldn't catch your dinner?"

"Yes," said Brady, with a toothsome smile. He was a bit chagrined at having been willing to tell more-or-less the truth when, with a little thought, he might have produced this very plausible lie on his own.

"There's a bit left of ours," the woman said. "I'll fetch it out to you, shall I?"

"I'll need more than a bit. I'm a heavy feeder."

The younger farmer laughed. "You look it. What'll it take to fill you, then?"

"A couple of loaves, a cheese about so big. Half a dozen apples. — That'll do me for supper and breakfast, too."

"I should think it would," said the woman. She looked to the younger man, who looked to the elder.

"Can you pay?" the older man asked. "We could spare a few scraps, for pity's sake, but you're asking for money's worth."

"I'm only a journeyman tanner." Brady roughened and stained his hands under cover of searching his nearly empty pack. "I only have a handful of coppers, but you're welcome to a fair reckoning of them."

The gray-haired man nodded and the woman ducked into the house.

Brady spent the next quarter-hour inventing the village he claimed to come from and populating it with caricatures of people he didn't like.

The woman returned and passed a sack to the younger farmer, who passed it to Brady.

The older farmer named a price – inflated, but not shockingly so.

Brady scooped a few coins from the purse he'd taken from Elsie and began to count them out into the young farmer's hand.

Two of them were silver.

"Hello!" said Brady, taking them back. "Where did you come from?" He dipped into the purse again and came up with one copper – the rest were silver.

He had palmed the wrong purse. Meaning to supply himself with plenty of coppers, he had gotten the silver instead.

"What's an apprentice tanner on vacation doing with coin like that?" the older farmer said, moving in on Brady from the side. "Robbed your master and run away, have you?"

The varier took to his heels. He kept his coloring and homespun but, under cover of movement and distance, dropped bulk and weight from his figure and picked up speed.

"I'll loose the dog!" he heard the woman shout.

Oh, to be a dog! A greyhound, streaking into the distance. But that would mean exposing his ability and losing the sack of food, not to mention his own things and Devona's money, and Brady wasn't yet prepared to make those sacrifices.

He ran on, leaving the farmers behind – but not far behind. The river glinted before him. The Fiddlewood gloomed ahead, leaves rustling as if in encouragement. He saw Elsie, or thought he saw her, just where he'd told her to be.

She probably thought she'd been right about him, that he'd tried to steal what he could have bought and brought this down on them, that a Kozabirian varier couldn't be counted on.

Well, he'd show her. He lengthened his legs, firmed his muscles, expanded his lungs, and pulled farther ahead. He turned more sharply north, leading the chase away from Elsie, though it meant staying in the open longer.

At last he reached the trees. He plunged into the shade and ran as far as he could before he stumbled. Then he shoved his things into some under-growth and huddled by them, panting and trembling.

He heard the men crash into the woods after him. He heard the distant barking of a dog. One of the men went back out, while the other cast about, striking at the growth with his foot or with a stick.

"Tiger!" The man outside the woods called. "This way boy! To 'im!"

The dog loped into the woods, circling and snuffling.

"What's the use of that dog?" one of the men said. "He knows he's hunting, but how's he to know what?"

"He's gone to ground, or we'd hear him," the other said. "Tige'll flush him, if only by chance."

It seemed that Tige would, at that, for Brady heard the circling and the snuffling come closer, until the dog's nose nearly touched the bush behind which Brady sheltered.

The next moment, the dog and both his masters were falling over each other to leave the woods behind. The men would spend many an hour during the balance of their lives, heavily armed, hunting the huge black bear with the white ruff that appeared as if from nowhere.

Brady sank back to his own form, weak with relief and weariness, and shaking with watery giggles.

"That dog's ears!" he whispered. "They stood straight up!"

He rested a moment while he imagined himself, returned from his mission, describing the scene to Devona.

As soon as he could, Brady took up his sacks and began to shuffle and stumble from tree to tree, heading northeast.

When he and the river met again within the Fiddlewood, he permitted himself to collapse. He hoped he was ahead of Elsie and that she would come up with him before dark, or else that she would come back for him. He piped a tune Devona had requested often, thinking Elsie might hear it and find him.

Night fell, and Brady was still alone.

Elsie would sleep hungry – which, Brady thought, might do her good. It wasn't his fault if she hadn't the sense to look for him. Even so, Brady was sorry to think of her, also alone in a strange wood and hungry into the bargain.

He went to sleep wishing her well, but his dreams were of the beautiful Kozabirian woman in the embroidered palla.

chapter 18
dream of a mandate

"Thane Guthrie is right, My Lord," said Oliva beren Audre. "Sorcery is in this."

Landry, his mother, and his Chief Sword were in private council in one of the small chambers off the Great Hall. It was late in the day of Elsie's disappearance; the door and windows were closed and barred, and scent from the oil lamps hung heavy in the air.

"The Sword who volunteered to search the woman's house never returned," said Guthrie. "All of my men are accounted for, and all swear they never left the bailey. The man was an imposter."

"Sorcery," Oliva repeated.

"Or lies," said Landry. "Bribery? This…Darcy…?"

Guthrie shook his head. "He's known in Bahari. He's unshakably loyal – to whoever happens to be in power. You may trust him utterly."

"His wife?" asked Landry. "Is she also known in Bahari?"

"Devona beren Valda," said Guthrie. "A shopkeeper. Nothing more, and thick-witted, at that. She couldn't seem to understand what I came for when I went looking for the missing 'Sword.' She offered me tea and gave me ale and babbled about the honor I did her shop by entering it. Hoping to get a Thane for a customer, you see. Just what you would expect of a shopkeeper from the provinces."

"We determined the parents to be harmless when you proposed the daughter as your consort, My Lord," said Oliva. She paused, pointedly not reminding Landry that he had made his choice alone, and against his mother's liking. "But one thing more we learned then that we did not discuss because it seemed mere trivia: This Devona beren Valda has a Kozabirian clerk. A young man a few years older than the girl. Kozabir is full of Hidden Matters. The Great Adept, Tarkastrus, spent many years there before he began his teachings."

"The clerk left for Kozabir several days ago," Guthrie told her. "I thought of him myself, and asked after him at the Roll-Keeper's manor."

"Who says he left?" asked Oliva.

"Devona beren Valda, two of the servants, the toll-collector on the Kudasad bridge...."

"He could have returned on the sly."

"It hardly matters," said Landry. "The girl – What was her name again?"

"Elsie, I believe," said Oliva, who knew the name quite well. She intended to expend time and energy – to say nothing of small, sacrificial lives – to learn more of the missing girl. The Divinities, properly applied to, would tell Oliva where this girl had gone, and how, and why, and what suffering she feared the most. One did not jilt a Sarpan, and one did not practice hostile sorcery in the stronghold of an Adept.

"– Elsie is gone," Landry continued. "If she managed her disappearance herself to escape marriage to me, there's many another maiden who would prove more tractable. If someone else managed it to deprive me of her, she's a loss I can easily bear. If it was done to make a mockery of me...." This was the only alternative Landry found insupportable. After a grim moment, Landry's delicate features eased into smiling satisfaction.

"We'll claim we still have her," he said. "We'll say she's ill, or that Corvina is schooling her in the manners of our class before we consider her fit to be Kinninger's Consort. Moder, you will pass the necessary orders to Rhu beren Robia."

Oliva inclined her head.

Landry went on: "In a few months, we'll declare the girl unsuitable and say we've sent her to a Waystation. Guthrie, see that the girl's parents are prepared to bear witness to this."

"Darcy will be compliant, as ever," said Guthrie. "We need only keep the mother away and let Darcy tell her what we want him to. Buy some of her parchment and she won't ask any questions. Who could doubt the word of the girl's own mother?"

"I'm not concerned that anyone believes the story," said Landry. "Let them believe what they will, just so they understand not to question what we claim. Let rumors dispute rumors; confusion is the best deceit. Before the year is over, I'll choose another bride – Moder, I will be guided by you when that time comes."

Oliva's face remained expressionless, but her eyes glinted behind her half-lowered lids.

"We'll consider the incident closed, then," said Landry. "I'm content that the explanation is this: One of the Swords, for whatever reason, claimed he saw Elsie vanish. While he rushed her escort back down the stairs, she hid in a room he had stocked with villein's garb. She changed her clothing and joined in the search for herself. He offered to search her home, but never left the grounds. He re-entered the tower, met her at a prearranged spot, and saw her safely away."

"Ingenious, My Lord," said Oliva, who believed something quite other. "But – away where?"

Landry shrugged. "It doesn't matter." He laughed. "How droll, to think of the little drab huddling somewhere in fear of my pursuit, as if a lion would chase a mouse for refusing to share his den."

"Well put, Your Grace," said Guthrie.

"Oh, if she should come into my hands, I don't say I wouldn't make her wish she hadn't."

"Rightly so," said Oliva. "But, My Lord, will you not consider that sorcery might be involved?"

"You're the only sorcerer I know of within the palisade, Moder," said Landry. "Corvina never took to it, I remember. Are you warning me against yourself?"

"N-No, My Lord. How can you say so?"

"Then let us hear no more of sorcery."

"No, My Lord."

"And one thing more," said Landry, to Guthrie.

"Yes, My Lord?"

"I want that Sword. The woman isn't important, but a Sword who would take something I claim as mine cannot be left alive."

"If he is to be found, My Lord, trust me to find him."

The Kinninger was obviously finished with the council, but Guthrie was not.

"May we not talk of Rhu beren Robia?" he said.

"What of him?" The shadow of a frown warned Guthrie to choose his words carefully.

"He ordered the villeins to search for the girl, and my men to stand aside. I agreed, to speed the search, but I protest. He was clearly suggesting that my men could not be trusted."

"And? It seems one, at least, could not."

"Begging your pardon, Your Grace, but that was an inspired conjecture – not a proven fact."

The frown was open, now. "You presume on your position, Thane Guthrie."

"Even so, My Lord, the Chamberlain –"

"I am aware of how matters stand between you and my Chamberlain," Landry said. "He resents your elevation to landed Thane and my reliance on you in matters of…security. You resent my reliance on his advice in all other matters. You sit at my right hand in the throne room; would you sit at my right at the bargaining table? Could you wring trade concessions from our neighbors, yet keep their good will? Could you have so impressed the Emir that, when that pestilential Kinnan beren Nobody came begging for an army, word was sent to us at once? Could you have gained the Emir's permission to allow Swords in Kozabir's very capital? And, after my Chamberlain had done all this, your Swords let the man evade them – again."

"Even a lion sometimes misses when he snaps at a gadfly," said Guthrie.

"Which is why," said Landry, "he often promotes a toad to perform the service for him."

Guthrie kept himself in his seat by force of will, his hand gripping the pommel of Deya beren Blotha as if only that pressure kept her from leaping from her sheath. It was not for this the Chief Sword had united himself to Deya's debilitating strength – not to be spoken to in this way, not by the man for whom he had bartered his peace.

"As for Rhu," Landry continued, "do you think I keep him landless and untitled because I undervalue him? Quite the contrary."

The Kinninger exchanged a wry smile with his mother. "Kinningers before me have underestimated and overauthorized their administrators, with results that were disastrous for the Kinningers."

Landry stood. He held out a hand to Guthrie, which the Chief Sword accepted.

"You're angry with me, my friend," Landry said, with his easy, beautiful smile. "I'm sorry for that."

Guthrie opened the door for his master and watched him down the hall. Oliva had risen when her son did, but had seated herself again under cover of a deep curtsey.

The Chief Sword pushed the door all the way back against the wall, knowing that nothing discourages stealthy listening like an open door. He returned to his fellow Thane and stood by her chair, his left hand fisted on the hilt of his sword.

"My son was harsh with you." Oliva laid a sympathetic hand on Guthrie's fist. "Perhaps he was more disturbed by the girl's defection than he thinks to show."

"He implied that my honors were a sign of disrespect."

"He's still a boy at heart. A boy who hides his embarrassment by striking at his friends. He would never have spoken so to a man whose faithfulness he doubted."

Some of the tightness in Guthrie's body relaxed. "I am My Lord's man."

"Of course you are."

"But, may I say, My Lady, I think His Grace could better use his friends by taking them less for granted. *All* his friends." He raised Oliva's hand and bowed over it.

"We must hope he learns that lesson, before much time has passed." Oliva rose, allowing Guthrie to help her to her feet. She smiled her thanks.

"Now," she said, "You must remember to speak fair to the Chamberlain."

"Apparently, we must all speak fair to the Chamberlain." Guthrie scowled. "And with great deference, too."

Oliva laughed. "Since we seem to be talking of animals today: Any jackal who causes a lion to guard his flank is a jackal to be reckoned with."

"I'll reckon with him, if need be."

"Gently, my fellow Thane. Landry is right in saying that the Chamberlain is useful; we have no quarrel with his utility, I think."

"Landry should not hold him above me."

"It isn't that. It's this: Landry thinks to hold himself above the rest of us." She fluttered a hand to show how little she regarded such an attempt. "Let my son play Absolute Monarch for a while, if it pleases him. For the good of the realm, let the two of us glean what we can from where we can and share it. When he does turn to us, he'll find us prepared. More heads make better management, though my son seems to have forgotten that for the moment. As for Rhu beren Robia – leave him to me."

"And the Sword whose life My Lord demands…. Would your Divinities tell you if such a man exists and who he is?"

"Between the two of us," said Oliva, "such a man is pure invention. You know your Swords – how could one be false and you not know it? And if you knew it, would you let him live?"

"Do you need to ask?"

"I do not."

"And yet, My Lord demands…."

Abruptly, he bowed and strode away.

At Guthrie's departure, Oliva's frailty dropped from her like loosened armor.

Toads, lions, and jackals, she thought in amusement. *And a spider or two somewhere about, as well.*

Oliva couldn't fault Landry for wanting to hold the crown alone; the son of a strong mother must be strong or nothing. But neither could she permit such a thing to happen.

She and Guthrie might speak of the good of the realm, but neither cared over-much for that except as it safeguarded their own well-being. What she and Guthrie wanted – and Corvina and Rhu, Oliva supposed – was some share in control of government.

Each of them, Oliva assumed, sought to indulge different urges. One might, for example, quite possibly wish to do the people good. Rhu had been bred as a servant and his highest aspiration was probably to render Landry his most efficient aid. Corvina was no doubt still struggling to prove to herself that she was her brother's rival. Guthrie…. Guthrie must be watched closely and handled carefully, like one of Corvina's choicer brews.

As for her own ambition, it was simpler than she knew. She thought it was to be privy to all the secrets of the state and indispensable in council – that, and to set her line upon the throne. It was, in truth, to not be packed away like an obsolete weapon that had once ruled the field. She had traded her Thanehold for the throne; she had never intended, nor would she now allow, that trade to be for the sole benefit of her son.

So, she must weaken him just enough to make him call upon her strength as he used to do. She must also take care to ally herself with the enemies he was making among the Thanes, Guthrie being only one among many. She must return them to Landry's fold with their fealty to him depending upon his deference to her, one of their own.

~*~

Oliva struggled for a week, for two weeks, to combine the right ritual, the right sacrifice, the right petition. There were dreams, but none of Elsie.

As elements of the dreams repeated, Oliva began to sort them out. A hunt. The Chamberlain. Landry exalted, sitting the throne with his mother's hand entwined in his hair. And a little scrap of something: A sack… a purse… a bag.

It was so old it crumbled, revealing its contents. But they, too, crumbled as Oliva tried to identify them. Then a new bag appeared and spilled what it contained: rare black coral for dominion over water, a diamond for dominion over fire, a sapphire for air, and a blood-red ruby for the earth. And one thing more: Shavings of alicorn.

"Alicorn"–An Adepts' term, not often used by others, for whom the more cumbersome phrase "unicorn's horn" sufficed.

Another term whispered through Oliva's dream: "Mandate."

"Know ye, by this," official documents of Layounna began, "the mandate bag of my people, that I am their chief."

That there had once been such a bag, Oliva had no doubt. That there had continued to be one, unknown to all but the royal line, she was not so certain. But that Tortoise was telling his handmaiden there should be such a bag again, Oliva was sure.

A new mandate bag for the new royal line, and alicorn in it. A hunt for a unicorn. The Chamberlain on the hunt. And would he turn up Elsie, by the way? Was this, after all, Tortoise's left-handed way of answering her question?

~*~

Oliva approached her son and curtsied. This time she had not had to await His Grace's sleeplessness, but had been sent for upon receipt of her request for audience.

Landry rattled the parchment he held. "What do you mean by this? 'Your reign will not prosper. Tortoise tells me why.'"

"I meant only that. The disappearance of your chosen bride is only a minor manifestation of your reign's decay. There will be other, more serious ones."

"Why? What does Tortoise tell you?"

Oliva was tempted to tease her boy, to twit him for his falling away from the faith from which he now sought answers. To have done so would have been a disastrous mis-step, and Oliva did not make it.

"Karol's body was never found. Neither was something else, for she would surely have carried it with her."

"What else?"

"The mandate bag."

"The m…. But that's nonsense. That's rubbish."

"My dreams tell me otherwise," said Oliva. "So do our own ancient writings. The mandate bag was – I don't say 'it was supposed to be,' I say 'it was' – what gave the royal line its right to rule. It not only legitimized the line in the eyes of the people, it gave them authority over the Mysteries Beyond."

Oliva listed the bag's contents and their powers. Then she named the final item, which bound and focused those powers, as the alicorn binds its own strength into a spiral and concentrates it into a sharp and savage point.

"The jewels will all be easily found in the treasury," said the Kinninger. "Well done, Moder! Well done, Tortoise! The alicorn may present some difficulty, but surely Corvina has some."

"Alicorn is far more rare than you seem to think. When was the last time a unicorn was sighted in Layounna? The year Karol was born – and that sighting was unverified."

"What do you suggest?" Landry liked this idea. He liked this mandate bag. It was the very thing to invigorate his régime. He would declare a week of festival – say, leading up to Midsummer's Day. He would present the bag to a carefully instructed committee of the people, and they would dutifully beg him to receive it back from them. He would consent with becoming humility….

"A unicorn must be found," said Oliva. "One man must hunt it and he must bring it back to you, living, and in secret. I'll sacrifice it to Tortoise and scavenge the body."

"Surely scrapings of the horn will be sufficient." This was, Landry never forgot, and Oliva never seemed able to remember, another line's castle and not Oliva's Thanehold. The older villeins here had been reared to follow the unled Way and the younger ones had grown up with that atmosphere undermining Oliva's Tarkastrian encroachments.

Landry made it his business to know what his people said of him when they thought themselves free to speak – and what they said of Oliva. They said that, with Karol gone leaving no heirs and with Sorcha refusing her duty, Landry would do as well as another – and another would do as well as he. They also said that, Landry being no better than he was, he was better than his mother, who had made the castle into a charnel house with her bloody sacrifices.

And this was in response to domestic livestock. Landry would have to be persuaded to permit the butchery of anything so reputedly beautiful as a unicorn.

"If the creatures are rare," he said, "killing one will only make them more so. You may sacrifice something valuable but less uncommon instead."

"There is great power in each part of the unicorn," said the Adept. "The chance to possess these powers must not be missed."

"What powers?"

Oliva had prepared her persuasion. "The horn, of course, is effective in all forms of mysticism and sorcery and is so poisonous that a cup made of it attracts any poison placed in it, rendering the poisoned drink harmless. The hooves are also potent and can be ground to powder; this powder, thrown into flames, will provide a clear vision of the future. The bones can be cast in divination or placed under the pillow to bring visionary dreams. The skull, hung in a stable, eliminates illness in horses and assures a high rate of birth and the best quality foals. A knife or sword inlaid with chips of any of these parts, whether on the blade or on the hilt, leaves wounds which never heal."

"Some of this, I knew," said Landry. "No wonder the beast was hunted to near extinction."

"These are only the brittle parts. Of the soft parts, only the flesh is useless; the flesh being sour and decaying within minutes of death. A mantle made from the skin renders the wearer invisible. Bracelets made from the hair of the mane and tail insure health and long life. The dried blood is more poisonous than the horn to the healthy, but heals the dying."

A commodity one would do well to control, Landry thought, *when one's sister is an alchemist.*

"And besides all else – mark this, My Lord – at the root of the horn is a ruby the size of my fist. With a mandate bag containing this gem and shavings from the horn of a still-living unicorn, the House of Sarpa will hold the throne of Layounna forever. 'Layounna' may come to mean more than the current Five Districts."

Landry was persuaded. "Let it be done. Choose the other stones and see to the bag's manufacture. Put the ruby and the shavings into the bag. Make me a cup of what's left of the horn And the blood – I want every granule, every grain.

"And the other parts I've cataloged?"

"Perhaps we should catch the beast before we divide its carcass. And if the search proves fruitless or continues too long, find me another ruby and other alicorn, however old; surely the horn in Karol's bag – if she had one – was weak with age."

"And Karol lost her throne, her life, and her line," said Oliva, giving Landry something to keep him warm of nights.

~*~

Landry had expected Guthrie to be Oliva's choice as huntsman. So did Guthrie, when Oliva spoke to him later.

"Rhu?" The Chief Sword could not keep the outrage entirely out of his voice, out of his expression.

"Rhu," Oliva said, "and no other."

Her vision had not shown the outcome of Rhu's hunt, but the sending alone could bring her only good. If Rhu succeeded, her line would have a powerful mandate and she would be rich in occult articles. She might even save Corvina some scrapings, in spite of Landry's order. If Rhu succeeded, he would be honored, and would be grateful to Oliva, who sent him on his quest.

If Rhu failed, a less powerful bag could be prepared, and Tortoise implored for access to the freshest available alicorn. If Rhu failed, he would be discredited, however slightly, leaving more room for Oliva near the throne.

In the meantime, the longer Rhu was on the hunt, the weaker his position with Landry would become.

"Why should Rhu be entrusted with this?" Guthrie demanded. "Is he Landry's choice? Was it not enough for him that I charged a loyal Sword with an invented crime; that I executed him, to satisfy the story My Lord spun about his bride's disappearance?"

"Rhu is my choice," said Oliva. "It must be Rhu."

"Rhu's no hunter. He sits a horse as well as another, but he's never been in on a kill."

"For that very reason, only he will do. A successful hunter can never catch a unicorn. Do you know why?"

"A unicorn can only be captured by a maiden. Everyone knows that legend. Take a young virgin into the forest and bind her to a tree. The poison in the unicorn is drawn to the maiden because of her purity and the beast is weakened. When the unicorn is helpless, the hunter snares it."

"The legend is a corruption of the truth. The maiden need not be pure, she need only be guiltless of an innocent's death. There are only three things a unicorn cannot abide: a poisonous serpent because of its venom, a lion because it will kill more than it can eat…."

"And the third?"

"Blood on the human soul."

CHAPTER 19
ELSIE BETRAYED

For five years, Kinnan "birn Matka" lived with the smith, Trahern, outside the Kozabirian village of Vatra. Kinnan was now in his thirties. His tight curls were a lighter blond in front, bleached by the heat of charcoal. Five years of chopping wood and working at the forge had hardened his already respectable muscle. Five years of waiting and brooding had done the same to his expression.

He fashioned rings, bracelets, necklaces, baubs, and bangles out of soft metal. These sold well, and would have more than paid for his keep, if he didn't already earn his keep with apprentice work. He pumped the bellows, fed the smithy fire with charcoal, and fetched whatever the smith needed. He cut wood in the Geiskeflor, and learned to turn it into charcoal for the forge.

"All my charcoal comes out of Geiskeflor," Trahern told him once. "Maybe that's what makes some of my work… unusual. Eh?"

Kinnan rubbed the bracelet Karol had given him and said, "Maybe." The bracelet was warm; it had grown so since Kinnan had come to live with the smith. It was always warm, whatever the weather. It held Kinnan's wrist like the hand of a friend, and life was in it. Not that the figures on it moved, which would have been merely a marvel; this was something one could not see or prove, but only know.

~*~

Kinnan never spoke of his past and Trahern soon stopped asking. It was enough for the smith to have companionship where he had, for so long, had none.

Trahern neither hoped nor expected that Kinnan would stay at the forge. Part of the pleasure of Kinnan's presence was the knowledge that it wouldn't last forever. No, a bit of company and a hand at the work was enough for Trahern; and the less he knew about this particular hand, he felt, the better.

Trahern birn Lona more than made up for Kinnan's reserve. The smith loved to talk of his ordinary childhood, his unexceptional apprenticeship, his search for a place of his own, and the ravishment with which he had set eyes upon the deserted cottage and smithy beside the Geiskeflor. "I saw it and I knew I was home. The folk in Vatra warned me off of it – said the woods were strange and dangerous – but I knew better. Not that they were wrong, see, but 'strange and dangerous' is only a little part of what that forest is. Do you feel it, too?"

"No. To me, it's only trees."

"Only trees…." Then Trahern shook his head, and talked of something else.

Trahern continued to make his pieces, some merely serviceable and some, as he put it, unusual – unusual, that is, in the hands of the proper owner. He continued to take his goods to market in Granitz while Kinnan minded the forge.

Kinnan asked the smith to keep a lookout for a battered child with red-brown hair and dark blue eyes and not let it be known he was looking for her. Trahern kept on the alert, but there was a sorry number of battered children in Granitz and Trahern could bring no word of the girl. There was no word of the trinket-woman, Salali, either. For five years now, and months beyond, Kinnan had buried himself in this pocket between the forest and the north-west curve of the Inland Sea. For more than five years he had suffered in safety, and the greatest part of his suffering was this life's comfort and delight. He had never wanted more than this: to work at his craft, to live unknown and uncelebrated, and to die with his father's dignity. The throne had been forced on him by Landry's taking of it, and he would count his own coronation among the worst of Landry's crimes.

Many times he convinced himself that Salali and Farukh had been minions of Landry Oliva, sent to imprison him with false promises. Then he would replay their meeting in his mind, and he knew the two to be honest.

One rainy evening, five years and more after Kinnan's coming, the two men sat before the fire. Both were fidgety, and had been, all day. They smoked, and talked, and fell silent.

Trahern kept looking from the fire to the door to one of the tin lanterns on the mantle. At length he stood, stretched, and lit one of the lanterns with a spill from the fire.

"Where are you going, on a night like this?" Kinnan asked.

"It's a bad night," said Trahern, and carried the lantern onto the porch. He put it down, watched the rain glitter in its light for a moment, and went back in.

"What was that for?" asked Kinnan, remembering his own coming. "Is someone out there?"

"Not now."

Evening had advanced to night when they heard what might have been a footstep on the porch.

Trahern opened the door. He saw only the lantern and the shadows beyond its small pool of brightness. The firelight and lamps in the room behind him cast his shadow down the steps and into the rainy night.

"Is anybody there?" he said, softly. When there was no reply, he repeated his question in Layounnan.

There was a cough and a sneeze; one of the shadows moved and came into the light.

Trahern saw a sodden figure – male, judging by the torn and muddy traveling clothes. Round brown eyes blinked up at him. A slender hand, the nails broken and mud-caked, pushed back the tunic's hood, revealing uncoiling braids of amber hair. The dirty little face was pinched and pale and wary, but there was no tremble to the narrow chin. Not a male, though.

"I saw your light," she said.

"Who is it?" Kinnan called, in Kozabiri.

"A stray kitten, half-drowned," Trahern called back in the same language. "A girl, traveling as a boy." To the girl, in Layounnan, he said, "Come inside, Little Stray Kitten. You've nothing to fear from us two. We're strays, of sorts, ourselves."

"I only want leave to shelter here till the rain stops. And news of any other young strays you may have seen lately."

"Something to eat and something hot to drink wouldn't come amiss, either, eh?"

"I don't ask it."

"But you wouldn't turn it down?"

The girl came close to smiling. "I haven't eaten in two days. I ran out of food, and had no luck at catching anything. I had nothing but dew to drink, after the river went east."

"No complaint of thirst today, though, eh?"

"No."

"Come in where it's dry. You're welcome."

The girl followed Trahern into the house.

"You can hang your tunic on one of those pegs just inside the door. Put your boots on that mat. Here's some water and soap for your face and hands. Let's see what you really look like."

Kinnan turned to see the "kitten" to whom the smith had been talking. His gray eyes sparked at first sight of the girl, then the intensity of his interest faded.

Her coarse linen shirt was as wet as her tunic, but was so thick and full of gathers it saved her modesty. She didn't seem overly concerned about it, but washed up with the unselfconscious ease of one who had grown up – or had become – used to the eyes of men to whom she did not appeal.

Kinnan stood and pulled his chair away from the fire to give her more room.

"She's come up through the Geiskeflor," said Trahern.

Kinnan said, "From Layounna...."

"I haven't!" said the girl. "I came from that direction." The way she pointed was due east.

"That direction is the Inland Sea," said Trahern.

"Well," said the girl, sheepishly, "I'm wet enough."

Trahern laughed. "You came from that direction." He pointed past the forge to the forest. "You said the river turned east within the last two days. The only river that close is the Fiddlewood, across the Layounnan border. It turns east, if you're traveling north. And, you understand Layounnan, but not Kozabiri."

Trahern swung a pot over the fire and fetched a bowl of crumbled bread. The pot began to bubble.

"Who are these other strays you're looking for?" the smith asked.

"Other strays?" Kinnan's interest revived.

"Have you seen any?" asked the girl.

Trahern shook his head.

"What sort of strays?" asked Kinnan.

"Any," said the girl.

Kinnan opened his mouth to ask again, but Trahern waved him quiet. "Let her eat."

The pot yielded just enough mutton stew to fill the girl's bowl to the brim.

"Sit," Trahern invited, pulling away his own chair and toeing a stool closer to the hearth. "I'm Trahern birn Lona, blacksmith. This is my journeyman assistant, Kinnan birn Matka. And you are…?"

The girl opened her mouth to answer. Trahern could see a lie trembling on her tongue. Then she said, "Elsie. Elsie beren Moder."

Elsie and Kinnan eyed one another, each obviously suspecting the other's lack of matronym.

"And what brings you up through the Geiskeflor," asked Trahern, "and lands you on our porch in the middle of such a night? How do you come to be traveling alone in the first place, Little Kitten?"

"I was with someone. We got separated."

"How?"

"We…." The girl stopped. She looked up, turning from one man to the other.

"I told you, Kitten," said Trahern, "we're all strays, here. Tell us a lie, if you like, or tell us you'll answer no questions. Or tell us the truth. All courses are safe with us."

He cocked a sparse eyebrow at his journeyman assistant. "Eh?"

Kinnan kept his answer to himself.

"I don't know how it happened," Elsie said. "We were to meet, and we missed each other. I hoped…. You've seen no one?"

"Male or female?" asked Kinnan. "Of what age?"

Elsie ate her stew as if she hadn't heard.

Trahern and Kinnan switched to Kozabiri.

"Why all the questions, my friend?" Trahern asked.

"She has the way of a fugitive. Anyone who runs from Layounna is of interest to me – and so are their friends. On the other hand, maybe she isn't a fugitive; maybe she's pretending to be one."

"To what purpose?"

"Spying out what someone else wants secret."

"What secrets would a whisper of a thing like that be after? And who would she be spying for? And who would she be spying on in Vatra? … You?"

Kinnan said nothing.

"And what sort of spy is it who sneaks into a country not knowing the language?"

"How do we know she doesn't know the language? Trust me, Trahern birn Lona, I have every cause for fear. So have you, having befriended me."

Still in Kozabiri, Trahern said, tipping Kinnan a wink, "Rest easy, my friend. I can snap this kitten's neck with two fingers. We can dump her in the Geiskeflor, and no one will ever find her or know she was here. Will that satisfy you?"

Elsie said nothing, but stared unmoving into the fire, the heat of the flames and of the stew beading her face with a damp glow.

Kinnan laughed. "I'm satisfied. She doesn't understand Kozabiri. Therefore, she isn't a spy."

But she was asking curious, guarded questions about someone. Could it be...? How ironic if she were an agent, not of his enemies, but of his friends.

Kinnan sat and watched the girl as she began to eat again. He had a feeling he could trade probes all night with this "Elsie beren Moder," and they would both end knowing no more than they did now. Someone would have to toss some information on the table, to get things going.

Trahern took his own seat, flicking glances from one Layounnan face to the other.

In Layounnan, Kinnan said, "Were you with a woman? A Nishite? Old but quick, and dressed in layers of bright...," Kinnan's hands fluttered, "...gauzy things?"

"No." Elsie looked at Kinnan as if he had lost his mind.

"Or a storyteller from Sule? With a red hat, and—"

"Farukh?"

"You know him, then?"

"Everybody knows Farukh. He's the best. Why would I be with him? Were you expecting him?" Then she said, "Never mind."

Kinnan worked his fists three or four times, and said, "We could do with a little entertainment, here, that's all. It's dull."

"It must be." The girl went back to her stew, keeping a watchful eye on the journeyman smith. When she had scraped up the last spoonful of food she said, to both men at once, "You've seen no stranger lately?"

"Not for some time," said Trahern. "Not here or in Vatra, the only village close-by. Your stranger could have come out of the Geiskeflor somewhere else or could still be inside, but no one other than you has come out here."

"Who are you looking for?" Kinnan demanded.

Elsie turned to Trahern for support, met only blandness, and said, "If I answer your questions, will you give me some bread and water and not try to hinder me from going back?"

Kinnan sat forward. "Back to Layounna?" he asked harshly.

"Back into Fiddlewood. To search."

"Let's hear the story," said Trahern. "We'll see about the other."

"Won't you promise? I'm supposed to take a chance on your giving me what I ask for?"

"We're supposed to take a chance on your telling the truth, Elsie beren Moder of the Inland Sea," said Trahern.

Elsie almost smiled again. She rubbed her thumbs thoughtfully on the rim of the bowl she held then said, "All right. My name really is Elsie. I was chosen by... a rich man, to be his bride. A varier from Kozabir helped me escape."

"Are you being pursued?" asked Kinnan.

"I don't think so. It was cleverly done. It was my m –" Elsie coughed. "– My mother's idea. We had no trouble, all along the way. But when we came to Fiddlewood – what you call the Geiskeflor – I sent Brady – the varier – to buy some food. Something went wrong and he... he didn't come back."

"He left you to shift for yourself?" said Trahern. "No wonder you're looking for him."

"No. It wasn't like that. He told me to go without him if there were trouble and he'd catch up later. But he didn't catch up. He didn't leave me. He wouldn't do that. Something went wrong. We missed each other, somehow."

"You really believe that?" asked Trahern. "So strongly you're willing to go back into the Geiskeflor for him?"

"Please. I can't leave him in there, alone and hungry and frightened. I have to help him. It's a matter of honor."

"Is it, now?" said Trahern.

Kinnan said, "This 'rich man' he saved you from must have been a monster, for you to feel such gratitude...." He looked at Elsie sharply. "And very powerful, if you couldn't refuse his suit. Who was it?"

Elsie looked just as sharply back. "Perhaps you know. Is he the one you're afraid of?"

"Afraid?" said Trahern. "Who says he's afraid?"

"Nobody," said Elsie. "It's just that he questions me so closely."

"All Layounnans have some cause to fear this man," said Kinnan.

"He is most powerful…," said Elsie.

"He is most monstrous," said Kinnan.

"Who?" said Trahern.

It was Elsie who gave in and said the name. "Landry Oliva beren Ada. Kinninger of Layounna."

"So-called," said Kinnan.

Elsie let out a short puff of breath, between a sigh and a nervous laugh. "Now, may I have the supplies?"

"Anything you like," said Kinnan. "I'll come with you and help."

"I only want what I asked…."

"Do you think I would miss a chance to aid someone who's frustrated Landry of Layounna?" said Kinnan, with a grim twist to his mouth. "I would go to a worse place than the Geiskeflor for that."

"Just food and water," said Elsie. "I can pay my own debts."

"Listen, girl, and see if I don't owe your varier a 'well done' of my own." To Trahern, he said, "You asked me my history and I told you nothing. I'll answer your question now."

"I don't want to hear it," said Elsie. "Brady doesn't want to hear it, either. I wouldn't have trusted you with my secret if you hadn't made me. Please don't trust me with yours."

But Kinnan raised his braceleted arm and said, "This was given me by my half-sister, Karol beren Ada, true Kinninger of Layounna."

Elsie said nothing, but Trahern said slowly, "I remember when Karol beren Ada sat the throne, and her mother, before her."

"*My* mother, before her. *My* mother, as well."

"Kinnan beren Ada," said Elsie. "They frighten children with that name – and the children threaten to run away and join your band."

"I wish I had one for them to join. As it is, I may have to take the children and wait for them to grow. I would be willing."

The room was still, except for the crackle of the fire and the patting of rain on the thatch.

"The Emir sent a formal protest when Landry declared himself Kinninger," said Trahern. "But no one of Karol's line or Ada's came forward to claim the crown."

"I did," said Kinnan. "Landry swore not to believe me. He's accused me of treason and of any civil crime committed in any of the Five Districts.

For years, I dodged back and forth over the borders, trying to raise rebellion. Dissatisfaction was the worst I could foster, and too much of that brought punishment down on my supporters."

Kinnan clenched his hands into fists again, and his face grew dark with rage. "Swords came after me in Kozabir! In Granitz! A little girl warned me...."

"The one you asked me to look for," said Trahern.

Kinnan nodded, and smiled at Elsie. "I thought *she* had found *me* when you came in. But you're older than she would be now, and don't really look much like I remember her. It was just a fleeting resemblance."

"But what does this have to do with Brady?" Elsie asked.

"He crossed my enemy," said Kinnan, with relish. "I want to shake his hand. Besides, a man so bright and brave, and with such a talent.... If he would agree to help me, I might not need an army."

"He wouldn't," said Elsie. "You're talking about more excitement than even he would fancy."

"You can't answer for the man."

"Yes, I can. I've traveled with him. I know what he's like."

She laid aside her bowl and stood to dry her backside.

"More or less a coward," said Trahern. "Saved you for the fun of it, drew you away with him and abandoned you, eh? Robbed you, too, no doubt."

Elsie flushed. "What do you know about it?"

Trahern shook his head. "Nothing. I'd better wash up."

He picked up Elsie's bowl and took an iron trivet from the mantle.

Elsie moved aside, right away from the fire, far out of Trahern's path.

Trahern seemed to stumble. Elsie and Kinnan both reached out to steady him. Kinnan caught his friend's elbow, but Trahern filled Elsie's hand with the iron trivet.

It wasn't Elsie's hand, now.

"You must be Brady," said Trahern.

Brady it was, in clothes as damp and hard-used as he had made Elsie's look. "How did you know?"

"I didn't know. I suspected, from this and that. I had a feeling."

Kinnan snatched the loggerhead from its stand and half-raised it. "Get from between us, Trahern."

The smith turned to Kinnan with surprise. "This is the man whose hand you wanted to shake."

"What makes you think any part of what she – he said was the truth?"

Brady gave Trahern his trivet. "It was all true, except that I'm me, Brady birn Ilka, not Elsie. I'm not a spy, for Landry Oliva or anybody else. I don't care who you are or who should rule Layounna. I made a promise to see Elsie safe to Kozabir and I lost her. This is where she would have come out if she followed the course we agreed on. You haven't seen her?"

"We've seen no strangers for many months," said Trahern. "Was that really her form you were in before?"

"It was. I meant to be somebody else – give a different story – but I couldn't put my mind to it. Elsie, cold and dirty and wet and hungry…. I couldn't think of anything else. I couldn't seem to be anyone else. I couldn't even think of a good lie."

"Poor lad," said Trahern, reverting to Kozabiri. "That must have been hard on you."

Kinnan lowered the loggerhead. "You believe him, then?"

"I believe him."

"In that case…." Kinnan put the loggerhead away and extended a hand. Brady took it.

"How did you do it?" Kinnan asked. "Manage the escape? Shapechanging, I suppose."

"I'll tell you some day, I hope. But Elsie's been in the Geiskeflor for nearly a week now; I can't spare the time." Brady's face, really pinched from his own real near-starvation, looked haunted. "I waited for her for hours in case she was behind me. When I was sure she wasn't, I went on as fast as I could. I thought I'd come up to her every day. I had just bought food, because we had run out. So I had the food and the fishing line and the tinderbox and the knife and… and most of her money. She had nothing. I wasted time circling around once the Fiddlewood turned, in case she'd lost direction, but…."

He turned to Kinnan. "Will you still help me? I won't help you – you see I'm being honest with you. But help me find her. I left my things on the porch; I can pay, in silver, if that's what it would take."

"Don't be insulting," said Kinnan. "I'd help, even if I didn't owe you for the blow you must've dealt Landry's pride."

"Thanks." Brady shuddered. "Let me finish drying. Then, if you'd give me the food and drink I asked for, I'll go back out tonight. You know what she looks like now; you start when you're ready and go back over the ground I've covered. I'll cross Fiddlewood and search the eastern bank."

"Wait till it's light," said Trahern. "The rain may stop before morning."

Brady shook his head.

"You must love her very much," said Kinnan.

Brady showed his teeth in distaste. "Love her? Elsie? I promised her mother. I love…." Brady lost sight of Kinnan behind a vision of a girl in Kozabirian costume. "I don't love Elsie."

But he didn't leave before morning, or after morning, either. The days without food had weakened him and the soaking had done its worst. He went out for his pack, and came back shaking. By dawn, he was tucked into a cocoon of blankets near Trahern's bed, delirious with fever.

"Will you look for the girl on your own?" Trahern asked Kinnan.

"I said I'd look. So I will."

"You won't find her. After this long, the most you'll find is…. And even if she were alive, would she let you find her? She doesn't know you."

"No, but she won't know that."

"Say that again?"

"I'll call out, 'This way, Elsie. It's me – Brady.' She'll come to me, if only to ask 'Brady' why he's hunting in another shape."

"How far will you go?"

"No farther than the bend in the river. If she lost her way, it would have to have been after she lost the river as a guide. And, at any rate, I think your first guess was the best: I don't expect to find her. But I will look."

And he did, quickly but carefully, the looking of a soldier trained, among other things, to hunt for hidden people. He looked for three days and returned to find Brady still in fever, sedated by an infusion Trahern had purchased from the Vatran apothecary.

Brady mumbled in his delirium. Other forms and faces took his place for seconds – sometimes for minutes – at a time. The most common of these forms was that of the girl he had sworn to lead to safety.

When the varier's fever broke, he woke to a numbness in his mind. The thought of Elsie fretted him and held back his recovery. Though Kinnan told him often of his own search and assured him, without believing it, that Elsie had probably made her way out and to a village, Brady forgot, and chafed.

Little by little, Brady grew stronger, while his hope grew weaker. By the time he could have resumed the search himself, he knew it was too late. More than a month had passed, and Trahern knew of no new arrivals in Vatra, nor had he heard gossip of any new arrivals anywhere round-about.

"I hope she knew," Brady said by the fire one evening, healthy once more in body but feeble in spirit. "I hope she understood, at the end, that I tried to find her. That I didn't just… leave her to die."

Trahern could only lay a heavy hand of comfort on Brady's shoulder.

Kinnan smiled in a most unpleasant way – though the smile was not for Brady – and said, "I know at whose door to lay her death. When my time comes, I'll strike a blow for her."

CHARACTERS

(MORE OR LESS IN ORDER OF MENTION OR APPEARANCE)

Darcy Aminta beren Valda (unmarried name: Darcy beren Aminta)	Roll-Keeper of Eastern District, then of Layounna. Husband of Devona, father of Elsie.
Devona beren Valda	Public scribe, wife of Darcy, mother of Elsie.
Elsie beren Devona	Chosen second wife of Landry.
Salvia Zglaria called Moder Zglaria	Old woman who lives in Fiddlewood.
Landry Oliva beren Ada (unmarried name: Landry beren Oliva)	Consort to Karol beren Ada.
Karol beren Ada	Kinninger (ruler) of Layounna. Chief of the House of Onagros. Wife of Landry.
Rhu beren Robia	Landry's Chamberlain.
Guthrie beren Melanell	Chief Sword under Landry.
Ada beren Cinnie	Mother of Karol beren Ada, Kinninger before her. Mother of Sorcha and Kinnan.
Gils Nara beren Ailith (unmarried name: Gils beren Nara)	Heart-husband and child-sire of Ada beren Cinnie and Osa beren Ailith, father of Cameron and Kinnan
Cameron beren Osa	Son of Gils Nara and Osa beren Ailith, half-brother to Kinnan, heart-husband and child-sire to Karol beren Ada
Kinnan beren Ada (birn Matka, beren Osa, beren Moder)	Son of Gils Nara and Ada beren Cinnie, half-brother to Karol, half-brother to Cameron. In line for throne of Layounna
Sorcha beren Ada	Karol beren Ada's younger sister, half-sister to Kinnan, wife of Hayward.

Oliva beren Audre	Thane of Sarpa. Mother of Landry, Hayward, and Corvina. An Adept of the dark Tarkastrian Arts.
Hayward Oliva beren Ada (unmarried name: Hayward beren Oliva)	Son of Oliva beren Audre, brother of Landry and Corvina, married to Sorcha.
Corvina beren Oliva	Daughter of Oliva, sister of Landry and Hayward. An alchemist specializing in poison.
Andrin beren Tooli	A Waymaster.
Biddi beren Anna	A kitchen maid, friends with Andrin.
Farukh Suria'Apa-Dan	A storyteller from the land of Sule.
Fala Salali	A trinket-woman from the land of Nishi.
Verrina beren Unna	Andrin's grandmother.
Chandler	A hen.
Trahern birn Lona	A blacksmith from the land of Kozabir.
Brady birn Ilka	Devona's apprentice from Kozabir.
Nerissa birn Matka	A slave.
Isa birn Isa and Barand Tara birn Isa	Nerissa's owners.
Audre beren Oda	Oliva beren Audre's mother. Thane of Oakwood.
Edelin beren Cinnie	Elsie's male disguise.
Vevay beren Sorcha Atwell beren Sorcha Joia beren Sorcha Blaine beren Sorcha	Children of Sorcha and Hayward.
Brina beren Moder	Waymistress of Kudasad Waystation.
Anshar "The Divine Spear" Redhand	A Layounnan rebel based in the land of Istok.
Janet beren Lana	Cook in the castle in Kudasad, capital of Layounna.
Bryan beren Basha	Captain of Landry's Swords.
Robeard Caitlin beren Regan	Thane of Leven. Spokesman of the Southern Council of Thanes.
Robia beren Dela	Rhu beren Robia's mother.

GENEALOGY

ONAGROS BEFORE INTERMARRIAGE

| husband (unnamed) | + | Ada beren Cinnie | + | Gils Nara beren Ailith | + | Osa beren Ailith |

| Karol beren Ada | Sorcha beren Ada | Kinnan beren Ada (Osa, Moder) | Cameron beren Osa |

No shared blood

SARPA BEFORE INTERMARRIAGE

| Otemar Sadira beren Oliva | + | Oliva beren Oda |

| Landry beren Oliva | Hayward beren Oliva | Corvina beren Oliva |

INTERMARRIAGE OF ONAGROS AND SARPA

| Landry Oliva beren Ada | + | Karol beren Ada | + | Cameron beren Osa |

?

| Sorcha beren Ada | + | Hayward Oliva beren Ada |

| Vevay beren Sorcha | Atwell beren Sorcha | Joia beren Sorcha | Blaine beren Sorcha |

www.ingramcontent.com/pod-product-compliance
Lightning Source LLC
Chambersburg PA
CBHW051656260626
47170CB00004B/1532